CLOCKWORK CANADA

CANADA

STEAMPUNK FICTION

Edited by

DOMINIK PARISIEN

EXILE
editions

Library and Archives Canada Cataloguing in Publication

Clockwork Canada : steampunk fiction / Dominik Parisien, editor.

(The Exile book of anthology series ; number twelve)
Issued in print and electronic formats.
ISBN 978-1-55096-579-7 (paperback).--ISBN 978-1-55096-587-2 (pdf).--
ISBN 978-1-55096-580-3 (epub).--ISBN 978-1-55096-581-0 (mobi)

1. Steampunk fiction, Canadian (English). 2. Short stories, Canadian
(English). 3. Canadian fiction (English)--21st century. I. Parisien, Dominik,
editor II. Series: Exile book of anthology series ; no. 12

PS8323.S73C56 2016   C813'.0876808356   C2015-908657-4
                                                   C2015-908658-2

Copyrights to the stories rest with the authors © 2016
Design and Composition by Mishi Uroboros;
Cover art "Autumnal Equinox" by Steve Menard;
Typeset in Fairfield, Copperplate and Akzidenz Grotesk fonts
at Moons of Jupiter Studios.

Published by Exile Editions Ltd ~ www.ExileEditions.com
144483 Southgate Road 14 – GD, Holstein, Ontario, N0G 2A0
Printed and Bound in Canada in 2016, by Marquis Books

We gratefully acknowledge the Canada Council for the Arts,
the Government of Canada through the Canada Book Fund,
the Ontario Arts Council, and the Ontario Media Development Corporation
for their support toward our publishing activities.

  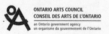

Canadian Sales: The Canadian Manda Group, 664 Annette Street,
Toronto ON M6S 2C8   www.mandagroup.com   416 516 0911

North American and international distribution, and U.S. sales:
Independent Publishers Group, 814 North Franklin Street,
Chicago IL 60610   www.ipgbook.com   toll free: 1 800 888 4741

For Ann, who made me love clockwork.

CONTENTS

INTRODUCTION
DOMINIK PARISIEN

Canada is often described as a mosaic, sometimes a patch-work. I would add that it might also be described as a great lumbering automaton; it is an absurdly large mass, a construct made of widely different cogs and gears that sometimes work together and sometimes don't, that is physically connected by the railroad – one of the great embodiments of the power, ingenuity, and crushing ruthlessness of the steam age. It is a perfect setting for steampunk.

Steampunk is constantly being reinterpreted, reimagined. Authors, makers, artists, cosplayers, and musicians are all breaking down the components of this seemingly infinitely malleable genre and reassembling them to explore new avenues, to tell new stories. What started as Victorian retro-futurist fantasy has gone global and now spans across multiple historical periods. With this anthology I wanted to bring steampunk to Canada, to give Canadian authors and readers a chance to see their stories told through a versatile genre, and reimagine our history in order to provide glimpses of other Canadas.

Many of the elements traditionally associated with steampunk are featured in *Clockwork Canada*. Some of the stories contain steam, others don't; clockwork frequently appears, as do automata, airships, trains, copper, brass, goggles, mechanical limbs; the works of Jules Verne inspire a character or two; the magical and the mechanical sometimes coexist; alternate history is often at the forefront; and great and fantastical inventions abound. While all these are important, they make up only the physical manifestations of steampunk. The grinding heart of the genre lies in the themes, in the communities we build, the drive of the maker movement and the do-it-yourself culture, the interrogation of industry and empire, the engagement with revolutionary and creative ideas, and the celebration of the adventuring spirit. Stories that focused first on the spirit of the thing, and then the thing itself, were what I looked for when I began assembling the book.

From stories like Charlotte Ashley's "La Clochemar," Holly Schofield's "East Wind in Carrall Street," Kate Heartfield's "The Seven O'Clock Man," and Colleen Anderson's "Buffalo Gals," to Claire Humphrey's "Crew 255" and Brent Nichols' "The Harpoonist," many of the narratives in *Clockwork Canada* take place on the edges of "high" society, of empires, of the great metropolises of the industrial world, and show us the lives of the working class, of aboriginal characters, of those out in the Canadian wilderness and in burgeoning villages, and of those striving to build communities. Other tales, such as Tony Pi's "Our Chymical Séance," Chantal Boudreau's "The Curlicue Seahorse," and Michal Wojcik's "Strange Things Done" revel in adventure and a sense of wonder.

As a movement that is both forward-looking and retro, steampunk also allows us to play with what-might-have-been, sometimes even what-should-have-been. It gives authors like Terri Favro, Kate Story, and Rati Mehrotra the chance to reimagine historical figures like Laura Secord and Isaac Brock in "Let Slip the Sluicegates of War, Hydro-Girl," Sandford Fleming in "Equus," and Gurdit Singh in "Komagata Maru," or gives Harold R. Thompson the opportunity to explore Canada's role in the American Civil War. It gives us stories like Karin Lowachee's "Gold Mountain" and Rhea Rose's

"Bones of Bronze, Limbs Like Iron" and helps us explore, even question, the idea of Canada as a safe haven for immigrants.

No story exists in a vacuum, so although these tales are set in The Great White North, they are nonetheless in dialogue with the global steampunk communities. With that sense of community in mind, it is my pleasure to welcome you to the world of *Clockwork Canada*.

LA CLOCHEMAR

CHARLOTTE ASHLEY

Here is what happened on Suzette's first run:

The living map they called the lifeclock – *manidoo-dibaigi-sisswaii* – woke her party up before dawn. Amidst the usual slow movements of the badges representing caribou, whitefish, rabbit, fisher, bear, lynx, and moose, the brightly beaded symbol of Mishiginebig, the Horned Serpent, had started to move. It was still distant, a spear of blood-red beadwork lancing over the lifeclock's mosaic face, but Mishiginebig was fast. At the rate he was moving, he'd be within sight of Baawitigong, their home, in less than an hour.

"Suzette and Makoonse, go. Now," their party leader, Shogamish, croaked. "Meet Mishiginebig here…" He pointed at the map at the crook of the Root River. "…and draw him up to the little lake—"

Suzette snatched up her gear and was out the door of the Hall of Migration before Shogamish could finish. When one of the big monsters moved, there was no time for curiosity or questions. There was only time to run.

With her rifle tight on her back and her partner, Makoonse, lagging in her wake, Suzette sprinted the entire way to the Root River. They caught sight of Mishiginebig at a narrow crossing where the tree line had been pushed back by spring flooding. His striped, yellow-and-green hide was nearly indistinguishable from the wall of pines, smooth scales locking together like bark. Only the motion of the lines, like a forest under the ripple of a paddle, gave him away. His head was obscured by underbrush somewhere to the north, but his forked tail lashed out of the tree line to the south, barely a half-mile back.

"Be the wind, Soofoo," Makoonse gasped at her, unslinging his gun once they'd forged the river. He raised the rifle and fired.

The bullet ricocheted uselessly off Mishiginebig's hide into a tree, kicking up a spray of splinters. The explosion from the shot did its job. The serpent's bulk slithered to a halt. Upstream, his four-horned profile, snouted and fanged like a wolf, emerged from the woods, his snake's body trailing behind it.

Suzette ran.

She bolted down the riverbank, ducking under Mishiginebig's tail as it whipped out at her. Her leathers were painted bright red and white, her face too; all the better to be seen when she wanted to be. The noise and the smell of the gunshot could attract a Mandimanidoo – one of the big ones – from miles off, as the first visitors from France discovered a hundred years ago. Keeping its attention and losing it again when you needed to – that was an art the Anishinaabeg had perfected. An art Suzette had spent the last ten years learning. An art that would be put to the test now.

She gained five hundred feet on the beast before it turned, and lost a hundred when she dove into the forest, taking a well-worn deer path. She ducked and leapt, a crazed jackrabbit without a hole, until her lungs screamed and her toes dragged. She tugged free the roll of camouflage secured about her waist, turned abruptly into the undergrowth, and fell into a crouch beneath it.

Then she closed her eyes and settled into niiyawaa, still-ness, as she had been taught.

Her heart slowed instantly. Her scalp prickled with an icy cold and her fingers went numb, but she willed her body to push further. Her laboured breathing calmed to a nearly imperceptible murmur as she felt her spirit lower deep into her self. She felt her consciousness waver, her constitution badly taxed by lack of air and an overabundance of excite-ment, but she held tightly to her spark of life. Niiyawaa was a dangerous state, but necessary if she was going to trick Mish-iginebig into passing her by. She had to be another lifeless thing on the forest floor.

For fifty long, slow heartbeats, Mishiginebig hurtled down the deer path past where she was huddled beneath her scant camouflage, then the rattle of the bush retreated. Suzette let another ten beats pass and, with a heave of her spirit, she pulled herself out of niiyawaa, surfacing with a gulp. Her head felt light and dark spots crowded her vision like night blos-soms, but that was all the rest she got.

Suzette ran.

She launched herself back towards the path, over it, and into the uncut bush. She ploughed through the sharp branches clasped in each other's grasps, letting them scratch her cheeks and tear her braids. In a clearing between two old beeches, she unshouldered her rifle, cocked the hammer, and fired into the air to draw the serpent back towards her.

But what roared in response to her rifle was not Mishigin-ebig.

Through the thick canopy, Suzette could see the shape of a mountainous moose's head with a distinctive crest of feath-ers rising up over the forest, no more than a league distant. The monster's angry cry was part bear's roar and part eagle's shriek – Pamolai, who should have been far east in the distant lands of the Panawahpskek this time of year. The earth shook as Pamolai clambered to a stand and began its lumbering progress towards her. Suzette's measured, trained breath rattled and accelerated as she realized she was trapped.

Suzette panicked – and ran. Wild, she tore herself on sticky-sharp pines thick with webs and fell over half-rotten cedars hidden under the rusty needle coating of the earth. She gasped for breath and forgot how to calm her heart and her mind. She ran faster than she had ever run before, away from Pamolai but towards Mishiginebig, heedless and lost.

A gun fired in the distance behind her. *Makoonse's?* Her partner was not as quick as she was, could not outrun these monsters. But he could gain her time.

Suzette stopped. She forced herself to breathe, to turn, to remember her training. Between the broken crowns of the trees, she saw the back of Pamolai's head. The beast was heading the wrong way, towards the gunfire – and the town.

The little lake could not be far.

Her rifle was still in her hand. Suzette regained control of her breathing as she reloaded it, keeping one eye trained on Pamolai's silhouette. She would fire again, she told herself; bring both monsters back towards her. She would draw them towards the lake. Then she would lose them with niiyawaa, as she had been taught. That was the plan, the technique she was supposed to have perfected. She pointed her rifle into the air.

Mishiginebig's tail lashed out of the bush like a whip, catching her completely unaware. Her body folded around it, limp with surprise, before being launched into the air by the impact. Her world became a bird's nest of shattering, stabbing, lacerating boughs followed by a crooked impact, bottom-first.

That was the end of Suzette's first run. But it would not be her last.

c   ⑾   c

Suzette woke to another thrashing. A thin man with horse-tailed black hair shook her shoulder with one hand, jostling her very tender skull. He was so preoccupied with the golden contraption in his other hand that he continued to shake her even once she had opened her eyes and convinced them to focus in the same direction.

"Oooh," she groaned, drawing his attention. He glanced at her only briefly, but ceased rattling her brains.

"Madame," he said to her in French, "if you can stand, you must come with me now. We are in great danger."

"Mishiginebig," she gasped, finding it difficult to speak. The man looked relieved.

"Yes, exactly. The serpent is…" The man studied his golden contraption. "…not two miles west of here, but on the move. We cannot stay here."

"How do you know that?" Suzette replied in Anishinaabe-mowin out of habit. She struggled to a sit, which she was pleased to find she could.

The man ignored her question. "Up with you, then," he said, placing his device in the pocket of his coat and wrapping his arm under her shoulder. "Weashcog is not far from here."

"Pamolai," Suzette blurted, almost an expletive, as a sharp pain in her chest robbed her of her breath again. "Pamolai was here as well. Did she—?"

The man's hand twitched towards the pocket that held his device, then he made a fist, scowling.

"She was headed north when last I saw her," the man replied. "Someone drew her up towards the little lakes. Can you walk?"

Suzette nodded. She took a few experimental steps and found it was not a lie. Her head ached and she could not catch a proper breath, but by sinking into a light niiyawaa trance, she could move well without requiring much air. She started to jog but soon found her rescuer was not following. She glanced back at him inquisitively.

"I'm not a runner," he said, gesturing at his outfit as if that explained everything. Indeed, he was garbed in the French fashion: a long woollen coat over hose with severely impractical heeled shoes, all sewn with beadwork. "I'm a map-builder. Dibaabishk," he introduced himself. *Weight Measure*.

"Soofoo." She gave him her own nickname.

"'Foo.'" Dibaabishk smiled. "From the French: 'An ill-considered journey.' A French runner. That's new."

Suzette shrugged. "Treaty," she said. "A dozen of us have been trained at Baawitigong. I was – young when my king sent me here." In truth, she had been a woman fully grown when she'd been caught poaching, arrested, and shipped off to the Americas. But she had long since learned that the Anishinaabeg did not like to hear an honoured role like runner conflated with a punishment for criminals. "This was my first run."

"You lived," Dibaabishk said. "Congratulations."

Weashcog was known to her, as one or two runners from her party had been recruited there. She had only stayed long enough to share a little food and drink those years ago, but she remembered the little place's sunny banks and rabbit-trimmed wigwams, rich and growing from the fur trade. Weashcog had its own lifeclock as well, smaller than the one at Baawitigong, but daintier. The badges depicting the area's lives slid smoothly over the map's surface without the rattle and grind she'd become accustomed to. The interlocking pieces on the lifeclock's backside were better made here, the metal friendlier with the spirits tied to it.

Dibaabishk's doing, she realized. He was the map-maker. She wondered again about the device in his pocket.

"Our midewikwe – Wazhindoon – lives just here," Dibaabishk said, breaking their long silence. "She'll get you medicine." They turned off the path they'd been following and pushed through a thick wall of ferns to reach a lone building in a clearing demarked with stark white birch logs. Suzette followed Dibaabishk in.

"Dibaabishk! Come, I need your little hands for – oh, huh, welcome." The woman inside was tall and as thin as knotted rope, wearing a sleeveless dress dyed bright blue with no underclothes or moccasins. She stood, paced in spot a few moments, studying Suzette, then returned to a crouch in front of an elaborate bead loom hanging from the wigwam's unusually tall ceiling boughs. "Well, what is it you need, then? Grooveburr?"

"Actually, I've brought you a patient." The map-maker gestured at Suzette.

The midewikwe swivelled on her heels and looked at Suzette again. "A runner. Only one? Where are the others?"

"She was separated from her party, hit by Mishiginebig. She needs something for her bones, I think—"

"Mishiginebig?" Wazhindoon interrupted. "You were out while the Great Serpent was prowling?" She squinted at the map-maker, her eyes finally coming to focus with a sharpness that betrayed her keen mind. "You've done it," she said suddenly. "You've got a manidoo-dibaigisisswaii."

"What?" Dibaabishk took a step back, eyes darting guiltily. "That's madness. You're barely sensible when you're fasting, Wazhindoon. A lifeclock is too big to—"

"Empty your pockets."

"Sorry? No. No, I won't."

Suzette caught a smirk flit over the tall woman's face before she affected a scowl. Wazhindoon stood, looming over the much shorter map-maker. "You haven't a drop of guile in your blood, my friend. I can see through flesh. I can see through stone. I can see through time – I can see through you."

"You need a good night's rest."

"God does not speak to the well-rested," Wazhindoon replied. She turned to Suzette. "You've seen it. What's it like? Beautiful? Elegant? Offensive? Tell me where he's hidden it and I'll mend your bones, no problem."

"I—" Suzette started, trying to tell herself she was unsure what the woman was asking for. But she knew. Her eyes moved to the pocket of Dibaabishk's coat where he had stashed his golden device. The map-maker threw up his arms in frustration as she did.

"Fine," he grumbled, producing the trinket. Held in one hand, it was no bigger than a goose egg, layers of gold and silver metal fitted together with a jeweller's precision. With a flick of his thumb, the smooth face swung open and revealed a mosaic of their surroundings in miniature.

Both women drew sharp breaths in unison, Suzette clutching her side in pain after. Wazhindoon did not appear to notice.

"You idiot," she breathed, though the expletive held no conviction. "Does Council know?"

"Of course not," Dibaabishk hissed, looking guiltily at Suzette again. "They wouldn't allocate me the parts. I – I obtained them other ways."

"Turn it over to them," Wazhindoon said. "Before you lose it."

"I won't lose—"

Dibaabishk's protest was cut off as Wazhindoon snatched it from his outstretched palm with the speed of a diving king-fisher. She stepped back as quickly, raised a pointed eyebrow, then handed it back.

"If anyone should take this from you—"

"I know, I know," Dibaabishk said, turning red and putting it back in his pocket. "But until now, nobody knew about it but me."

"Pardon me," Suzette wheezed, only now recovered from her unwise inhalations. "Perhaps a discussion of such secrecy – whatever it is – could be held after I'm able to hold more air than a mouse's bladder? I'll leave you be and—"

Wazhindoon caught her by the forearm with her unexpected speed and ran her other gentle hand over her side. When Suzette coughed in pain, she nodded.

"I'll mend you," she said, "but you're privy to this secret now. You can not go anywhere until we have sorted out what to do about that."

Suzette tried to pull back her arm, but the other woman's grip was strong. "I don't even know what it is," she protested. "How can I tell a thing I do not know?"

"It's a lifeclock," Wazhindoon told her, pulling her firmly and smoothly towards a furred rug warmed by a puddle of sunlight. "Just like the one in your Hall of Migration. It will help guide a hunter to her prey or a traveller to his destination. It will tell you when the bears are coming out of hibernation, when the trout have come to spawn, and when a Mandimanidoo is coming to crush your boat and dash your family across the rocks of the lake's shore."

"I know what a lifeclock is," Suzette protested as Wazhin-doon guided her to a sit, and then laid her flat on the floor. "But you've already got one. Why would anyone care that he's got another?"

"Nobody has to ask Council to confer with this one, do they? Anyone could use it, anywhere."

"That's why I built it," Dibaabishk put in. "Everyone would be safer with lifeclocks of their own. If Soofoo had had one, Mishiginebig would never have taken her by surprise."

"For such a smart man, Dibaabishk, you are a fool, born and blooded." Wazhindoon cut the laces of Suzette's robe and rubbed a numbing ointment on the flesh over her pained ribs. "If anyone could navigate these lands without permission, guide, nor running party, we'd be overwhelmed with unin-vited guests before next season, even as half the fools were eaten by Mandimanidoo. Council keeps the lifeclock's secrets for good reason."

"Council would never give any unscrupulous person the metal nor the means to bond it," Dibaabishk scoffed. "Who would craft them but me?"

"They would take those things." Wazhindoon gave Suz-ette's side a pat and pulled her up to a sit. It took her some effort to draw breath, but the pain had subsided. She found both the midewikwe and the map-maker looking uncomfort-ably at each other. Finally, Wazhindoon sighed. "Well, it has been made. There's no unknowing a thing. Runner, what do you think?"

Suzette stood to avoid the tall woman's uncanny gaze. She thought of the sway the lifeclock had over her life, the lives of everyone in Baawitigong. Hunters who could not set out, trav-ellers who were forced to stay at home. Ships that could not be turned back in time and gatherers who were caught unawares. She thought of all the times runners had come home broken and bleeding, or never came home at all.

"I think Dibaabishk's little lifeclock could save a great many lives," she replied quietly. "To know, always, where the Mandimanidoo are, and to be able to avoid them? I cannot think that is a bad thing for anyone."

The map-maker smiled and raised an eyebrow at Wazhindoon. The midewikwe scowled.

"The Mandimanidoo are part of God, same as anything," she said. "They have their piece in the big story. It's a fool who thinks they are our enemy. Smarten up, Dibaabishk, my friend."

"Come, Soofoo," Dibaabishk said after a pause. "We'll feed you before you return to Baawitigong. I think you and I might have more in common than I thought."

Together, they left. Over a spring supper of fish and leeks, Suzette tried to consider the midewikwe's misgivings and found herself recalling the French word for the Manidoo-dibaigisisswaii: *clochemar*, or nightmare-alarm. Her party leader forbade her from using it. It was disrespectful, he told her. And yet how smoothly it fell from her tongue when she recalled the looming monstrosities with death-calling howls who had so nearly had her life.

C   ⟨⟩   C

Dibaabishk liked the word: clochemar. He adopted the term for his pocket lifeclock. *La Clochemar*, he called it, as if it were a wife who watched out for him and with whom he had to consult. La Clochemar says I'm to go fishing. La Clochemar woke me when Mishibizhiw stirred last night. A game of bones? Let me ask La Clochemar.

Suzette learned Dibaabishk was a Francophile who spoke German, English, and Dutch in addition to French, Mohawk, and several varieties of Anishinaabemowin. He had been trained as a jeweller and clockmaker in Nuremberg as a youth, around the time Suzette was a wild child racing barefoot around the king's forests near Toulouse. Yet it was Dibaabishk who began inviting Suzette on clandestine journeys into the wilderness, as if it was he and not she who was at home where the trees were thickest. In truth, he wanted the opportunity to test La Clochemar and Suzette could not resist exploring the woods unhindered by the constant threat of Mandimanidoo.

The Autumn came with it the news that a large delegation from Versailles was bound for Baawitigong the following spring. The French had begun to fulfill their treaty obligations by supplying runners to assist with the protection of the area, and so Council had allowed a French representative to sit among their number. Suzette was assigned to the new ambassador's retinue, much to her chagrin. She could not see the value in helping an aristocrat polish her *Academie* Anishinaabemowin, but Dibaabishk could.

"I think we understand each other in matters of moral philosophy, Soo," he said to her one day as they sat on the bank of a murky little pond. "Council cannot be everywhere. It is the responsibility of every individual to protect and defend his neighbours when he can."

"Did Council deny you resources for parts again?" Suzette guessed, knowing her friend by now.

Dibaabishk stiffened. "They granted me leave to work in Baawitigong for two moons, with the new forge there."

"Well, that's something."

"Pretty lot of nothing it will do me. I need fusee chain and springs. Gold and copper. Loowe's shop isn't ready for that kind of work. I'll need it from France. I *needed* credit."

"So get Loowe's shop ready." Suzette tossed a stone into the pond. "He needs tools only you can make him."

"I need *money*," Dibaabishk insisted. "Soo, you will have the ambassador's ear. You must petition her for me."

"But you just said Council denied you—"

"Not Council, Soo. The ambassador. The French."

Suzette was startled by the distinction, but considered it. "Council would not like it," she decided. "Wazhindoon is right about that. They want to control the lifeclocks. You sell even one to the French and they lose that."

"Yes, they would," Dibaabishk replied. "But to try to control who can and cannot protect themselves – Soo, that is not good. It is not just. Control cannot come at a blood price. Our Council is wise, but they have lost their way with baseless fears on this point."

Suzette could not help but agree.

When the first ships drew up after the long journey down Lake Karegnondi, Suzette met Ambassador LaRonde with a generous and sure smile. A full moon of celebrations flowered in the excitement that the new French presence brought, rosy-cheeked as they all were with affection for their new friends and neighbours. Within a quarter moon, the new French were adorning their belts and sashes with Anishinaabe beadwork and the Anishinaabeg were singing French tunes to their babies before bed. When Roman, of Suzette's party, was killed after a fall during a patrol, they mourned together and thanked Roman for his protection of the homes and lives they all shared.

In this time of hope and joy, Ambassador LaRonde grasped Dibaabishk's hand and promised him she would write to her king personally on his behalf. He was a genius and La Clochemar a wonder, the perfect alloy of French and

Anishinaabe arts, she said. They would all flourish in Baawit-igong once they could perfectly anticipate the comings and goings of the Mandimanidoo. No price was too high for that dream of harmony with the land.

But the reply that arrived with the next ship was not what they expected.

c (l) c

Suzette, like everyone, watched the mid-summer ships pull up at the docks, disgorging their passengers. Along with the usual Odawa, Mississauga, and Anishinaabeg traders and artists was a lone blonde woman with the washed-out look of laundry left out in the sun. She was well dressed in the French fashion and carrying her own small trunk. She vanished into the crowd of gawkers without speaking to anyone.

That evening, Suzette visited Dibaabishk at Loowe's blacksmith. Her friend sat on the floor in nothing but a breechclout, leaning against the wall in deep thought.

"I've had a visitor, Soo," Dibaabishk replied after a silence. "From over the seas."

"From the king?" Suzette's heart skipped. Even all these years and miles later, the idea of reaching out to that august personage awed her.

"From France," Dibaabishk replied evasively. "But she does want a clochemar."

"Oh! That's wonderful!"

"Yes…" Dibaabishk seemed cautious. "But the lifeclock she wants…is not for here. She wants one to take home."

"What? That's plain silly. There's nothing in Europe to track. Rabbits, badgers, deer. They haven't got Mandimanidoo."

"Soo," Dibaabishk said in a voice that brought an ominous gravity to the conversation. "She wants to track *people*."

Suzette opened her mouth to respond and closed it again in confusion. Eventually she managed a second attempt. "But there are people everywhere over there. It would be meaningless."

Dibaabishk sighed. "In the same way the lifeclocks know different herds or flocks, it would know different people. Odawa from Potawatomi, French from German. That kind of thing. She – she will pay very handsomely." He locked eyes with her. "She says her homeland is plagued with bandits and this will help her."

"Bandits," Suzette echoed. That was perfectly plausible, but something had begun to rot in her belly. She remembered hunting rabbits for stew as a child – rabbits the clerks at Toulouse said were the king's. They'd run right through her mother's garden, eating the greens off her turnips; tiny taxmen. But Suzette had been fast and clever even then, and it was years before she was caught in the woods with the limp conies in her satchel. Years of freedom from the eyes and laws of the king... "You cannot do it," she heard herself say.

Dibaabishk said nothing for some time. "Her affairs do not concern me."

"Yes, but—"

"And her money will buy me what I need to build more, to learn more. I could make a clochemar for you, Soofoo. It would be folly to refuse."

"You cannot build a map that treats people like – like herds. Like prey. No matter who they are. Dibaabishk, come, this is not what you want to make!" Suzette pleaded.

"No, prey deserves better respect than bandits do. I *did* question her, Soo. I am not a fool," Dibaabishk's voice rose in frustration, becoming defensive. "These are murderers and thieves, terrors in their own right. Should a traveller afar not have the right to avoid highwaymen, to flee from plunderers? Tell me why human lives should be any more sanctified than herds?"

"You don't know her," Suzette pointed out. "Do you trust her word that a clochemar will be used only to avoid harm and bring about justice?"

"Yes," Dibaabishk said, standing. His reply was blunt and irrational, a sure sign he felt guilty. Suzette pressed on.

"Go with her, then," she suggested. "You need to – to bond the pieces to their spirits. Go meet these bandits. Then tell me if you still believe that."

"Council would never let me go," Dibaabishk responded airily. "I'm disappointed, Suzette. I thought you understood how important it was that the clochemar sees production. It's a tool of survival. It is not for anyone to say who does and doesn't deserve to protect themselves."

"Dibaabishk—"

"I'm going for supper," he cut her off. Without meeting her eye, he pushed past her and vanished into the evening's gloom.

Suzette knew little enough about how the lifeclocks were made. The secrets of the map-maker's art were well kept. Even Dibaabishk guarded this secret tight. His willingness to simply give his mysterious client some instructions came very close to a great betrayal of his craft.

It was easy, then, for her to intervene on his behalf, telling herself she was doing it for him, for his honour. She found Ambassador LaRonde in her room at Baawitigong's first and only European-style building; a long, stone-framed rectory that served as both the French administration centre and parish. She told the ambassador that Dibaabishk would have to return with the pale woman to France in order to get what he needed to make a clochemar.

She did not need to say anything more. The speed with which LaRonde agreed to collude in keeping the affair secret from her fellow Council-members turned Suzette's stomach. LaRonde promised Dibaabishk would be given the time to work in Europe and that Council would never know the true purpose of his visit.

Even Dibaabishk was sobered by this quick and inexplicable display of power, tempering his anger at Suzette's meddling. He was cold and formal when she turned up at the docks ten days later to see him off, but he squeezed her hands in friendly farewell. His lingering glance seemed to hold a warning for her, something that could not be said out loud. She struggled to understand what it might be, but he was departing for a world unfathomable to her. She could only hope he would make sense of the danger she felt lurking behind the smiles of those who ruled by pen and law, while she focused on her unmistakable world of moon-crowned giants roaming their shared earth.

c ⦿ c

In fact, she was kept so busy during Dibaabishk's absence that she could hardly spare him a thought. The moose-headed menace, Pamolai, remained within a few days' travel of the big lake, Gichigami. They had to run her off no fewer than three times in four moons.

Dibaabishk returned on one of the autumn's last ships with the pale woman at his elbow. Suzette waited for him at the docks, but he ignored her completely. He led the woman arm-in-arm to LaRonde's residence.

Later that night, a young messenger met Suzette outside the Hall of Migration. "The map-maker wants to see you," the girl told her. "At Wahzindoon's, he says. As soon as you can." She handed Suzette a heavy purse. Within was the original clochemar.

Suzette crept a little ways into the bush until she was sure she could not be seen, and then flipped open the little map. It was as she remembered it: the familiar paths and rivers of the area rendered in delicate coloured seeds; badges tinier than her fingernails symbolizing vital herds, packs, and Mandimanidoo crawling over the surface like beetles. Mishiginebig, the serpent, was there, unmoving to the north of the little lake, and Mishibijiw, the sea cat, still motionless at the heart of Lake Karegnondi where she had slept these last years. La Clochemar did not show Pamolai, whose constant presence had only become a fact of life only after the little map had been built. She had recently been drawn west towards the Mississagi River and had not been seen since. A pack of wolves appeared to be hunting north of Baawitigong, but these she could avoid easily. It should be safe to travel.

The night was young and the sky still a deepening lilac, but the woods curtained even the scarce light. Suzette, as much a creature of that place as the chipmunks and centipedes rustling through the forest floor, navigated by touch and memory more than sight, avoiding this tree or that, half-submerged shards of granite and sopping depressions of mosquito-infested mud. The trail from Baawitigong to Weashcog was well travelled but tended to be reclaimed by other creatures at night. She had no more desire to startle a wolverine than one of its giant cousins, and indeed, several times she heard the unmistakable crunch of larger, bolder creatures; too close to settle her nerves.

She smelled Wazhindoon's wigwam before she caught the glimpse of the white birch trail glowing in the moonlight. The midewikwe was burning something to smudge, something protective that reminded Suzette of runs gone bad; vigils for fallen runners. She entered the hut to find it dimly lit; just bright enough for the wide eyes of Dibaabishk and Wazhindoon to shine orange embers in her direction.

"You were right," Dibaabishk said by way of greeting. He stood, ill at ease, as Wazhindoon sat placidly nearby with a familiar disk of fire-coloured metal in her hands. A second clochemar.

"*I* was right," Wazhindoon put in. "You should never have made this thing."

"You were both right," Dibaabishk admitted, his habitual defensiveness absent. "I should never have made La Clochemar. And this—" He gestured at Wazhindoon. "We must destroy this."

"You made it? For the pale woman?" Suzette guessed, her heart sinking.

"La Comtesse Martine de Champchevrier, yes, I did. I had no choice!" he stressed. "She was there, always, and her master's swords. I tried to beg that my work was secret, to work alone, but I needed – that is, the pieces needed to be bonded. You were right," he sighed. "It's – a complicated process. But I needed access to the lives the clochemar was supposed to track. They had prisons. I was never alone there. Guards, swords, and always, her eyes and ears somewhere in the shadows." Dibaabishk stopped pacing and faced the wall. "Her 'bandits' – well. Corsicans, mostly. Mussulmen. Jews. If it is banditry to want to defend your villages and herds, your family and neighbours... No, you were right, Soo. I met men who hunt other men for sport, and now – now I have helped them."

"She doesn't have this clochemar yet, my friend," Wazhindoon said. "Break it on the anvil."

"She would never allow it. It is only because I told her some nonsense about requiring a midewikwe's blessing for the thing to work that she does not have it already. Even so, I am not sure she believes me. No, Soofoo, you must take it to Loowe, in secret—"

Suzette had begun to nod her assent when her keen ears heard the footsteps of someone outside the wigwam. She held up a hand for the others to fall silent and recognized the same bold gait she'd heard on her way here. Her heart fluttered when she realized her mistake. *I have been followed*, she tried to warn her friends with a look.

"Mr. Nebahahquahum," the pale woman said, striding into the hut calm as June in her dark blue wools the colour of night. It took Suzette three heartbeats to realize she was speaking to Dibaabishk. "You will not destroy anything. I have your money, and you have my map. I'm disappointed to find you are as sentimental as my masters feared." She appraised Wazhindoon, Suzette, and the room with a quick glance that displayed a well-seasoned talent for evaluating threats. Nothing in her body language indicated whether she took any of them for a credible one.

"I'm sorry, Madame, but I have changed my mind. I thank you and your masters for your hospitality, but I must decline to close on our arrangement. The clochemar will stay with me." Dibaabishk stood stiff as ice, like a creature about to bolt.

"No, it will not," the woman called Champchevrier replied. "One way or another, it will come with me. The simplest way is for you to honour our agreement."

Her contemptuous demeanour flared Suzette's anger, but Dibaabishk's eyes grew wide with fear. Wazhindoon climbed slowly to her feet and moved to her friend's side. "We will fight for the clochemar, strange woman," she said. "We do not fear your masters here. You've overextended your reach."

"Have I?" Champchevrier sighed, looking bored. Her hand dove into the folds of her skirts kingfisher-quick, drawing out her gleaming, silver prize: a pistol no bigger than a clochemar. Suzette gasped.

"You cannot fire that here," she blurted. "It will draw Mandimanidoo. You'll be killed. Put it away this instant!"

"We will, won't we?" the woman smiled, teeth yellow by the firelight. "Perhaps this whole village as well. That would be a shame. The map, if you please."

Dibaabishk reached out and took Wazhindoon's hand, the one holding the clochemar, in his own. He stared hard at Suzette. "No," he said, refusing to lose her gaze. "I will not allow you to conduct your conquests with my art."

"Idiot," Champchevrier said, shrugging. "You are nothing to me." She squeezed the trigger.

Smoke and sound filled the room in a fiery burst. Dibaabishk recoiled, hit, but remained standing. A moment later, a second shot caused him to crumple around the wet slick blossoming in his belly. He clutched Wazhindoon's hand, and the clochemar, to the wound. He held it there as he fell to his knees, unyielding as stone, even as Wazhindoon lowered him to the ground.

Champchevrier strode towards them and pointed her gun at Wazhindoon. "I will take the map now," she told her.

A terrible, familiar cry rang out through the night, drawing all their attention. Pamolai.

Suzette seized her moment. In the half-heartbeat Champchevrier looked away towards the smoke-hole Suzette threw herself at the other woman, laying her weight into her body as her hands took hold of the little gun. She pushed the muzzle back towards her face with her wrist in an iron grip until she felt one of Champchevrier's fingers pop. The woman's grip loosened for only one moment. Suzette wrested the weapon from her hands, sprang to her feet, and backed across the room with lightning speed, raising the gun in rage.

"Soofoo," Dibaabishk groaned. "No. Just run."

Suzette ran. She threw aside the door hangings and ran blindly into the night, eyes straining against the starry treetops for any shadow or shape that might be a waking monster.

There, blocking the thin sliver of the waxing moon, was the dread tower of feathers growing taller as their bearer stood straight. Pamolai, the Mountain's Anger, with her crown of feathers and horns, and her hatred for the people of the lakes.

Pamolai raised her equine muzzle to the stars and shrieked, as many as ten miles away. Far enough to ignore on a calm day, but right now bound directly for the gunfire she hated so much, and the town of Weashcog.

Suzette ran towards Pamolai barely armed and unprepared. She was not painted, but wore nonetheless the warm leathers of autumn that would protect her from the branches and boulders she could not see. She had no rifle, but neither had a thousand years of Anishinaabeg runners before the French had arrived and she had, at least, the little pistol. She had no partner, but she had the determination that comes with knowing nothing else will save your friends and neighbours if you do not. She could not read La Clochemar in the dark, but she found she had no desire to.

She knew this terrain well enough to know Pamolai must have been slumbering under the cliffs by Crooked Trout Lake, north and west of where she was. The area was spotted with hundreds of little lakes and swampy ponds, each as black and sudden as the last, but these broke up the forest and the sky, letting in enough starlight to guide her. She raced from shore to shore, never losing sight of her quarry. As Pamolai closed the space between them twice as quickly as Suzette could, she wet her lips and forced herself to breathe, for she would need every muscle of her lungs very soon.

Suzette ran until she was less than a mile from Pamolai. She stuttered to a stop on a flat rock next to a lake too small for a name, pointed the tiny gun at the sky, and fired.

The bird-crested beast slowed its stride as if taking notice, but did not turn. Suzette cocked the gun and fired again. How many bullets could such a little thing have? Surely, not many more.

Pamolai stopped and looked in her direction, eyes little lakes in their own right. Suzette stared back. Pamolai started towards her.

Suzette waited. Her training told her to run, now, while she still had a lead, but she could not risk losing Pamolai. For all she knew, the gun was barren already. She was lucky enough to have gained the monster's interest – now she needed to keep it.

Two hundred heartbeats was all it took for the creature to come so close, Suzette could feel the gusts of Pamolai's feathered arms pumping, the heat of her angry breath. She was too close to outrun, not with her stride of fifty feet and taste for human blood. The run had to end here.

Pamolai had nearly reached the clearing when Suzette leapt into the lake. The monster's great, taloned feet crushed the stones of the shoreline to sand as Suzette kicked water as hard as she could, flailing clumsily for the deep, impossibly cold heart. Pamolai's long, moose's face opened to reveal a forest of bladed teeth when she howled in anger, reaching out with a great feathered arm to pluck Suzette from the lake.

Suzette dove. She curled into a ball and let herself sink, letting the icy water weigh her down. She dropped into a niiyawaa state so deep that her held breath slipped from her lungs and her consciousness slipped under the folds of her mind. Unbreathing, unmoving, unthinking, she was still sinking when she forgot the world completely.

c   ⊕   c

Suzette woke up.

They had pulled her body, still and frozen, from the lake just a shade before dawn, almost a whole night since Pamolai had grown frustrated dredging the murky water and moved on, prey forgotten. Makoonse, her partner, and the others of her party had wept thinking her as dead as her body itself believed.

But the keen attention of Wazhindoon found her heartbeat, each thump an eternity from the next. Though there was little they could do about the blackening joints of her fingers and toes, little by little they coaxed her self out of its hiding place and returned her to the world. Nobody was more amazed than she when her eyes fluttered open, when her mind was unchanged.

"But, Dibaabishk?" she finally found the courage to ask. Wazhindoon's smile turned sad. Suzette looked away.

"It was for nothing, then. Champchevrier has the clochemar and I could not save Dibaabishk. Ooh," she moaned. "That you had left me at the bottom of the lake!"

"Hush, Soo, hush," Wazhindoon cooed. "It is not for nothing Dibaabishk spilt his life's blood," she murmured. "That clochemar won't work. Not for her purposes. It was forged anew in our friend's blood. It has his spirit now," she chuckled. "And where he has gone, even Manidoo-dibaigisisswaii cannot track him." Wazhindoon squeezed her shoulder as Suzette began to grieve.

Suzette did not run again. For some time, people of science arrived from Europe with coy questions on their tongues about pocket maps and blood-spirited metals, but, in her new capacity as interpreter to these folk, she had become a wall. La Clochemar had never existed.

And in the wilderness, a rough morning's travel north-west of Weashcog, was a lake they named Fooniiyawaa – Foolish Stillness. It was said to be a particularly good home to mosquitoes in summer, though legends persisted about a woman who once lay half-dead in its belly. Both were causes to give the place a wide berth, keeping well the other secret sleeping undisturbed at the lake's bottom: La Clochemar.

EAST WIND IN CARRALL STREET

HOLLY SCHOFIELD

Wong Shin pulled down on a lever, scraping his elbow against the metal framework within the clockwork lion. The lion obediently approached Margie where she stood in his family courtyard. Over and over, he made the lion step forward, then retreat, keeping a light hand on the crucial levers. When Margie shot a guilty look over her shoulder at the brothel behind her, Shin copied her glance, awkwardly peering upwards through the screening above the lion's broad nose. Margie's aunt was not at the second-storey window. He let out his breath. Fully four years older, he felt responsible that they not be seen together. Practice time was short so he gave all his attention back to the controls, completing the sequence of dance steps, as focused as if he were performing a traditional Chinese lion dance in front of his father's business associates rather than for the amusement of a ten-year-old White girl.

From his cramped spot behind the lion's eyes, he twisted a bamboo rod, snapping the lion's mouth open and closed, imagining the traditional drum beats. As cables tightened, a pulley triggered another line attached to the puffy silk balls mounted on the lion's papier-mâché face. He let the silk decorations waggle a bit then he pressed a ceramic spring-loaded button next to his knees, sending the clockwork lion's gears ratcheting noisily. As he pumped his legs in the iron stirrups, the lion's front feet followed suit, dancing a complex jig. Dust billowed up between the gaps in the stirrups, making him cough.

He pranced again toward Margie, his knees reaching up around his ears. "Go away, Mah-jee, go away!" he called out, laughing.

Margie giggled and twirled out of his way. "You mean run away! Or flee!" she called back, eager to improve his English, as always.

He chased her across the unkempt courtyard, picturing the layers of colourful cotton swaying behind him. This morning's improvements meant the lion's iron framework was now the length of a large horse – fully a dozen *chek* long. There was nothing like the clockwork lion in the city of Victoria's Chinatown, nor in British Columbia, nor perhaps in all of the Dominion of Canada – despite it being a complete sham.

Tomorrow, across Carrall Street at Teck Woo's new bakery, the drummers would play: at first, slow beats, then becoming gradually faster and faster. The crowds would yell encouragement and, as the excitement grew and the lion danced, Shin would snatch the all-important red envelope of money through the massive lion jaws. And no one would know that it wasn't a true clockwork lion.

Shadows crept up the brick wall of his father's grocery store as the afternoon wore on. A dial on the lion's interior panel indicated that the clockwork's energy coil was almost spent. Shin's arms and legs began to ache from the repeated motions in the confined space.

As he sashayed one more time across the yard toward Margie, making the ears wiggle and the beard shimmy, she looked past him toward the store and her eyes grew wide with fear. He stopped, in confusion, just as his father's voice rang out.

"Shin-Shin, neh jow mat yeh, wah?" Shin-Shin, what are you doing?

Shin laboriously turned the lion fully around to face his father, hoping the cotton-clad framework would shield Margie's escape. She would need time to climb the fence and his father blocked the only front exit that led between brick buildings out to Carrall Street.

"Doy em jee, Baba." I'm sorry, Father.

"Why are you practicing out here? The neighbours must not see!" His father's village-accented Cantonese harshened in displeasure.

"Sorry, Baba, the workshop floor is not big enough anymore for the full routine." Shin let the lion's knees sag, relieved that Baba hadn't caught sight of Margie; his father was simply worried that the clockwork lion would be seen by the neighbours. No one in Chinatown, aside from Shin and his father, knew that the boy steered the lion from within. In the two years since the lion had been completed, Shin's father had convinced the Chinatown businessmen's association that the lion was truly clockwork-run. The scale and complexity of such clockwork had been attempted without success since the start of the Qing Dynasty and his father had quickly grown famous. If the businessmen knew that this lion was controlled by a boy pulling levers, they would not pay the ten-dollar fee for an opening good-for-tune ceremony; instead they would hire Lee Chan and his brawny son to provide the two-dollar, man-powered version.

"Since you are already out here, practice the lettuce-retrieval ceremony. Grab that maple leaf up there." Shin's father pointed at the woodshed roof, cluttered with twigs and debris. "Balance your front legs on the old chicken coop."

"Yes, Baba." Shin steered the lion to the dilapidated wooden structure that hugged the woodshed. They hadn't had chickens since Mama had died during childbirth seven years ago. Now, thistles filled the coop, spilling out the top and sides through wire mesh. Shin pressed a lever to raise the lion's left foot onto the top corner of the rickety structure, praying to the earth god *Dabo Gong* that the chicken coop could withstand both the lion's and his weight. He knew he'd grown taller since Baba had designed the lion head when he was twelve – he was now up to Margie's shoulder – and he must have put on a few *catties* of weight too. He almost blurted out that this stunt would be more difficult than placing the lion's front legs on two pre-positioned barrels as he would tomorrow, but he bit the words back. Baba would know all that and have factored the risk, like men did. If it was fated to collapse, it would. Shin clamped his mouth shut, even as the huge lion foot made the top board creak. If he didn't attempt difficult things, Baba would never call him Ah Shin and treat him like the adult he was.

He eased his weight forward, the energy coil unwinding with a squeal. An indicator on the left panel said he had about ten *fan* of energy left – just enough to make the lion grab the large green leaf and drop down to kneel in front of Baba.

The chicken coop creaked again. Thistles rustled. Shin looked down between his leg stirrups. A wisp of blonde hair was caught among the thistles. More rustling and blue eyes peered up at him.

"Hurry up!" Baba's voice came from behind, near the grocery's rear door. His father must have stepped back, most likely expecting Shin to fail and fall. He hadn't seen Margie.

In the chicken coop, Margie's eyes filled with tears. The lion weighed as much as three men. If the chicken coop couldn't support its weight, it would surely crush her just as being born had crushed his little sister. The baby that was to be Shin's little sister had only lived a few days, not long enough to name.

Should he tell Baba that Margie was in the coop and save her life? She could run home. He glanced upward at the building behind. A woman with a mound of hair on her head stood at the brothel window, scanning the alleyway. His father would thrash him with a bamboo stick if he knew about Shin's friendship with Margie, but that was nothing compared to the beating Margie's aunt would give her for associating with filthy heathens such as himself.

Perhaps he could pretend to roll to one side, as if he wasn't in control? Surely the lion, made with his father's sturdy workmanship, could handle such a fall? But Shin would bring shame to his ancestors if the controls got smashed and were unable to function for tomorrow's ceremony.

Shin balanced on the left leg for so long, his thigh muscle trembled.

He heard his father hawk and spit on the ground in disgust at Shin's delay.

He couldn't crush Margie, he couldn't. Perhaps he could fall to the left, very slowly and gently, controlling the lion's iron spine. He raised the lion's right foot and placed it close, deliberately too close, to the left foot. He slowly eased the main lever upwards, arching the lion's spine, placing the centre of gravity slightly over the paws. Too much! The lion overbalanced and crashed forward. Shin quickly threw his body leftward. His head hit iron bars and the lion hit the ground. He closed his eyes for a moment until the dozens of sewn-on bells stopped jingling.

It was almost a relief when Baba, still swearing, opened the neck hinges so he could scramble out onto the dirt of the courtyard. The left side of the chicken coop was smashed to bits, loose boards dangling at all angles. Snapped cables littered the ground near the lion. The giant head was crushed and broken in several places. The far end of the chicken coop appeared undamaged but it was hard to tell.

He listened for the rustle of thistles as he helped Baba carry the broken pieces into the grocery-cum-workshop but heard only the inauspicious caw of a crow. He gave a final look back, the lion's bright horsehair tail dragging in the dust behind him, but there was nothing to be seen.

c   ◑   c

After a meal of rice and dried salmon, accompanied by unsellable black-edged greens, Shin crouched on the floor of the workroom. The lion head lay on a workbench and his father hunched over it, cursing loudly and slamming various hand tools around. The bakery opening would happen at first light. The almanac had been consulted and it was an auspicious day. The ceremony could not be delayed.

Shin's offers to help were ignored so he did his evening shop chores, including winding the springs on the little shop heaters needed to ward off the springtime chill. Shin's failure to do his duty to the family drummed through his head even as he took pride that his fingers no longer bled during the endless turning of the tiny keys. Small gadgets like the heaters could be human-wound, unlike larger coils that required teams of men trotting in circles, or oxen like the White Men used. The lion's clockworks were powered by a mid-sized coil and Baba had arranged delivery of a new pre-wound one at sunrise. The fee – a fifty-cent coin – gleamed under the oil lantern by the door.

Shin tinkered for a while with a clockwork monkey he had been working on for Margie. Over a period of months, he had taken apart an old tofu-maker and he had reassembled the sprockets and gears. He had shaped the framework from cedar, rather than the more traditional, and more expensive, bamboo. Daringly, he had travelled six blocks, his first foray outside Chinatown, giving his Spring Festival money to a dark-skinned Indian down by the stockade in exchange for a raw beaver pelt. After soaking the skin in an oak stump, he had softened it to a felt-like material that he thought might resemble monkey fur. He had crafted robes and a headband from scraps of Mama's dress that Baba had been using as a window covering. The shade of yellow matched the cover of Shin's proudest possession, a book of tales about the Monkey King's many journeys.

The rebuilt clockwork mechanism functioned well enough to make the monkey wave its hand; however, Shin wanted to do better. He took a used wax cylinder – its grooves blurred by overuse – and began to cut new and intricate lines with his pocketknife.

The day that Margie had shown him the White Men's wax cylinders had changed his life. She had snuck him into the whorehouse's laundry room to show him the shoe-polishing machine, thinking he would be impressed. Shin had opened the machine's repair hatch and been appalled at the White Man's crude and clumsy clockworks. "Like a beast would expel," he had told her. But, he had been fascinated with what had conveyed the wondrously precise instructions to the poorly engineered clockworks: wax cylinders, each grooved with a thousand tiny lines. Even the richest Chinese didn't have such marvels. When Margie had given him dozens of spent cylinders, he had clapped his hands in glee.

He put down the knife and opened a page in his second proudest possession, a programming manual that Margie had stolen for him last month. He had been explaining to her that the last new moon was the beginning of the Year of the Monkey and, later that day, she had brought him a slice of bread dripping with salt pork fat. She had some concept of birthing day anniversary gifts that made no sense to him. He had politely eaten the bread. Baba had told him many times that the diseases White Men got by drinking unboiled water and eating uncooked greens were many and complex, challenging even for Chinatown doctors and pharmacists. Shin had carefully watched his bowels for days but there appeared to be no ill effect from the treat.

He flipped a page in the book, looking for a certain coding sequence that would help the monkey move its tail in synchronization with its hands. Margie's aunt had boxed her ears soundly for the book theft but then covered for her, telling the irate customer it had been taken by one of the maids. Margie had spent hours teaching English numbers and coding symbols to Shin, as well as all the algebra and geometry she learned in the school for White children. In return, he had patiently drawn diagrams of simple clockworks on scraps of butcher paper, explaining them in his broken English, sitting cross-legged beside her in their favourite spot atop the greengrocery roof.

He tossed the monkey aside, not in the mood to work on it when all of his dreams were being dashed by his foolish actions. He watched Baba grapple with the broken lion as fresh waves of shame washed over him. Over the past few

months, the yin and yang synergy of elegant Chinese clockworks and White Men's wax cylinders had filled his thoughts.
Ideas had poured out of him faster than he could form the
English words to tell Margie: how wax cylinders could perhaps someday be used to guide abacus beads, making giant
calculating machines. When he was old enough to run Baba's
greengrocery, he would investigate such things in the
evenings, like men did, much as Baba tinkered nowadays with
clockworks.

"Come." Baba pointed at the bicycle in the corner. Shin
squeezed between crates of carrots and gear parts and
mounted the bike. The length from the seat to the pedals had
become too short for him. With a strong push, he started the
pedals turning, then settled into a fast, even pace. In front of
him, the lengthy bike chain spun and the friction welder
started up. His father grasped an iron rod with bamboo tongs
and pressed it in the collar of the welder. He touched the
lower end of the rod to an interior brace of the lion head,
which lay wedged in a vise below.

As Shin kept up a furious pace, the rod began turning fast
enough to blur. It would take a long while to heat enough to
form a proper weld. He let his thoughts drift. There was no
point in buying Margie *bao* or other pastries for her birth celebration, whenever it might occur; her calendar was too
strange to have much meaning. Plus, she had smilingly refused every piece of food he had ever offered her. The thought
of food made his stomach growl, empty again. As acrid smoke
swirled around him, he imagined the wonderful contents of
Teck Woo's market cart, soon to be a full-fledged bakery in a
new finely styled brick building across the street. Businesses
were springing up every day. White Men might refuse to hire
Chinese for even the worst jobs at Roger's Sugar Mill, but that

would not break the businessmen's spirits; the community would build their own new China here in the Dominion of Canada.

"Steady, Shin-Shin," Baba said, as the end of the rod began to glow a cheery red. By the time the sun had set and the automated oil lanterns clicked on, the many necessary welds were completed. Shin stepped down and dried his sweat on his too-short jacket sleeve. His stomach rumbled again. The store's income was not enough to live on; without the lion ceremony earnings they would be hungry next winter, like they had been before Baba had built the wonderful mechanism.

Coming to the "golden mountain" was to be a new start for the Wong family. Baba had come first, earning money labouring in the fields on the mainland to the east, paying off his head tax and landing fees. Years later, Mama had left her small village and travelled in what she had called "in fear and boredom," along with several other women in a large stinking ship. Both had worked hard at the greengrocer business as baby Shin played on the store's splintery wood floor amid clucking chickens and broccoli stems. His first toy had been a broken abacus. His second was a broken automated wok-stirrer he had first turned into a toy warrior, then a stick-like doll for Margie.

Margie's story was similar. Her mother had come from a mountainous place over the ocean to the east, where people slid on snow with boards tied on their feet. Margie wanted to be an architect, designing buildings like the new brick Driard Hotel where fine ladies drank tea. Meanwhile, she did kitchen duty at the brothel, saving up customers' tips for an architecture mail order course from the Simpson's catalogue. Once she had shown Shin a paint set a customer had given her. She had swirled powders together, yellow and blue. "That's like you and me, together we can make the Dominion of Canada better than either of the two alone." Shin had answered in his stumbling English that Canada was more like the many colours of vegetable fried noodles – a mixture of everything but a blend of nothing.

"Come. Try this." Baba's wiry body swung the lion head to the floor, not bothering with the hoist. Together they reattached the long body to the head in the cramped space, laying the drooping middle over some barrel staves at the rear of the shop and looping the legs and back feet towards the head by the big door at the front.

Shin swung his short queue over his shoulder to his front as he examined the rebuilt lion. It would be a tight fit. Baba had reinforced the head with more cross supports, threading iron rods past the leg braces to the back of the head. Shin hastily reattached the yellow cloth, sponging off the dirt from the yard, and brushing out the red and gold horsehair fringes while his father repositioned cable housings every which way. Baba was a competent craftsman, but Shin suddenly realized his designs were less elegant than the sturdy oxen White Men used to wind coils.

"You, east wind, get in." His father gave an impatient gesture and Shin got down on his knees beside the head, a second insight flooding into his head. His father's continual reference to the famous battle in China that depended on a late-arriving east wind – a wind crucial to the success of the fire ships being sailed toward the enemy – was not a compliment to Shin. Instead, his father was ashamed of their deception to the community and ashamed of the necessity of using Shin to operate the lion. Shin studied the stern line of his father's mouth. There was no time to dwell on the matter.

Shin bent his head so that Baba could lift the lion head over him. Bowing his head had not been necessary even three months ago. He must have grown a full *tsun* – a hand's breadth – since then. His wrists jutted out from his jacket as he helped lower the lion head over his own.

A gasp, a grunt, and the head – now probably weighing as much as Baba himself – came down hard on his thighs, cutting off all light but for a faint glow though the nose screen. One of the new iron rods crushed down on Shin's knees. He shoved a leg out the side of the head and under the huge rear paw on the side away from his father. He tucked his other foot under his buttocks, where it was useless to power the leg controls.

"Good, it works." In relief, Baba waggled one of the lion's silk balls, the connected bamboo handle striking Shin on the ear. "Now, get out. A short sleep is still possible."

Shin quickly tried various other positions as he clambered out from beneath, Baba holding the lion head aloft. In the poor light, Baba hadn't noticed Shin's struggles, how his legs stuck out. His failure.

Shin's mouth tasted like raw bitter melon.

He no longer fit inside the lion.

A small part of him thrilled at the thought that Baba's shameful fraud could not continue. He pushed the thought away. The red envelope money would go unearned. He had let down Baba and all Wong ancestors. And Teck Woo's bakery would forever have bad luck.

As his father climbed the narrow stairs heading to the sleeping mats, Shin stayed huddled on the cold dirt floor. He didn't deserve to sleep tonight.

c ⑴ c

The lion weaved and dodged, as graceful as bamboo in the wind. It danced closer to the barrels, surrounded by smiling, dark jacketed men who nodded with delight. Lucky green onions tied to its horns waved merrily. The drummers intensified the beat, luring the lion closer and closer to the leafy green lettuce hanging over the bakery doorstep and the red envelope tied within. The lion approached, cocked its head at the lettuce, put a foot on a barrel, then stepped off again, turning its head to wink coquettishly at the crowd.

A toddler emerged from between a man's legs and headed for the lion, probably attracted by the glittering metal discs sewn to the red and yellow layers of cloth. The lion continued to dance, oblivious, stepping forward and back in a tradition as old as gunpowder.

From his perch atop the greengrocery roof, Shin wrapped his arms around his bruised knees, the clay tiles cold under his thin slippers.

Finally, a woman scuttled from between the men and grabbed the child's arm, dragging it back into the crowd.

Shin let out his breath. The monkey's cylinder programming was set to a specific pattern. There was no altering it, for toddlers or anything else. He pictured the energy coil unwinding in the body of the lion, powering the mechanism even as the monkey pushed and pulled levers and switches in an intricate pattern; its hands and feet, even its tail, manipulating the lion in a dance more complex than a Chinese acrobatic display, all seven cylinders spinning madly. With wooden blocks tied to its feet and a wire hook embedded in its tail, the monkey had fit inside the lion perfectly. He had used the yellow robes to tie it securely to the framework.

"That's charming, that is." Margie settled beside him on the roof, tucking her green skirts immodestly under her. Her right arm hung in a sling made from a paisley scarf and a long scratch ran down one cheek.

"Therefore no birth present for you," Shin answered tensely, keeping his eyes on the lion.

Margie giggled. "I never understand you even when I understand you. Here, I brought you a present because you saved me. Don't worry – I waited until dark yesterday then I told my aunt I fell from a tree." She shoved a pastry in his hand, ruby and gold in the morning sun. "It's called rhubarb pie."

"Rhu-bah pie," Shin repeated absently and bit into it. He hadn't had time for rice porridge this morning and working hard all night had made his stomach hollow. Baked wheat flour and tart juice filled his mouth, sliding down as pleasantly as Teck Woo's sweet red bean *jian dui*.

The clockwork lion grabbed the lettuce in the final dance sequence, as the drumbeats grew staccato. From his vantage point above, Shin saw the small brown hand flash out and draw the red envelope inside the jaws. The crowd cheered, Baba loudest of all. For the first time since he'd seen Margie hiding in the chicken coop, Shin began to relax.

Finished, the lion lumbered back across the street, the crowd parting way. A grinding noise drifted up as the grocery's large workroom door opened, its escapement mechanism perfectly timed. The lion marched steadily toward the grocery as the door rose higher and higher. Several *chek* before the workroom entrance, the lion turned sharply to the right, stepped up onto the wooden sidewalk and rammed face-first into the grocery's brick wall.

"Ah Shin! Ah Shin!" Baba rushed toward the lion as it made a horrid grinding noise and the front legs collapsed.

On the roof above, Shin bit down on his knuckles. Baba's use of "Ah Shin" – the adult form of his name – shone through the awfulness of the crash.

Below, his father prodded the ruins of the lion. He gave a start then, just before the other men reached him, pulled off the yellow restraints and shoved the monkey beneath his jacket. He made calming gestures at the men and laughed with an open mouth. His words drifted upwards – assurances that the lion could be repaired. After all, he said, it was clock-work-run and the best technology in all the continents.

Shin licked blood off his knuckles, careful of the large blister on his hand – a result of winding the monkey's coil for many *fan* last night. He felt his chest swell with pride. Combining the White Man's cylinder technology with tradi-tional clockwork meant that the shameful deception of the lion could stop. And, equally importantly, his father saw him as a man.

He looked out over the rooftops as a gentle rain started. In the distance, Chinatown's clay tiles blurred together with the White Man's cedar shingles.

He grinned at Margie and crammed the rest of the pastry in his mouth. "Two countries, both east wind," he said, around oily crumbs, and laughed when she shook her head in confusion.

THE HARPOONIST

BRENT NICHOLS

Building factories was a lot more work than burning them.

Henry McClane grinned ruefully as he lifted a pine board from the wagon bed beside him, set it on a pile beside the wagon, and stepped back, wiping his brow. A kid half his age, eyes shining with enthusiasm, stepped in to take his place, and Henry got out of the way.

He'd been a woodsman once, able to run through the forest for hours in pursuit of a buck. Now he was puffing and panting after a couple of dozen boards. Still, the building would go up even if he wasn't much help. The sheer enthusiasm of the two dozen people around him was irresistible, and Henry found himself unable to sustain his usual irritable mood.

"This is going to be terrific," said a voice at his elbow, and he turned. Alice O'Reilly was spearheading the Cotton Cooperative project. She was a few years older than Henry, a solid, practical woman who worked harder than anyone Henry had ever met, and managed to be cheerful and enthusiastic the whole time. "Just think," she said. "Building our own jobs! A factory without bosses."

Sure, Henry thought. *She says that now. But who's in charge of construction, and who'll still be in charge when the factory is complete? Alice, that's who.* He couldn't object, though. Alice was a great boss.

Her eyes went to his right hand, and her voice softened. "Did you get that in a factory?"

He glanced at his twisted fingers and thought of French Murphy pushing his hand into the spinning gears of a cotton gin. "Yeah."

"We'll have proper safety equipment here," she said. "And no children, and no bloody fourteen-hour days."

He nodded. Gastown was filled with workers hurt or crippled by the ravenous machinery of the Industrial Revolution, and most people assumed he was just one more victim. Mostly, he let them.

"What were you?" she said.

He knew she meant, what position did he have in a factory. He wasn't about to say "wrecker," so he pretended to misunderstand. "I was a hunter and a trapper," he said. "Lived in the forest alone for years. Then I decided to try out life in the city." He held up his hand. "Now I can't use a bow any more, and I never did like guns. So I'm a city man now. There's no going back."

Alice nodded solemnly. Her spirit was too lively, though, to hold a sombre mood for long. She grinned. "Well, we'll find a place for you here. Build a place, if that's what it takes. That's what this is all about!" And she left his side, wading into a crowd of men and women, bawling commands and drawing order out of chaos.

Henry left her to it and walked over to lean against the boiler. They'd lugged the vast iron tank in first, and were putting the walls up around it. After that would come the machinery.

The crowd of people before him, unlikely partners in an unprecedented business venture, were about as motley a group as Henry ever expected to see side by side. Molly had organized one union after another until there wasn't a factory left in the city that would take her. Some of the others were former spinners and weavers, made redundant by automation. Likely they'd protested factories just like this one, or tried to burn one or two. Gotten themselves blacklisted, so they couldn't even change sides.

Now they'd bowed to the inevitable. As it was too late to go crawling to Joseph Cottonwood or Mike Tremblay for a job in an existing factory, they were stuck building their own.

He'd cursed people just like them, and fired a musket not too far over their heads, in his job as a factory night watchman. He'd stood shoulder to shoulder with people just like them, and egged them on to greater acts of violence, when French Murphy had hired him to get the Cordova Street factory shut down. He'd been ignored by people just like them after he betrayed French Murphy and found himself begging in the street, his hand a mangled mess.

Now he worked beside them. He swung a hammer until his fingers ached, then held boards steady while others did the nailing. They framed all four walls by sundown and left them splayed around the rectangular shape of the floor.

He hit the Blue Barnacle after sunset, hoping to find an old acquaintance and cadge a drink. It was a rough bar, the kind of place he intended to avoid once his new respectability took hold. In the meantime, it was just the sort of rat's nest he needed.

"Hank! As I live and breathe. I haven't seen you in ages."

Henry turned, hiding gritted teeth behind an affable smile. Archie Wigman was a petty crook and a two-penny con man, an irritating, whining little rat and good for nearly nothing, but he drank to excess and might not notice one pint more on his tab.

They clapped each other on the shoulder, and Archie glanced at Henry's hand with a grimace. "Heard about the paw, mate. Bad bit of luck, that."

Henry nodded. "That's life in Gastown."

"Too right." Archie gestured at a greasy table near the side wall. "You'll join me, of course? Us being old pals and all." They weren't old pals. Clearly, Archie wanted something. Henry smiled wider and sat down.

Leaning in close, Archie said, "You don't mind treating an old pal to a pint, do you? For old times?"

"Sorry, Archie. I'm skint."

"Ah, well, no matter. We'll stay a while and see who turns up. Maybe Frenchy'll come by. He's always good for a glass of something." His eyes went to Henry's twisted fingers. "Oh, sorry, mate. I forgot."

Henry waved the apology away. "Maybe his conscience will tweak him, and he'll buy us each a pint to ease his remorse."

That sent Archie into paroxysms of laughter, and Henry grinned in spite of himself. The idea of French Murphy feeling remorse was pretty funny.

When Archie had himself under control he leaned close and murmured, "Speaking of Frenchy, there might be a bit of coin in the wind, if you think he's not still sore." He looked at Henry's hand. "You're still alive, so he can't have been *too* put out."

Henry shrugged. "I disobeyed him. There was this girl trying to get shut of him. He sent me to the airship station to bring her back." He sighed, remembering the fear in her eyes when she saw him. "I gave her a fiver instead, and wished her good luck." He rubbed the scars on his hand. "Frenchy didn't really care. He just had to make an example of me."

"Cor!" Archie shook his head. "What'd you do a stupid thing like that for?"

There was no good answer for that question, not one that Archie would understand. Henry chuckled instead. "It was pretty stupid." He looked at his hand and felt the familiar wave of regret. It rose and then quickly faded, as it always did. His hand had hurt – it still hurt – but the look on that girl's face when she saw him? That had hurt more.

Archie shrugged, losing interest. He glanced left and right. "We've got a bit of a job on tonight. A torch job, and there's always room for another fella who's been around a bit."

Henry felt his stomach tighten. In the dark days when he couldn't find work he'd been both angry and desperate. He'd done ugly things for French Murphy, things that still haunted his sleep. A torch job meant burning some factory to the ground. It would look like the work of Luddites, but French Murphy probably had a client footing the bill. Another factory owner, most likely, getting rid of a competitor and stirring up resentment against the hated Luddites, all in one blow.

"It's a sweet little job," Archie continued. "The place is all wood. No brick. And the walls aren't even up yet. We're supposed to burn whatever will burn, and bash a hole in the boiler." He cackled. "Place will never open."

Henry's skin went cold. How many half-built wooden factories could there be in Gastown? He was willing to bet there was just the one.

"We're meeting behind Smith and Sons," Archie said. "Around midnight. Frenchy prob'ly won't be there. He's getting to be the fancy man these days. Likes to keep his hands clean." Archie made a rude gesture with his own filthy hands.

"So they'll likely take you on." His grin was mostly a leer. "I'll vouch for you. And you can buy me a pint, after, in exchange."

Before Henry could figure out how to reply, a barmaid stopped at their table. Archie ordered a couple of beers, she demanded cash up front, and a moment later the two men were in the street.

"Behind Smith's," Archie reminded him as they parted ways. "Around midnight."

"I'll remember," Henry said, and slouched into the darkness. His head was spinning, but he already knew there was nothing he could do. The communal factory would burn this night. The boards he'd laboured over would go up in flames, and the expensive boiler, brought in with such effort, would have to be hauled away and junked.

He thought about the police, but Gastown's solitary constable would be no match for one of French Murphy's mobs. He thought about rousing Alice and her people. They would fight to defend their new venture, he knew. But they'd be up against experienced skull-thumpers. The only person they had with experience at street violence was Henry.

"I can't do it," he muttered at the dark cobbles under his feet. Half the mob would know him by sight. If he fought alongside Alice they'd come after him later. They'd come to the little blue house on Wickham Street, and if they didn't find him at home, they'd vent their rage on Widow Cready and her daughter. That would be her reward for believing in Henry McClane and letting him stay when he didn't have the week's rent in advance. He imagined Widow Cready watching her house burn and knew that he couldn't get involved.

For a bad couple of minutes he even thought about going to the clandestine meeting behind Smith and Sons. If the factory was going to burn anyway, he might as well get paid, right?

He ran his fingertips over the scars that covered his right hand like a lace glove, and spat. "Be damned if I'll work for that bastard," he muttered. "Be damned."

He called on the town constable. He went with his collar up and his hat pulled low, slinking like a thief into the little storefront that doubled as an office for Gastown's one-man police force. As recently as nine months earlier, a lone constable had been perfectly adequate. The town was growing at an explosive rate, though, and the luckless man was now overwhelmed.

He was not in. A young woman dispensing patent medicines sighed and produced a notebook from under her cash register when Henry asked for the police.

"Name?"

"Er, John Smith."

"Right." She rolled her eyes. "What's it about?"

Henry gave her the details of the impending raid, including the meeting at the warehouse, and added, "Tell him not to go alone. This is a rough bunch."

He expected another eye roll, but the look she gave him was thoughtful, and it made him wish that less of his face was showing. As he walked out he heard a strange clicking noise. He glanced back, and saw the woman with one hand concealed under the front counter. The clicks continued, sounding remarkably like a telegraph set.

Bemused, he shrugged and headed out into the street.

Now that the ball was rolling he realized he couldn't stop. The constable might actually show up in time for the burning, and whatever happened to the man was on Henry's head. So he jogged to a boarding house near the construction site and banged on the door until a suspicious-looking woman let him in. Tenants were gathering at the top of the stairs by this time, and Alice came down to speak to him. He poured out the story, making it sound like something he'd overheard, and she marched off to get her bonnet.

By midnight eight people had gathered at the construction site, including Henry. There was no sign of the constable. Alice unlocked the tool shed and passed around hammers and crowbars. He took a framing hammer, the leather-wrapped handle slick against the scars on his hand.

The nearest streetlight was well down the block, and Henry moved to the far side of the group, keeping himself in their shadow. The minutes crawled past, and then a mutter of voices rose in the distance. Henry could make out a flicker of torchlight on the walls of the row houses several blocks away.

The mob was coming.

There were a dozen men in the group, half of them carrying torches. They wore bandanas over their faces. Henry knew Archie by his greasy coat and slinking, furtive movements. The others were just anonymous shapes.

"Good idea," Henry muttered, and took out his handkerchief. It wasn't quite large enough, and by the time he got it tied his nose was mashed to the side. Some of the closer workers gave him curious looks, and he shrugged.

"Clear out!" shouted a man at the head of the mob. "Move on and no one gets hurt."

"Oh, someone's getting hurt, all right," said Alice, shouldering a board almost four feet long. "Someone's getting hurt very badly indeed."

The approaching mob didn't slow down, but the torches wobbled as men pulled weapons out from under their coats.

Henry saw chunks of pipe and lengths of chain, blackjacks and brass knuckles.

This was going to be ugly.

A fearful muttering rose from the little knot of workers, but they were drowned out by Alice's rising voice. "You think you can take a livelihood away from honest working people!" Her voice echoed from the buildings around them. "Well, not tonight. Tonight we protect what's ours!"

The muttering fell silent, men and women squaring their shoulders, exchanging nervous glances but standing firm. Henry groaned. She was going to get someone killed.

He looked past his friends to the approaching men and tried to gauge how much damage he could do before he went down. Archie was of no consequence. He'd slink away as soon as the fighting grew hot. The big-bellied man who had told them to clear out – he would be Henry's first target. If someone struck down the leader, and did it with enough brutality, the rest might break and run.

"We don't have nothing to worry about," Alice said, her voice reflecting an unshakable confidence. "When they see we won't be frightened, they'll scatter like rabbits."

Henry didn't know if she believed it. He only knew that her implacable will was keeping the group together, and that blood would flow in the street tonight.

The two groups were a dozen paces apart, the masked men looking confident and unstoppable and utterly ruthless, when the blast of a steam whistle froze them in their tracks. They turned, gaping in confusion, and Henry heard the rumble of wheels on cobblestones. There was no corresponding clatter of hooves or jingle of harness, so he wasn't surprised when a steam-powered wagon rounded the corner. It was a blocky machine with a glass window in front, a shadowy figure just visible at the controls. The back of the wagon was a big enclosed box. The machine rolled forward, moving at the pace of a sprinting man, and clattered to a halt beside the gap between Alice's crew and the mob.

"It's the Justice Wagon."

Henry wasn't sure who had spoken, but people stiffened in both groups. He'd dismissed tales of the Justice Wagon as the worst sort of sensational journalism, entertainment for the gullible masses. Could it be real?

A moment later he had his answer. A slim figure in a long black coat and a leather mask slid from the front of the wagon, and a door at the back of the wagon crashed open, tipping down to form a ramp. The wagon rocked from side to side, and a huge mechanical shape came lumbering down the ramp.

"Get 'em before they're ready," cried the thick-bellied man, and took a single step forward. The slim figure in the dark coat moved with impossible speed, a foot lashed out, and the leader of the mob staggered back into the arms of his followers. He hung in their grasp, red-faced, his mouth opening and closing as he fought to breathe.

"It's Typhoon," someone said, and Henry remembered the stories. Typhoon was worth ten men in a fight. They said he could dodge bullets and put a fist through a brick wall. That was absurd, of course, but the truth was still pretty amazing.

Henry felt the ground tremble as the mechanical shape came trudging around to stand beside Typhoon. That would be Crusher, the man in the steam-powered suit that could lift a thousand pounds. The suit was a gleaming marvel of brass and steel, with articulated arms and legs and pincher-like hands. A perforated grill covered the face of the man inside.

"Disperse," rumbled a bass voice from inside the suit. "Go home or face the consequences."

The thick-bellied man regained his feet, one hand pressed to his stomach. He wore a look of murderous rage, and he wormed himself backward, putting several of his men between him and Typhoon.

Then he drew a nickel-plated revolver from under his coat.

Henry bellowed and charged, pushing his way past his friends, and hurled himself at the man with the gun. Men clutched at him, he drove a fist into a masked face, and a swinging chain curled around his left forearm. He used his right hand to throw the hammer he was carrying, and it caught the gunman on the side of the head.

Men shouted, a woman screamed, and metal clashed against metal. Henry didn't see the blow that hit him, he just felt an explosion of pain above his ear. The world lurched around him, and when he became fully aware again he was lying on his back with a cluster of worried faces peering down at him.

Half a dozen torches lay sputtering in the street. The Justice Wagon was gone, and the mob had scattered. The battle was over.

For now.

The others applauded when Henry climbed to his feet. He was the most serious casualty. Alice had a black eye, and a young man had a bleeding nose and a line of welts across his face where a chain had struck him. He wore his bruises like a badge of honour. All of them were chattering excitedly, flushed with the thrill of victory.

It's not over, Henry thought. But he kept the thought to himself as he slipped out of the group and headed home. His handkerchief was gone, and there was no discreet way to ask if any of the gang had seen his face. It was a relief to find the little blue house standing quiet and intact, and he breathed a prayer of thanks as he let himself inside. French Murphy might still take a terrible revenge, but for now Widow Cready and her daughter were safe.

He was exhausted, but he lay awake reliving the battle. It should've gone much worse. Only the intervention of two masked fools had saved them all from disaster. Henry was intensely curious about Crusher and Typhoon. They were remarkably effective together, like a hammer and an anvil, but they were vulnerable to gunfire. Oh, Typhoon could dodge the shots, and Crusher could deflect them, but the innocent people they were trying to protect could be gunned down before the two heroes could react.

What they needed, Henry reflected, was a ranged weapon. He fell asleep dreaming of joining them, wearing a mask and using a bow to round out their defences.

c   ⦿   c

The next morning, he dropped a knife while spreading jam on a slice of toast. It was a bitter reminder that his twisted fingers would never hold a bowstring again. He was good for stacking lumber and busting heads, and that was about it. He left the house in a sour mood and headed for the factory site to see if it had burned yet.

He found most of the crew already there, getting ready to raise the walls. Alice's shiner had blackened and spread into a magnificent blossom that covered a quarter of her face. If it bothered her, he couldn't tell by looking at her. She was as indomitable as always.

When she saw Henry, she said, "I want you to put in a short day today. Take a nap in the afternoon. You're our new night watchman." She handed him a familiar-looking nickel-plated revolver. "Pick up some ammunition for this. It probably needs a good cleaning, too. I don't think that oaf took very good care of it." She grinned. "If they keep dropping guns for us, we'll have quite an arsenal soon."

He bought a pouch of lead bullets, some powder, and a box of percussion caps, and hiked to the outskirts of the city. He fired off half a dozen practice rounds, wincing at the noise the gun made, and reloaded. His aim was bad, the gun felt clumsy in his hand, and reloading took forever. Being on the edge of the forest reminded him of the life he had given up, and he was in a bleak mood by the time he returned home. The night was going to be cold, lonely, and dull. Until French Murphy's men came back and finished him off.

He wasn't looking forward to it.

c   (l)   c

Three days later he was almost resigned to his new position. He was finally able to sleep during the day, so he no longer spent the nights yawning. The factory building had a roof, and there was a little wood stove big enough to keep the office at the end of the building warm. That took care of his creature comforts. He prowled the factory floor, looking for a cure to his boredom.

He found a machine shop. There were lathes and bending machines and cutters, everything you would need to repair or create a tool for the mill's machines. He strolled up and down, thinking of the possibilities, thinking about what a man could do if he'd didn't like guns and couldn't use a bow.

When he arrived the next night, the stove was cold and there was a fire banked in the boiler. "Keep it warm, please,"

Alice told him as she left. "We need the gears turning tomorrow while we set up the Ginny."

By midnight he was standing in a pile of brass shavings watching a steam-powered harpoon launcher take shape.

Over the course of the next week he constructed his weapon. The first design, a brass tube with a hole down the centre for a harpoon, was a dismal failure. It would lob a three-foot wooden spear slightly farther than he could throw it, at which point the pressurized air in the cylinder was exhausted. He finally settled on a brass tank that he wore strapped to his back. The factory boiler had the power to compress air to the point where he feared the tank would explode. A rubber hose connected the tank to a hand-held launcher that fired a harpoon with enough force that the harpoon shattered when he fired it into the side of the boiler. The tank held enough pressure for a dozen good shots.

He had some ideas for a backup launcher, a spring-powered device that he could reset by cranking. It would need to be reset after every shot, but it would never run out of air. Before he could work out the details, though, fate caught up with him in the form of another raid.

The attack took place just after sunset. The target this time was a sawmill a couple of streets over. Henry heard shouts and screams in the distance, and he weighed his options, then ran to get his things. He had a dark coat, reinforced on the shoulders and elbows and along the forearms, and a cloth mask that covered his entire head. He strapped the tank to his back, shoved harpoons into the quivers on either side, and set off at a run.

The mill was on fire by the time he arrived. There was a canal close by, and dark figures lurched back and forth near the water's edge. Men cast giant shadows as they fought around the bulk of a pump beside the canal. Not satisfied with torching the building, the gang was trying to stop the gathering crowd from fighting the fire.

The mob was smaller this time, but the quality seemed to be higher. There was no Archie, no cowardly wharf rats. Six or eight men, brawny figures with determination in every line of their bodies, formed a ring around the pump and held back a belligerent crowd of locals. One man kept the mob together – a tall, broad-shouldered figure in a long dark coat and a white mask. The mask glowed in the light of the burning mill, giving the man an unearthly look that lifted the hairs on the back of Henry's neck.

"French Murphy," he muttered. "You bastard. It's time for you to pay your tab." He flexed the fingers of his mangled right hand and charged into the fray.

The harpoon launcher, he was dismayed to learn, was impossible to use with a crowd of civilians in the way. He shoved his way through the crowd, and when he reached the front he used the launcher as a bludgeon, clubbing down the first masked thug he saw. He could see the bulk of French Murphy a dozen paces away, just one masked figure in the way, and Henry started toward him, lifting the harpoon launcher in his hands, snarling under his cloth hood.

A rustle of movement behind him and a grunt of effort were the only warnings he got. Pain exploded through the back of his head, he felt cool grass against his hands, the world spun around him in a kaleidoscope of fractured colours, and then a blast of cold water snapped him back to full consciousness.

Water filled his mouth and coughs shook his body as dirty water trickled into his lungs. He squirmed and thrashed, arms flailing, utterly disoriented. He was on his back, submerged in dirty water, the surface a pale curtain above him. He tried to rise, to turn, but the weight of the canister on his back held him pinned. His fingers, clumsy in the cold water, went to the straps across his chest.

He couldn't budge them.

The urge to breathe was overwhelming. He pressed his lips together, fighting a rising panic, his whole body convulsing with the need to inhale. Then the surface exploded into ripples as something splashed into the water. He saw legs beside him, then a pair of strong brown arms. A moment later his head broke the surface.

He was in the canal, with Typhoon standing over him, holding his head and shoulders above the surface. The water was barely past waist-deep, and Henry soon got his feet under him. With Typhoon's help he trudged up the bank and onto dry ground.

Crusher stood with steel hands planted on vast metal hips, watching the last of the mob disperse. A crowd of people worked the water pump while others played a hose over the wall of the mill. The fire was nearly out.

"Come to Justice Wagon," Typhoon murmured into Henry's ear. "We need to talk."

c ⬥ c

"That should do it," Dan Carter said. Without the steam-powered suit he was an unassuming middle-aged man confined to a wheelchair. His body was strangely out of proportion, with broad shoulders and a thick chest that didn't go with his withered, stick-like legs. "Now you've got something for close-range fighting."

Henry looked down at his hands. He wore black leather gloves with copper disks attached to the palms. There was a

capacitor strapped over his heart, able to hold enough charge
to knock a man off of his feet. He could insert a hand crank
into the capacitor to recharge it.

"I talked it over with Wu," Carter said. Wu Lee was
Typhoon's real name. Or perhaps it was Lee Wu. Henry still
didn't have it quite straight.

"We think now is the time to go after this French Murphy
character you told us about." He glanced out the window of
his sprawling, extravagant house, where dawn was lightening
the sky. "He'll be in bed. Sound asleep, if we're lucky. But
honest citizens will be off of the street and out of harm's way."
Carter stretched and yawned. "What do you think? Are you
ready for another dust-up?"

Henry flexed his fingers in the leather gloves and checked
that the capacitor switch was open. It was safe to touch things
until the switch was closed. "I'm ready," he said. "God only
knows what Murphy will get up to if we give him another
day."

"Splendid." Carter moved his hands to the wheels of the
chair. "I'll need you to help me into the suit. We can do it on
the road. Wu will drive."

c ⑴ c

They hit Murphy's house at six in the morning. Henry's job
was to cover the back door, and he crouched in the garden
with a harpoon gun in his hands, listening to the crash of
wood as Crusher demolished the front door. Henry heard
loud cries and sounds of breaking furniture, then a stealthy
metallic rasp as a window on the back of the house slid open.
A freckled leg appeared on the sill, and a bulky form came
sliding out. A dirty yellow nightshirt covered the man, and
Henry smiled to himself as he took careful aim.

The harpoon missed the inside of French Murphy's leg by a couple of inches, punching through a loose flap of nightshirt between his thighs and sinking into the wall of the house. Murphy, in the middle of dropping out the window, had to clutch the windowsill and balance on one leg, the other leg resting on the shaft of the harpoon. He reached down to tear at the hem of his nightshirt.

"I wouldn't do that, Murph," Henry said, making his voice low and gravelly to disguise it. "I have more harpoons."

The gangster gave him a red-faced glare over one beefy shoulder. The back door swung open, Typhoon stepped out, and Murphy grabbed the windowsill in both hands. His nightshirt tore as he sprang back into the house.

Three gunshots rang out. By the time Henry made it to the window it was over. French Murphy lay sprawled on his kitchen floor, a small hole in the fabric over his heart. There was a pistol in his hand and an expression of startled dismay on his face. His legs were twitching, and they went still as Henry watched.

Typhoon stepped into the room. "What happen?"

"He caught a bad ricochet," Crusher said. "Damned fool. Let's get out of here."

C ◌ C

When Henry showed up for work that evening he was expecting a quiet shift. Alice greeted him with a cheerful smile. "We may not need you much longer, Henry," she said. "Things are changing in this town. Look, we've put in an alarm bell." She gestured at the wall of the mill. "Haul on that rope if there's any trouble."

Henry gave the rope a dubious glance. "All right…"

"Don't worry," she said, "someone will come. Things are changing, I tell you. The mayor called an emergency meeting this morning. They're putting together a task force to deal with these mobs. His Worship has decided that enough's enough." She grinned. "About time, too. We've been spreading the word in the neighbourhood. There'll be a bell like this in every mill in Gastown by the end of the week. You ring it and half the neighbourhood will come running. And if you hear a bell from some other mill, wherever you are, you go running too. Right?"

"Uh, right."

She clapped him on the shoulder. "Good man. There's talk of incorporating Gastown as a city, and getting a proper police department. The mobs won't be running things for much longer, you mark my words."

c   (1)   c

He was tinkering with the capacitor weapon an hour later when a voice from outside the mill made him look up. Shadows moved on the wall in front of him, and he stiffened. Either a bird had flown in front of the nearest streetlight, or there was someone outside with a lantern.

Henry ran to the window and peered outside. And swore. Torches flickered in the hands of a small crowd outside.

He pulled on the long coat, strapped on the pressurized tank, and hurried for the door, pulling his mask on as he went. The capacitor, due to his tinkering, was discharged. He'd have to rely on harpoons and the strength of his arms. He thought about the bell. If he rang the thing, the Harpoonist would have to explain the absence of Henry McClane, night watchman.

He shrugged. So be it. Shutting down the mob once and for all had to take priority.

A kick sent the door flying open, and he stepped outside. And froze, superstitious terror sending icy fingers across his skin.

It was French Murphy, surrounded by four of his hired thugs.

"No..." Henry shook his head. What he was seeing wasn't French Murphy. It was simply a big man with a white mask. There was no magic here, no wizardry. Just a bully who was about to get a bloody nose.

He headed along the wall of the mill, and one of the torch-bearers raised a pointing arm. All five men came toward him as Henry reached the bell. He hauled on the dangling rope, heard the bell peal loud across the dark neighbourhood, and then he let go of the rope and turned his attention to the harpoon launcher in his hands.

The closest man was a dozen paces away when a thick wooden harpoon with a blunt end caught him in the pit of the stomach. He folded up with a hoarse grunt and Henry shoved another blunt-tipped missile into the launcher. The next man was no more than half a dozen paces away when Henry fired again. The man threw a hand up to protect himself, and the harpoon broke two of his fingers without slowing. The missile slammed into the man's rib cage with an echoing sound that was as startling as it was horrible, and the man screamed as he doubled over.

One man threw down his torch and ran. The remaining thug froze, and the big man in the white mask grabbed him by the shoulder of his coat. "Come on! We can finish this!"

Henry, his eyes on the men, grabbled blindly for another harpoon. He could feel that this missile was smaller, a slender steel shaft with a barbed metal tip. He raised the launcher, took aim at the big man's chest, then lowered the muzzle of the launcher and fired.

The barb tore through the big man's foot and pinned him to the ground. He screamed, and the thug beside him took off running. There were people gathering between the buildings, women with lanterns, men with cricket bats and hammers, and the running man circled wide around them, throwing down his torch.

For a time there was a confused crowd jumbled together on the lawn and street in front of the mill. No one seemed to know quite what to do. A thug with a bandana over his mouth and nose rose gingerly from the grass, pressing a hand to his ribs. Henry stepped forward, raising the harpoon launcher like a club, and the man shrank back down.

Alice pushed her way through the crowd, and order formed from chaos in her wake. She marched up to Henry, looked him up and down, then turned to the tall man in the white mask. He was moaning, stooped over, hands clutching his leg. It made him short enough that she could drag the mask from his face.

The man was in his fifties, with white hair and a craggy face that looked aristocratic and severe through the pain. Henry had never seen him before, but Alice gasped. "Joseph Cottonwood! You miserable bastard! You mean that's what all this has been about? You wanted to shut down your competition?"

Beside Cottonwood a dark shape moved in the shadows, and Alice pounced. The man Henry had shot in the stomach was trying to crawl into the darkness, and Alice booted him in the ribs, then hauled him back by the collar and dumped him beside Cottonwood's feet. "You're not going anywhere."

A whistle blew in the distance, a sure sign that the constable was on his way, and Henry edged back from the crowd. He reached the wall of the mill and set off at a brisk pace, heading for the nearest corner and the chance to disappear.

Alice caught up with him just around the corner. "Henry?" she said. "It's you, isn't it? What in Hell are you playing at?"

"Keep it down," he muttered. "And keep it to yourself."

She planted hands on her hips. "Are you barmy?"

Henry shook his head. "So long as the mysterious masked Harpoonist is behind this, no one's going to come after Henry McClane, or Alice O'Reilly."

She scowled up at him. "I can take care of myself."

"Sure," he said. "And when they burn your boarding house down around your ears, and some of the people make it out alive, and some don't?"

The scowl slowly faded.

"You don't know who the Harpoonist is," he said. "The Harpoonist did this, and then he faded into the night. Understand?"

Slowly, reluctantly, she nodded.

"Now boost me through a window," he said. "I need to get out of this outfit."

When her fingers were laced together and he was scrabbling for the sill of a window she grunted and said, "Will you still work for the mill? Or will there be more of this masked crime fighter business?"

He got the window open and hooked a leg over the sill, taking the weight off of her hands. "I don't know," he admitted. "Maybe when Gastown is a city there won't be any more need for people like me." He thought of Crusher and Typhoon and their lonely crusade. "People like us." He shook his head. "I've got a feeling, though, that crime will just get worse."

"It doesn't mean you have to do something about it," she pointed out.

He looked down at his right hand, the scars hidden by the glove. It felt good to be the Harpoonist. To hold back a mob. To look past his bitterness and self-pity for a change. To do what was right. There was no way to tell Alice how he felt. What could he say? That he'd saved more than a mill tonight? That he'd saved himself? He didn't need her laughing in his face.

"I'd like to just work at the mill in peace," he told her, and it was largely true. "But if the city needs me, I'll answer the call." And he dropped inside and closed the window.

CREW 255

CLAIRE HUMPHREY

Emiliana's first sight of Toronto was the crater. No longer smoking, ten days after the wreck, but ash still drifted like fine snow in the draft of the airship's propellers. Emiliana saw the ghostly foundations of some of the buildings that had been – or maybe the curbs of streets – straight lines here and there laid bare amid the rubble and the windblown char.

"Our boys on the ground have moved a thousand train-loads of brick already," said the young man in the next seat over; he was called Manuel, unofficial leader of a dozen fellows from the same Azorean village. "I was worried they wouldn't leave us any," he added, and all his lads laughed and elbowed each other.

They were squeezed onto narrow fold-down bench seats, butted right up against the inner curve of the airship's passenger compartment, these dozen wide-shouldered lads, their heads ducked uncomfortably or hooked over each other's shoulders like they were all puppies from the same litter. Emiliana, at the end of the row, looked down at all the heads of dark hair and all the square, tanned hands – not a single hook or grasper among them.

"My friends," she said, "there is always more labour."

No one answered her. Eyes flicked down and away; heads tilted awkwardly. A minute or so later someone made a joke

Emiliana's altitude-dull ears could not pick up, and the lads went back to shoving at each other, or yawning hugely to relieve the pressure in their heads.

Emiliana caught a gangly fellow looking at her, and she smiled and then yawned in sympathy, but he only flushed pink and pretended he had not seen.

When the airship moored at a station north of the crater, the young men jammed shoulder to shoulder in their hurry to get to the ladder, not looking back.

Emiliana offered to carry Manuel's luggage for him. He refused her politely enough, but she saw the downward flash of his eyes toward her graspers, the whitening of his knuckles as he clung to the canvas strap of his bag. He hefted it over one shoulder, turning away already. The fine muscles of his forearm pulled taut beneath the skin.

Emiliana lifted her own carpetbag, hearing the winding of gears and the hum of wire beneath the leather of her arm as her right grasper clung to the handle. Her left steadied her, grappled to one of the cables criss-crossing the inner wall, as the airship rocked gently against its moorings.

Her arms were more than a decade old now; they needed oiling each night, and the brass was scarred bright here and there with the scratches of heavy work, just as the boys' hands showed the white scars of fishing accidents. They were not so different. Time left marks on metal just as on flesh.

As Emiliana descended the ladder, though, she felt the ache of the bones within her knees, and the swelling that came and went about her ankles. And her graspers, painlessly locking and unlocking on the rungs, bearing most of her weight.

She gained the solid platform, and followed the young men out of the wind, into the station tower, and down a few narrow stairs. She caught up again at the end of a queue before a red-hatted immigration official: he was stamping papers busily, with the same crest that had decorated the airship's curved flank, a Union Jack surmounted by a red leaf.

"How many in your party?" he asked Manuel. "Are you all together?"

"Everyone except her," Manuel replied, as if he did not even know Emiliana's name; maybe he had forgotten it already, although she had told him only that morning.

Emiliana waited until the herd of young men had stampeded out into their new country. She had her papers stamped alone by the official whose pale gaze lingered on her arms. He slid the packet back across the counter to her and said, unsmiling, "Welcome to the Canadian Territories, Miss Da Silva. Proceed through the gates."

c   ⊙   c

The young men sat shoulder to shoulder on the tram exactly as they had on the airship, jostling, giggling. None of them looked at Emiliana when she boarded. She took the last seat, right behind the driver, who nodded, and did not meet Emiliana's eyes.

She dropped her bag between her feet and used one of her graspers to poke at the ever-present ache in her lower back. The tram rang its bell and belched out a gust of steam and rumbled off southward down twin steel tracks. Over the driver's shoulder, Emiliana could see the clinging pall of ash and smoke over the heart of the city, shrouding the pale sun.

Their boarding house turned out to be in the west end, in a grid of streets where each block was a solid row. The roofs were lower, the lots narrower, than the others the tram had passed. Chimneys clustered together in threes and fours.

"Oldest gets dibs on the best bed," Manuel called out to a chorus of groans. The youngest-looking one on the tram, a raw-boned boy with lips too soft for his face, theatrically covered his eyes and said it was just like living with his sisters. No one laughed.

The tram stopped on a corner where the tracks curved lakeward, and everyone piled out, slinging cases to each other. Emiliana grabbed a trunk before anyone could stop her, passed it out to the nearest lad and bit back a smile when he staggered under the weight.

The boarding house had four bedrooms, each with several cots. Manuel bulled his way into the largest, and tossed his kit on the cot by the window.

Emiliana followed him in, puffing a little from the steep stairs, her own carpetbag clutched in one of her graspers. She deposited her bag on the window cot, plucked up Manuel's and set it on the floor nearby.

He was staring at her, mouth open, looking not so much angry as utterly bemused.

"Oldest gets dibs on the best bed," Emiliana said.

Manuel grabbed up his kit bag from the floor. For a moment Emiliana wasn't sure where he was going to put it.

"I didn't realize you were with us," he said finally, face stiff. "Of course you should have the best bed, ma'am."

He turned and left, taking his bag with him.

Emiliana sat down on her cot, kicked her feet out of her elastic-sided boots and rotated her stiff ankles. Her stockings were torn again; her graspers didn't have the smoothness of hands. She rooted through her carpetbag for her ancient sheepskin slippers.

As she was bending stiffly to put them on, the raw-boned lad came in, sidling along the hallway, ducking his head as if to hide his height.

He glanced at Emiliana, eyes half-hidden by his unruly hair, and placed his case – a kicked-in, rotted leather suitcase – on the smallest of the room's cots, closest to the door. Then he disappeared again.

At sundown, when Emiliana returned from a solitary dinner at the nearest public house, the bedroom's wood stove had a log in it, but the other two cots were still empty.

C ◑ C

Morning in Toronto, late March, proved to be blisteringly cold. A tram took the crew downtown, over roads white with ash and the remnants of winter's salt. Emiliana saw some of the young men tucking their fingertips into their armpits or blowing steaming breaths over them; her own graspers didn't have feeling, but she could see the brass dulled over with frost, could sense the stiffness to the mechanisms as their oil congealed.

The factories along the lakeshore sent up billowing towers of smoke into the clear cold sky. Emiliana had no idea what they were making, or who was working in them now, with so many of the working folk committed to the massive rebuilding of the downtown.

The airship crash, so she had heard, was the largest to occur in the world. Two zeppelins, each with a hydrogen capacity of sixty thousand cubic metres, had become entangled while trying to dock in high winds. One had collided with the mooring mast and caught fire; the other had nearly freed itself, but was set on fire by the explosion of the first.

The first had been a passenger ship; fifty civilians had been aboard, all killed.

The second, though, had been carrying explosives. Each of the rival newspapers had a different story, the bartender at the public house had another, and the charwoman at the boarding house still another: civilian explosives destined for the Sudbury mines; Allied munitions en route to the depot at Downsview; some kind of contraband shipped under a faked manifest destined for an enemy strike on New York.

Casimiro – the young man who was the only one either brave enough or unimportant enough to share Emiliana's room – thought it was not explosives at all, but some new and fearsome fuel, something that would give airships the run of the globe if it could be made less volatile.

Up close, it all became irrelevant. The crater had looked much deeper from the air, but it looked much wider from the ground. Churches, banks, office buildings, and a brand-new department store: how many million bricks had been thrown down by the blast? How many square metres of construction laid waste, how many beams and trusses shattered, how many windows blown to shards?

How many people were still missing?

Casimiro didn't know that one, and Emiliana didn't press him.

Their tram stopped a good half-mile from the epicentre, and they walked from there to a command post where they were issued lunch bags and heavy leather gloves.

"No, thank you," Emiliana said, brandishing her graspers, which were pincer-shaped, lacking the complex fingers of a fleshly hand.

"You want mittens instead?" the quartermaster asked cheerfully. She was a woman maybe the same age as Emiliana, round-faced and fat. She didn't wait for an answer, just hauled a pair of scorched leather mitts out of one of her bins and handed them over. They were shiny and stiff with use, bigger than Emiliana's graspers needed. Emiliana slipped them on anyway, an extra layer between the world and the most delicate bits of her metalwork.

"Which one of you wants to be foreman?" the quartermaster said.

Manuel stepped forward, shouldering in front of Emiliana even though she had not moved.

When no one objected, the quartermaster tossed Manuel a whistle and a timepiece, and said, "You're Crew 255. You'll be clearing rubble. Wait by the yellow flag and someone will come fetch you."

So they waited by the yellow flag. Some of the lads stood flush up against each other for warmth, chest to back. Not Emiliana. Not Casimiro, who seemed to have been elected keeper of everyone else's belongings, and stood alone over a heap of lunch bags.

Other crews gathered, too, in eights or twelves, many of them bearing resemblance to each other in the same way Crew 255 did: people from the same village or county, people from the same extended family. Emiliana saw two others with mechanical limbs – one a very young man with a grasper like her own for his left arm, and one a severe-looking fellow with both legs brass from the thighs down. This man stood a half-head above the rest of his crew, and Emiliana wondered if he had been so tall on his old legs too. She thought so, from the length of his arms and torso. While she was measuring him with her eyes, he happened to look over and he scowled; the scowl leavened a bit, though, when Emiliana drew off one mitten to give him a wave.

Her attention was shattered a moment later by Manuel's whistle-blast, completely unnecessary and right beside her ear.

"Crew 255!" he bellowed. "We have our work order. Follow me."

And Emiliana followed, all the way to the rear, behind even Casimiro, who was burdened with everyone's lunch.

She inched up behind him and said, "You won't make friends that way. They'll just give you more to do."

"You won't make friends at all," Casimiro snapped.

"No," Emiliana said. "But I'm not trying."

"Aren't you?" Casimiro said, halfway between sulky and honestly curious.

"I do only what I want," Emiliana said, "and I want from others only what they give freely. Not scraps that must be begged."

She saw him recoil at that, and bit her tongue on whatever she would have said next.

And here was their little square of the work site, anyway: their mounded rubble, their hand-trucks and dump-bins, and a tiny kerosene heater for them to take turns warming themselves on their breaks.

Emiliana wiped her streaming nose on the cuff of her leather mitten, and listened to Manuel over-explain their day's work.

C   ()   C

The tram ride back to the rooming house was quiet, apart from the rumble of iron on track, the hiss of steam and the occasional clang of the bell. Even Rafa, wiry, pranking Rafa, smallest and loudest of the crew, had run out of things to say; he was drowsing in his seat now, head drooping toward his friend's shoulder.

All of them were grey with ash from foot to thigh and from hand to bicep. Emiliana's graspers had taken in some grit, and the left one especially made a grating sound when she bent her elbow. Her left knee felt nearly the same, as if the kneecap scraped against the butt of the femur when she bent. Twenty-odd years of heavy lifting took a toll on flesh and bone and metal alike.

She was well tempered to it in her mind, though. In her will. It was what kept her moving when some of the lads had gone glassy-eyed and stupid and slow near day's end.

They were quick enough to pile out of the tram and shove each other into the rooming house, but they stopped and milled about uncertainly when they saw the unlit stove, the dark kitchen.

A couple of them looked to Manuel. Manuel looked to Emiliana.

Emiliana crossed her mittened graspers over her chest and looked back.

"Casimiro," Manuel said. "You know how to make biscuits?"

c ◑ c

The work got harder as the first week went on. Muscles and ligaments strained, joints compressed, feet chilblained, faces chapped. Little pains compounded and bigger ones took root. Emiliana began to wrap her knees with bandages made from torn stockings.

The lads ate like starving hounds and Emiliana wasn't far behind them. Casimiro could not cook worth a damn, really, but they all crumbled their burned biscuits into their over-salted stew and tucked it away uncomplaining against the next day's work.

At night Casimiro slept hard until the small hours, but then began to whimper in his sleep. Emiliana put up with it at first, not wanting to embarrass the lad after she'd already insulted his pride. But, when on the fourth night she was awakened, she threw a slipper at him.

"What?" he said, snuffling. "What did you...did you just—"

"You were whining like a pup," she said, "and I need my rest."

Casimiro turned over; in the darkness all Emiliana could see was the long skinny shape of him, feet extending off the end of the cot.

"I get hungry," he said, through a yawn. "It wakes me sometimes."

"Then learn to cook better," Emiliana snapped. "And there are two apples in my kit bag. Eat them and go back to sleep."

Casimiro caught his breath. "Are...are you sure?"

"I don't like them. My graspers get sticky," Emiliana said. "Chew quietly." And she stuck her head under her pillow, not waiting to see if Casimiro would take her up on it.

After that, at the end of each workday she set her apple out on the windowsill, and each morning it was gone.

c ⬙ c

The crew had Sundays off. A few blocks away through the streets of workers' houses, there was a church with services in Portuguese twice a day, where they would let lads in sooty jackets fill the pews.

Not all of the crew went. Emiliana preferred to stay back and work on her graspers. It was a slow business, going over the joints with a rag to get the grit off and then applying oil with a dropper, which was difficult to squeeze delicately with the strength of her machinery. Half the time the oil dislodged more tiny cinders from within the joint, and then she had to rag everything all over again.

Casimiro was devout enough that he had talked Rafa into taking over Sunday dinner for him, or else maybe the lads had done so in protest of Casimiro's still-terrible cooking. Rafa would spend the morning and early afternoon on a spread of roasted meats, a soup of potato and kale and sausage, and a pot of rice with flaked fish and raisins.

Manuel did not attend the church either; he spent his Sunday mornings composing letters to a sweetheart back home, who he said he was going to bring over if the crew received a second contract.

Emiliana found Manuel alone by the stove as he finished up a letter, and she sat herself down in front of him and laid one of her graspers on the page to get his attention.

"Some of your lads are being bullies," she said.

Manuel actually laughed a little, disbelieving. "You mean Rafa? I told him your stockings would tear if he tried to fit them over his damn goat-feet..."

"Oh, was that him? I tear them myself all the time," Emiliana said. "No, I meant Casimiro."

"Him, a bully?" Manuel shook his head definitely. "Not him."

"I'm glad we agree. No. I mean someone's bullying him. He's not getting enough to eat."

Manuel blinked.

"Fix it," Emiliana said. "You wanted to be foreman. They're your crew."

She lifted her grasper off the paper then, but Manuel didn't take it up right away.

"I can't make them like Casimiro," Manuel said. "He's always the odd one out. He was the one who put himself in your room. The rest of them chose to recognize your seniority."

"Does that still rankle?" Emiliana said, laughing a little. "I don't care where he sleeps, as long as it's his choice. But you can make sure he doesn't eat last every meal, and you can stop the other lads taking his share and then tossing it on the midden."

"Do they?" Manuel said. "Well."

He stayed in his seat, letter forgotten, while Emiliana pulled her chair closer to the stove to warm her joints, both flesh and not.

c   ⊙   c

Slowly the work began to get easier. Arms and legs and backs grew accustomed to the motions of work. The chill lifted. Instead of huddling over the kerosene burner for their breaks, the crew could choose to sit on overturned buckets to play cards, though the cards grew almost illegible with soot.

Emiliana, who had been fearing that her strength was beginning to wane, found that it was not. It came with a bit more pain these days but she could lift more than ever, the long bones of her legs dense with years of work, the muscles of thighs and calves grown heavy and practiced, the webbing around her spine not quite as supple as it had been, but just as sturdy. When the crew needed to move a massive beam or a cornerstone, Emiliana was one of the ones who always stepped up. Many of the lads had stronger legs or shoulders, but the muscles of their hands couldn't hold as fast as Emiliana's graspers.

Neither she nor Manuel could quite figure out what was going on with Casimiro, though. Even after Manuel put a halt to anyone messing with his food, Casimiro stayed gaunt, the fleshy lips looking almost grotesque on his hollow-eyed face. He kept carrying lunches and ferrying water from the tanker that drove slowly between all the crews around the crater, but the other lads didn't speak to him the way they spoke to each other, and they left a careful space around him on the tram and in the rooming house.

He kept eating Emiliana's apples in the night, and he kept awakening her with his nightmares.

She began to feel too much sympathy for him to throw slippers any more. She did not want to frighten him with the touch of a chilly pincer, either. She settled for reaching her foot across the gap between their cots, and prodding him, very gently, with her wool-socked toes.

Sometimes he woke; sometimes he quieted. Once he wrapped his hand around her foot and held on.

"No one's messing with him any more. I would swear to it," Manuel said in one of their Sunday conferences, while Rafa sang to himself in the kitchen, chopping onions. "You've seen it, haven't you? They save him a bowl now, even when he's still in the kitchen."

Emiliana said, "I've seen him eating it, too. But no one treats him like one of the crew yet. And he doesn't write home."

"He might be lonely," Manuel said. "But aren't we all? Don't we all miss our sweethearts?" Maybe it was intended to be judgmental, but his eyes welled up as he spoke, and so Emiliana left him to his letter and went back to her own rags and oil.

c ⬦ c

As the rubble-clearing grew closer to completion, Crew 255 moved on to building. The blast had crumbled so many struc-tures right down to their foundations, fissuring stonework that had been made to last centuries. Earth had to be shored up and framed, cornerstones had to be laid, then foundation-stones and supporting walls. The work was going to take years, and the workers were ready and willing.

Manuel, when he saw the next set of orders, was so jubilant he actually hugged Emiliana and shook her by the graspers. "I can bring Paula over!" he said. "I can marry her at last!"

Emiliana kissed him on each cheek and hugged him back, in the stiff way her graspers would allow. "Will you still live with the crew?"

"Paula can cook much better than Casimiro," Manuel said. "Maybe she can sleep in your room until we're married."

Emiliana laughed at that. "If we're going to move people around, doesn't Rafa have seniority?"

"Rafa's been sharing with Jorge so long they can't sleep when they're apart," Manuel said, grinning, and that was that.

Emiliana did not tell Casimiro that he was going to lose his post as cook, but someone must have, for he came to her that evening, as she laboriously trimmed the lamp and rolled the sleeves of her nightgown down over her graspers.

Casimiro sat on the edge of his cot, long hands wrung tight together, and ducked his head between his shoulders. He did not usually come to bed so early; Emiliana did not even know what he did in his evening hours. She rolled her sleep-socks onto her feet and waited for Casimiro to speak.

He took forever about it, too, taking in deep sighing breaths and then letting them out again without finding any words.

Finally Emiliana said, "Paula might be a wonderful cook, but you will still be part of the crew after she arrives."

Casimiro lifted his head, eyes wide, lips open. "Manuel's wife is going to be our cook?"

"I thought you had heard," Emiliana said.

"Thank the Lord," Casimiro said. "I was never going to get the salt right."

Emiliana touched her pincer to her mouth so as not to laugh. "If it isn't that…then what has you worried?"

He didn't bother to deny there was something. He only ducked his head again.

"I won't tell anyone," Emiliana said. "Whatever it is. I'll find you more apples, since you like them. Buy you bread. Whatever you need."

Casimiro hunched further into himself, hands over his face. "No," he said. "You told me not to beg for scraps. You said that."

Emiliana did not remember saying that. "It's not begging," she said. "I'm offering."

"Why?" Casimiro said, looking up at her, brows twisted.

Because you're part of my crew, Emiliana almost said, and that was true – the crew was hers now, in a way, hers as well as Manuel's – but that was not the whole of it.

Because you're my friend, she thought next, and that was also true. But that wasn't all of it either.

"I want to," she said finally, simply. "When I give, I give freely. If I want to say no, I will say no. But I might say yes."

"I'm afraid of what will happen," Casimiro said. "I'm afraid either way."

And he shuffled off his cot to kneel before Emiliana, and he laid his cheek on her thigh, and she could feel the heat of his breath in heavy quick bursts through the flannel of her nightgown.

And she saw what he was asking, and it was much greater than apples.

She reached out with her graspers and lifted Casimiro's shirt from his shoulders, and the fabric tore apart.

"I am not afraid," she said. "And I am strong enough to carry you, if you'll let me."

c ⑴ c

The rooming house was full to bursting: one room for Manuel and Paula and the babe on the way, another for Emiliana and Casimiro, the other two rooms with four cots each for the crew, and then Rafa and Jorge on a makeshift cot in the pantry.

"We'll build an addition," Manuel said, rolling out a sheet of plans on the table by the stove, while he and Emiliana stayed back from church. From the kitchen, Emiliana could smell thyme and onions, and hear Rafa teaching Paula a new song in English he'd learned from someone at the work site.

"Build it ourselves?" Emiliana said. "We've got enough brick workers, that's for certain."

"We'll need plumbing. And another stove."

"And conduits for the wiring Casimiro is always talking about."

"Then we'll have better light," Manuel agreed.

"Even though you don't have to write letters any longer," Emiliana said, "it will be better for you when you read to the baby."

Manuel's face went soft. "And you?" he said. "Will there be a baby for you?"

"A baby is not what I wish to bring into the world," Emiliana said, shaking her head and smiling.

She laid one of her graspers on the sheaf of plans to hold it open, while she pointed out where they could put the third chimney, and how the new rear wall would cast warmth onto the earth, and how in the next spring Casimiro might plant an arbour there.

THE CURLICUE SEAHORSE

CHANTAL BOUDREAU

"We're making land," Captain Roberta Rogers declared in a booming voice. "Prepare for descent."

She liked feeling the wind whip about her shoulder-length hair, even if it occasionally brought tears to her eyes. She also enjoyed listening to the hiss and whoosh of the steam engine that propelled her airship as she strolled across the main deck. She didn't know much about the mechanics that made it work – she was an adventurer, after all, and not a technician or an engineer – but she still found the shifting steel and chrome that churned at its heart impressive. It glittered in a divine way, a living, breathing metallic beast.

"In Lunenberg, Captain Ro? You can't be serious. We just left Halifax. It's a long trip to Bermuda. It'll be far longer if we stop for every whim along the way," replied Lorna, one of Roberta's most forthright crewmembers.

Captain Ro, as her crew of nine liked to call her – all women at her father's behest because travelling with men would be unseemly for an unmarried woman of her status – could be intimidating at times. Her voice was enough to cow the shyer ones in the bunch, like the mousy Marian or the mild-mannered Beth. That never stopped Lorna, her second-in-command, from speaking her mind though. The stout, brassy-skinned woman wasn't afraid of much.

"Not just a whim, my friend. I received word from Father by wireless that Grandfather has a gift for me, one that might sway me to postpone our voyage to the islands. You know he's not fond of me straying so far from home. Apparently, he doesn't understand the nature of an adventurer. The whole point is to leave home far, far behind me when the inclination strikes."

Roberta wasn't about to offer her father too much resistance, however. If it had not been for the efforts of her father and grandfather to convert the family's sailing ship construction business to the manufacture of steam airships instead, at the most opportune of times, her family would not possess the wealth that it did. It was that family wealth that funded her high-minded excursions. Her father had gifted her the *Evangeline*, the prototype of their most successful line. She could never have afforded such a lavish vessel, sizable for an airship, using her own earnings – she wasn't the type of adventurer who carried home plunder and riches to support her travels. Her finds were more of the scholastic kind – ancient artefacts with historical value.

Her father had never understood her interest in items of historical significance or her love of adventure, travelling when necessary for business, but rarely for pleasure. Then again, he had never been confined to his house. After a riding accident at the age of eight that had her housebound, Roberta had sought solace and escape in a scattering of books. Mostly school textbooks, history, geology and science, though she had uncovered a few fictional adventure novels and some travelogues as well. In these, she lost herself in stories of pirates and treasure islands, treacherous mountain treks, and journeys into the darkest depths of the oceans.

When she had tired of reading books, she had used the knowledge she had found within them to imagine her own adventures to pass the time. She found that far more exciting than learning to needlepoint or staring longingly out of her window at the world denied her. Eventually, she didn't just want to dream of such things – she wanted those dreams to come true.

Roberta's latest plans had been to investigate the supposed site of a shipwreck down in the Caribbean, one that had been transporting important academics as well as their goods. Her father hadn't enjoyed that notion. The quest for lost collegiate relics somewhere underwater would require the use of untested diving equipment and put Roberta and the *Evangeline* at risk of pirates, both in the water and in the air. She knew he would find a way to divert her if he could.

"Then again, he would have me married off to the first high-society elitist willing to take me, if he could. Safe at home birthing his grandchildren. Like that would really be any safer for me," she harrumphed to herself.

While schucking her skirts and ascending into the sky for the sake of her latest expedition might not be a proper lady's pastime, Roberta had never considered herself, nor any of her crew, a proper lady. She was brash, impulsive and strong-willed. Not all of the women working under her were similar in temperament, but they all shared her love for adventure.

"Postpone our voyage? But we have all this new underwater equipment to test and one good storm out there could shift our salvage site marker out of place – or even drift the salvage itself," Lorna protested. "Besides, if we delay, someone else might beat us to it."

Roberta laughed inwardly, but noted that Lorna's words had drawn the attention of crusty, old Marguerite who had been scrubbing a portion of the deck. The steely-haired deck-hand frowned. They all knew that the expected recovery would offer less potential return than risk to the typical bounty hunter. No one else would be willing to put in the work required to steal their claim.

Roberta believed they could spare the time, and she knew Lorna was aware of that. The real reason for Lorna's protest was that she longed to bask in the island sun, partake in the abundant rum and maybe even have a delightful roll in the sheets with some dark-skinned stranger – man or woman, it had never really mattered to her. The area was flush with its own particular types of indulgences. The other crewmembers had also been looking forward to some time spent in the sun.

"Give me the chance to at least inspect Grandfather's offering. I didn't say the detour would be a given. But Father seems to think once I see what's there I'll be willing to wait… So, we'll have a look."

Lorna made a sour face before returning her attention to her duties, and Marguerite went back to scrubbing as well, but that was the last of the objections. Roberta's father had sent a cryptic message that had intrigued her: *He has a key to a mystery long in need of solving.* Once her curiosity was piqued, there was no turning back. She suspected her unyielding persistence would be the death of her some day.

When the *Evangeline* was settled within town limits, Roberta ventured off into Lunenburg to meet her grandfather, taking Lorna with her for both company and camouflage. "You make me look good when we're together," she insisted. "You're mouthier than I am and less tactful too. I'm a demure flower next to you."

She gave leave to the other eight women for the afternoon also. With their voyage delayed, she could at least offer them the consolation of time to relax.

It was easy to pick out Grandfather Rogers' home from a distance, the most ostentatious house in all of Lunenburg. A servant met them at the door and guided them to the sitting room where they would partake of tea and blueberry scones with their host. Grandfather did not leave them waiting for very long. He hobbled in soon after them, his cane in one hand and a neatly wrapped package in the other.

"This was meant to be your birthday gift, Roberta, but your father requested I give it to you now. He mentioned something about wanting to keep your treasure hunting closer to home. It comes in two parts. Here's the first."

When Roberta plucked the box from inside the paper, she wondered how the contents of something so small could have any bearing on a treasure hunt. She cracked it open to find a tiny metallic seahorse charm inside, one decorated with fine filigree and curlicues.

"This is lovely, thank you," she remarked, letting the chain of the delicate trinket dangle from her fingertips. "But I don't see what this has to do with any treasure—"

Before she could finish her sentence, Grandfather Rogers reached over and gave the charm a gentle prod. Movement followed, along with the subtle whirr of miniature clockwork within the seahorse as it reshaped and transformed. In the end, Roberta was left holding a little silver key. She gave her grandfather a questioning look.

"What's this for?"

"You've heard of Oak Island and its cursed treasure?"

Lorna spoke up in response. "Of course. No person legitimately calling himself an adventurer doesn't know about

Captain Kidd's legendary treasure. Trying to find it is more trouble than it's worth, however. The venture has proven lethal to many a man crushed, drowned or suffocated. None of them pleasant ways to go."

"True – but none of them possessed this key, nor had the information and the wherewithal to use it. Your father says you have prototype mechanisms with you to keep divers safe?"

"I do," Roberta agreed. "But I wouldn't know what to do with it or this key, in this instance. Without knowing more, I wouldn't run the risk of attempting to retrieve the treasure. I'm not in this for riches and too many others have already failed."

"You needn't follow in their footsteps," her grandfather insisted. "There is a failsafe within the pit, a mechanism that will disarm all of the traps Kidd had put in place, but it will only work for the wielder of this key. Of course, you have to know where the keyhole is located, and it happens to lie underwater at this point, thanks to the blundering efforts of those attempting to excavate the treasure before you. But the opportunity and the advantage are yours if you choose to use it. That's where your diving equipment would come in."

"The intent was to use it to search underwater in a safer way, yes. But how am I expected to find the keyhole for something so small? It would take forever, down there in the depths of the pit." She held up the tiny end of the key, scrutinizing it.

"Well, that's where the second part of the gift comes into play. I bought this at a special auction. It belonged to a young man who happens to be a descendant of Captain Kidd's Nova Scotian mistress. This gentleman claims that Kidd left the key in this woman's care, declaring the treasure to be hers if he and his crew did not return for it. He also left her a journal with directions on how to locate and disarm the failsafe should they not return. Apparently, she never chose to follow through and fetch it back from the island. An antiquarian has authenticated the signature of Kidd that accompanied the instructions and dated both the journal and key to the appropriate time. Plus the seahorse bears the maker's mark of an artisan known to run in the same circles as Kidd. He likely crafted that failsafe mechanism and key on commission."

Lorna's dark eyes lit up, her slight smile broadening into a full grin. "So the journal is the other half of the gift then? Come on – out with it. Let's see it."

"Not exactly. The young man was not willing to give up possession of the journal. He considers it an important part of his family history – that it serves as proof he may be descended from Captain Kidd himself. But while he won't let the journal leave his possession, he is willing to accompany any treasure seekers wishing to attempt to retrieve the treasure. I told him I might be sending you out his way. Your arrival wouldn't be unexpected."

Roberta's excitement faded at this news. She now eyed the key with reluctance. Lorna caught the look and immediately started in on her.

"Captain Ro – you're not about to turn this one down are you? I'm willing to forego sun and surf in the Caribbean for this. This isn't just any treasure. This could make us rich."

"You know I'm not doing this for wealth. I don't see why I would add this to my agenda. It's not my kind of find – not my type of claim. And I don't want some overgrown boy worming his way into my salvage excursion. There's too many problems to this. Too many complications. Perhaps I can just wear my gift as a proper keepsake and return to our original plans. Or if

Grandfather thinks that would be an opportunity wasted, perhaps it can be resold to someone more willing to make proper use of it." Roberta glanced his way, her eyes questioning.

Her grandfather chuckled.

"A gift is a gift, my dear. You can do with it as you please. But you shouldn't cast aspersions upon Mr. Briand without meeting him first. He left a positive impression upon me with our auction encounter. He's a clever one and a man of scruples. I think you and he would get along just fine, and I don't think he would prove to be any sort of impairment if you brought him along while pursuing the treasure. I hope you wouldn't do him the dishonour of dismissing him without even giving him a chance. If he's not up to snuff, you're perfectly free to abandon this quest and return to your southerly travels."

By the end of a sometimes heated discussion over tea and scones, the captain was convinced by Lorna that they should follow through on the elderly man's suggestion and at least meet with Mr. Briand. Roberta would still be wary regarding any scheming on his part. Authenticated journal or not, she wasn't entirely convinced that this "mistress's descendant" wasn't orchestrating a scam and her poor grandfather happened to be his unwitting prey. Nevertheless, the pair returned to the *Evangeline* and set off to meet with the journal's owner, less than an hour's travel away.

Mr. Briand's cottage on the shores of Oak Island looked like a little wooden box in comparison to the Rogers' Lunenburg estate, but the grounds surrounding it were well kept and the home had a rustic charm to it. Roberta was pleased to see enough cleared land to dock the *Evangeline* rather than having to set down in water. Most of the island was covered in trees.

The gentleman who answered the door took Roberta somewhat by surprise. She had been anticipating someone rakish, with the air of a snake oil salesman. Instead, the man who greeted them had a bookish look, a slender, pale individual with dark hair, spectacles and conservative attire. While well groomed, he had not gone out of his way to embellish his appearance, wearing neutral-coloured clothing with no stylistic flair.

"I'm looking for Mr. Briand," Roberta said, lifting the seahorse that hung at her throat. "I was told he would have some information I might find useful."

"I'm Mr. Briand – Louis Briand, to be exact. You must be Miss Rogers," he replied.

"*Captain* Rogers," Lorna corrected with a growl.

He gave her a leery look. "Pardon me – my mistake. I wasn't aware. No disrespect intended."

Roberta elbowed Lorna, giving Briand a cheerful smile. "No offence taken. Don't mind Lorna. We encounter disrespect far too often and she can be a little overprotective at times. Her bark is worse than her bite."

"Says you…" Lorna mumbled.

"I'm pleased to meet you," Roberta continued. "My grandfather says you are insisting on joining us if we follow through on this venture. Is that so?"

Briand waved the two women into his humble abode, waiting for them to take their seats before speaking further. "I really can't afford to let this journal out of my sight. If the wrong people get their hands on it, I'll never see it again. It could bring ruin upon a few families with stellar reputations, any of which would go out of their way to destroy it if given the chance. I wasn't inclined to part with the curlicue seahorse either, but I'm a man of letters and it was my only means of raising the funds I needed to continue my studies. Selling it at auction was my concession. I will not be so liberal with the journal."

Roberta noted that his otherwise cold grey eyes glimmered with warmth when he mentioned his studies. She found that appealing. She could certainly appreciate a learned man, even if he was a tad on the scrawny side.

"You do realize how dangerous this could be? The cursed treasure has already killed more than one man. I don't expect to be held responsible for you if things don't go as hoped. I will already have enough to worry about. I figure that's plenty."

"I can mind my own person, Captain Rogers. I'm not ignorant of the risks involved. Removing the failsafe requires more than just the turn of a key. First of all, you need to know where to excavate to reach the deactivation device. And then there are a series of knobs and levers that also have to be manipulated in the proper order. One misstep is likely to trigger one or more of the many traps surrounding the treasure, possibly resulting in death. I doubt that any of us would wish to see that as an outcome."

A small crease furrowed Roberta's brow. She shot Lorna an unhappy look. "It sounds like it's more trouble than it's worth. We don't need that money. I have no plans to retire early and I pay my crew well enough for them to respect my wishes. I really want to get to those scholarly artefacts down south. Are you dead set on this, Lorna?"

"This will have rewards the likes of which our crew has never seen. I don't want to retire early either – I love the airship life – but setting a nest egg aside for when I do would be a good thing. Whatever you decide though, Captain Ro, is good with me as it will be with the others. We trust your judgement."

"If it's scholarly artefacts you're after, I can guarantee you such finds in this treasure," Briand told them. "Captain Kidd left an inventory in the journal. I'll let you review it and you can consider that in your decision. To be honest with you, that's what interested me in this treasure in the first place. Sure, I need the funds to further my education, but that's not my primary motivation. These historical gems ought not be left to rot in the dirt. They belong in a museum. I've dedicated my life to history. I'd risk my life to preserve it."

The grin on Lorna's face when he said this suggested the man of letters had just struck gold. Roberta knew she didn't have to show her the contents of that inventory. By nature, it would prove incentive enough for her to agree to Briand's terms and postpone the *Evangeline*'s trip to the Caribbean, as Lorna was no doubt aware.

Roberta eventually sighed and nodded, returning the journal to Briand.

"I hate to agree with you but I must. We'll postpone our voyage to the south, but I want to limit any delays. Since we need you and your journal for this recovery, I expect you to be ready to go first thing tomorrow. We'll be examining this 'pit' from the surface and readying our equipment. We brought with us a special submersible that works as an extension of the ship. I understand the area we need to venture into was flooded during the last excavation?"

"That's right. The treasure hunters triggered one of the traps. I'll be ready."

Morning couldn't seem to come fast enough for Roberta. She waited with anticipation on deck as Lorna fetched Briand. He looked fresh faced and far more eager than he had the day before. At least, he did until he caught sight of the submersible.

"That? That's your diving equipment? It looks like a giant brass potato dangling from a pair of chains and hoses."

"With arms," Lorna pointed out. "Don't forget the arms. The person inside the submersible can insert their own arms into them from the inside of the vessel and use them to manipulate things in the water on the outside."

"There's barely enough room for one of us in there, let alone two," Briand said, continuing to gape at the egg-like encasement.

"That's because it's only supposed to be a single person device. Who said anything about two?" Roberta gently pushed her way past the pair, making for the brass hatch. "I'm the one trained to use this. I'll be going down to disable the fail-safe."

"And how exactly do you plan on doing that without the journal? Because even if I were to let you take it down there without me, I doubt you are agile enough to hold it open with your toes and read from it while you work the key and levers with those mechanical hands."

Roberta stood up, pursing her lips. "I suppose you have a point." She eyed him and then the submersible. "I guess it will have to be a tight squeeze then. I hope it can withstand the additional weight."

Briand's pale face turned a brilliant shade of red. "The two of us pressed into such a tiny space?" he sputtered. "It wouldn't be proper. Certainly not for a lady of your status."

"I never claimed to be proper," Roberta said with a grunt, as she spun the wheel to open the hatch.

"Nor a lady," Lorna added, smirking.

"Take it or leave." Roberta swung the hatch out with a lurch. "It's not like we have a lot of options. We get cozy, or we abandon this altogether. You go home with your journal and we head south with my decorative but otherwise useless sea-horse trinket."

Perspiring more than he should in the morning cool, Briand mumbled his consent to proceed with a slight nod, his face even more flushed. Roberta allowed him to step in first.

"I have a feeling I'm more flexible than our man of letters," the captain said to Lorna over her shoulder. "I'll manage to contort myself as best I can into what little space he leaves me."

The fit was so tight it left little room to breathe and even less for movement – enough to open and page through the journal and insert arms into the holes provided for external access. If it weren't for filtration through the hoses, the air in the cramped submersible would have gotten stale fast. Briand's laboured breathing didn't help matters any.

"I'm going to Hell for this," he muttered.

"If I deflower you before we're through here, I guess I'll just have to marry you. Now stop being so anxious and take a slow deep breath," Roberta said. "We just have to relax and sit tight until we spot that marker you mentioned through the porthole. When I knock, Lorna will stop our descent. If I knock twice in rapid succession, that's the signal to pull us up as soon as possible."

"I can't do any of that as long as your elbow is wedged into my diaphragm and your hipbone is threatening to penetrate my thigh."

"If it's that much of a bother it would take no trouble to have Lorna yank us out again." Roberta raised her fist to knock.

"No, no – I've already suffered enough embarrassment and shame. Let's just get this over with, all right?"

Their vessel continued to drop until Roberta caught sight of the marker. She knocked hard, with a great *clang!* and the submersible jarred to a sudden halt.

"What now?" she asked.

"Dig to the left of it. The failsafe device is buried about a foot past it, so be careful when you're getting close."

Thrusting her hands into mechanical arms, she started clawing into the compacted earth with the left one only.

"It will go faster with both. I'd prefer faster." Briand leafed through the journal, looking for his next reference point.

"Lorna and I rigged the right one with the key. I wouldn't want to knock it out of place before I've had the chance to use it," Roberta said.

Briand glanced up from his pages, somewhat surprised. "Right – it would have to be outside the submersible, wouldn't it...that required some foresight."

"You say that as if you're surprised."

"Well, you do strike me as rather impulsive."

Roberta snorted. "And that precludes me from thinking things through? I may be impulsive at times, but I never embark on an adventure unprepared." She paused. "I think I'm almost there. The soil is getting looser." A silence came from Briand in response. "Did you hear me?"

"Captain Rogers – I think you need to work faster. My feet are getting wet."

Roberta froze. "Wet?" She glanced down and noted the puddle forming at the bottom of the submersible. "Damn it. One of the seals didn't hold, likely because of the additional weight."

The dirt where she had been digging gave way in a cloud of newly formed mud, and when it cleared it revealed a strange-looking box with a keyhole and a variety of levers.

"That's it! That's the failsafe device. Let's resurface, repair the damaged seal and then return to finish the job," Briand said.

"Are you kidding me? We need to finish this. Can't you see that entire area is unstable? It could collapse at any moment because of the water, and if it does, it could take the entire tunnel with it. We have to do this now. Circumstance won't allow for delay."

"My soggy ankles beg to differ."

Roberta scowled at Briand, perched above him. The water had yet to reach her. "It's now or never. So either give me those directions or it's over."

Briand hesitated, precious moments ticking by while he decided if staying was worth the risk. Then, with an anxious sigh, he began listing off the steps.

Roberta followed his commands diligently, echoing word for word to make sure she had each step right. It felt as much like a dance as it did a disarming, a plethora of varying flicks and turns. Arriving at the end, there was a shudder accompanied by a grinding sound. She glanced down. Briand shivered beneath her, waist-deep in cold water. Her legs were also wet now, the dampness encroaching on her as well.

"That's it," he confirmed, teeth chattering. "The traps have been disarmed. The water should start receding now."

"Let's just hope it does so fast enough. Just in case it doesn't, I'll have the ship raise us as well." She slipped her arms out their mechanical extensions and gave a solid pair of knocks upon the submersible's brass frame. "Hopefully we'll be out of the water before the interior of this can is entirely immersed."

In response to the knock, the submersible did begin to ascend, but progress was painfully slow. Roberta grimaced.

"They must be having trouble lifting us with all this extra weight. This is going to take longer than I would have liked."

"You and me both," Briand said. He gasped from the cold, the water now reaching his chest. "I think the breach is worsening – the water is rising more quickly. Here – take the journal. You'll be able to hold it out of the water higher than I can. Maybe you can keep it from getting the kind of soaking that would destroy its secrets, where I would fail."

"I'm more concerned with preserving you, my good man. The book is secondary."

"Not to me. It's my family's legacy. Besides, there's little you can do for me now. I'm in the hands of faith and fate. Lift that journal as high as you can and pray for me."

Roberta did as he asked, raising the book as far up as she could. Only slightly elevated above Briand, it was enough to allow her to watch as the water spilling in surrounded Briand's face while she still had her mouth and nose above its surface. Bubbles rose up from his position a few moments later, slowing as time ticked by. At the point Roberta feared she would follow him into a watery grave, the water finally stopped rising and started to regress. The man of letters' head lolled against her, seemingly lifeless, as soon as it lost its liquid support.

"Briand? Briand!"

Despite the urgency in her voice, he offered no reply. As the water continued to recede, she propped the journal under one arm and clutched his bluish face with both hands. No breath escaped his nose or mouth.

"Damn it. We should have gone up as soon as the leak started."

With worried eyes and frantic gestures she decided she could not just abandon him for dead. She had watched a native woman breathe life into a drowned sailor once before. She could at least attempt that herself before giving up on him.

Unsure exactly what to do, she pinched his nose closed and tilted back his head, as she had seen it done. Then she pressed her still warm lips to his frigid ones and blew in. She attempted this several times, blowing harder when gentler puffs drew no response.

Without warning her own mouth suddenly filled with brackish water as Briand began to regurgitate massive quantities. She pulled away, watching helplessly as he wretched up almost all he had swallowed. He then clung to her, eyes unfocused and limbs trembling, as he attempted to borrow as much heat from her as he could manage. Roberta was so distracted by the entire affair that she did not notice they had reached the surface and that her crewmembers were scrambling to extricate their captain and the man of letters from their watery capsule.

Briand still held her in his shaky grasp, his head resting in the crook of her neck, when Lorna threw open the hatch.

"Well now – you two are even cosier than you were when last I left you," she remarked.

"Don't be foolish," Roberta snarled. "One of the seals gave way and he almost drowned. He's freezing. Have someone round up blankets and hot tea, then help me get him somewhere better suited for his recuperation."

"Aye, aye, Captain." Lorna disappeared from view.

Briand groaned, returning to his senses. "I'm not dead? The journal?"

"Safe, as per your bidding. And by some miracle, so are you."

"Thank you," he whispered, before lapsing into a faint.

Roberta sighed, hugging him close. It no longer seemed like an awkward or uncomfortable thing to do.

"Don't thank me just yet. The treasure's not in hand. But first, we get you secured and then we see what that pit has to offer us now that its traps are disarmed."

c   ⋒   c

Roberta crept into Briand's current quarters to check on the *Evangeline*'s only treasure-hunting casualty. Fortunately, the Oak Island curse had not claimed him along with the others. Perhaps it was destiny that had overridden it, God's will, or plain dumb luck. They would never know.

Briand stirred upon her approach. He started, sitting up abruptly in bed.

"Be calm," Roberta insisted. "You're safe. Your journal lies securely beside you. My crewmembers are retrieving the treasure as we speak. There is no more need for worry. Rest."

He gently lowered himself back into the bed, an action accompanied by a rattling cough.

"It'll take some time before your lungs return to normal, but that's better than the alternative. I wasn't sure what I was going to say to your family if we returned with the treasure but without you. I'm sorry that my persistence nearly brought you to an early end."

Briand appeared unfazed by the incident, more interested in confirming the presence of the journal, safe and sound. He glanced around until sighting it, then relaxed

"I heard you right? Your crew found it – the treasure?"

"Indeed they did. It was hidden just beyond the failsafe mechanism, locked away exactly as your journal described it. It was far more impressive than anything else we've managed to recover. I'm sure my crew are already contemplating their plans for their cut. I likely won't retain them all. Lorna will stick with me, and several of the younger women, but a few, like Marguerite, will retire as a result of this. I'll have to recruit replacements before resuming our trip to the Caribbean." Roberta sat on the end of the bed.

"You're still planning to travel down south?"

Roberta nodded. "This was an entertaining and rewarding detour, but we still have other adventuring business to attend to. Don't worry – we'll leave you with a sizeable share of the profits. I doubt you'll ever have to auction off another of your family heirlooms to fund your studies ever again. Speaking of which..." She pulled the curlicue seahorse from her pocket and passed it to him. "I retrieved this from the submersible arm. I thought you might like it as a memento of your near-death experience."

He took it from her tentatively, his expression uncertain.

"I was actually hoping I might be able to propose another venture. I wasn't lying when I said this journal held many secrets. There are other treasures, other relics, to be found – other mysteries to be solved. I was hoping I might convince you to find them with me. I certainly can't do it alone."

"I will be needing to replace some of my crew. I suppose I could consider you if you're willing to be trained to help run the Evangeline. You'd actually be interested in coming along? After all that just happened? What if next time we run into trouble and I can't resuscitate you?"

"A chance I'm willing to take. Besides, you owe me." Roberta still displayed her reluctance, so Briand continued. "Did you forget, you offered to marry me if you deflowered me? I won't expect you to make good on that promise, but I'd at least expect you to oblige this whim – a partnership of a different sort."

Roberta cocked an eyebrow. "Are you trying to have me believe I deflowered you? I mean, I know those close quarters left little to the imagination but…"

"You were my first – I am no longer a treasure hunt virgin." He smiled with more vigour than he had shown since she had met him.

"And then there's my father's demand of a female-only crew."

"You can tell him my name is Louise, if that's what it takes, although I won't wear a dress for his sake. It amazes me. I never anticipated enjoying this. Despite the near-death experience, I've never been quite so thrilled in my life. I've been missing out on that. I want more of those experiences. I want to follow through on my family's legacy." Briand tapped the journal's cover.

"Let me think on it," Roberta said, rising from her perch on the bed. "I'll need time to decide."

She smiled as she left the cabin, closing the door behind her. Truth was, she had already made up her mind. The idea of tracking down the other treasures in Briand's journal excited her as much as it did him, a historical scavenger hunt. Plus the man of letters and his scholarly ways intrigued her. But he did not need to know that just yet.

As for a man on board for the trip, she would find a way around her father's rules. She always had before, when so inclined.

"Back to the city," Captain Rogers instructed her crew. It would not be a terribly long trip – just over a couple of hours. None of them seemed to mind. After the treasure find, all of them were in good spirits. Even Marguerite wasn't her usual surly self. "We'll need to cash out and settle up before we head out on our next venture. We'll have repairs to make to the submersible too. And I'll want to know who's still with me on the *Evangeline*'s next outing by the time we make land again. The next course I'll be plotting will demand full hands and a solid commitment. The curlicue seahorse was just a beginning."

With that, Roberta strode over to the best vantage point of her ship and waited for the *Evangeline* to begin her ascent. The new thrill that ran through her veins matched the rush of the winds that met her as they climbed into the sky.

STRANGE THINGS DONE

MICHAL WOJCIK

Gold sings a strong song – led all these men up over the Chilkoot Pass with their bundles bound tight on their backs, sledges bound tight to their waists while they slogged through the snow. Women followed soon enough, some of them heading for the dance halls and opera houses and taverns. They were tough women, even tougher than the men, and a good many weren't looking to sing songs or spread their legs. They smelled other opportunities: mills, hotels, public houses. Build a comfortable business in that wood-and-canvas town and let the gold come to you instead of burning and breaking your way through the permafrost.

Then there are some women, like me, who didn't come for gold at all.

Sam Steele was strict about bringing guns into the Yukon. That is, none, if he could help it. But Mounties were a bit less discerning when it came to lone ladies, especially young things telling tales of husbands who'd abandoned them in Vancouver and sailed off clear to Hawaii. Meant the North-West Mounted Police didn't go routing through my things, didn't find the pistol there or the ammunition scattered all through my smallclothes. Not that it looked like any pistol they'd have ever seen. It was made special someplace in

Germany, packed more bullets than any revolver and had lot more wallop too when it started spinning and spitting. Lady Sabina Amery gave it to me in Vancouver along with a knife, its handle all white and silver, a clutch of ferocient canisters (which meant the job was serious) and instructions to memorize good and well: find Jack Sheldon's claim and take whatever the man found there. Maybe off him, if he got in the way, which he most likely would.

I don't need to tell you Jack found no gold in that icy soil, though Sabina kept mum on what it truly was. "Rumours," she'd said. "Just rumours."

c ◌ c

Before I ever got here, I was just one of many kids coming on the boats from Suffolk over to Montreal. Father was a soldier of the British Empire discharged and ready to make a new life for himself presiding over some vast estate in the new-formed Dominion; Mother was a gentry lady married below her station for love and maybe a bit of foolishness. Truth was, they weren't cut out for frontier life. Father didn't last so long trying to clear that plot by the Rockies. He just up and hanged himself when the crop failed that one year. Or maybe he was hanged – the French lord next to us wanted to expand his holdings and Father was in the way.

Mother did the best she could, but she wasn't in any state for wilderness life and we ended up starving. We kept on starving even when we went to Calgary and she took on a job as a seamstress (she wasn't a very good one). Oh, she tried to raise me and my sisters, but the youngest got some sickness where you puked your guts out and then Mom fell to it too. She was stuck in her bed while we had to go out in the dusty streets and beg, go out and find odd jobs just to stay alive. Not much of a life.

Lady Amery, she stepped off the train from who knew where – English, definitely, and I'm sure she wasn't lying about the baroness part. She sure dressed like one: elegant promenade dress and shawl, a charming silk bonnet, purple-ribboned and frilled and feathered, blue-tinged spectacles to protect her eyes. It's not like she prowled through the run-down tenements in the labourer's part of Calgary looking for girls of twelve in desperate straits. She had others in her pay sent to seek us out. Find the ones with just enough hunger in their eyes, just enough cruelty. Survivors.

One of them found me.

I was in a scrap with some boy who'd tried to take the flowers I was hoping to sell. I was rangy and had a knife, and gave him a good cut that sent him running. When I wiped the blood clean with a rose a woman came to me – I don't know how long she'd been waiting there – and asked about the book I had in my bag, *The Adventures of Captain Hatteras* by Jules Verne.

Did I like it? Did I often read Jules Verne? Where did I get it? I said it was a gift, which wasn't true; I'd nicked it after I'd finished *Twenty Thousand Leagues Under the Sea*. A gentleman left it on the bench while he was finding a place out of the wind to light his pipe.

"Your name, if I may take the liberty of asking?"

"Tessa Fitzpatrick," I told her.

"You like adventure?"

Her voice was crisp as a school ma'am's but she didn't look like one, not one bit. She was in her thirties, I think, and she could break you if she wanted. Even under all those layers and almost formless dress, you could see she was well-stocked with muscle. Her eyes were grey like cast iron, stern. Later, I'd find out her name was Annabelle, Annabelle Leigh, not a name that suited at all.

"Fantastic voyages, extraordinary encounters to lands undreamed of," she finished.

I nodded. Those were the stories I liked best of all.

"How would you like to go on such adventures?"

I had my flowers crushed up against my chest with one hand, the book crushed there with the other. I admit I was afraid of her at first, thought she'd drag me to the constabulary for what I'd done to the boy, but when she asked the question, she was smiling with warmth I didn't see from any but my mom.

"I'd like that," I told her.

You'll ask me how I could just up and leave my mom and sisters. Well, I didn't, not quite. Annabelle took me to the quarters of Lady Amery first. Already told you how she dressed, and she had that sort of face as well, all hard corners. She interviewed me, trying to get a grip on how well I read, how much I knew, but mostly my sharpness and my strength.

"Hmm, not an orphan," she said, "but I see why Annabelle brought you here."

It was Annabelle who talked to Mother, saying I'd have a patron who'd taken it upon herself to educate young women across Canada. I'd visit Calgary every summer, and most of all, they'd give her money too, to support my sisters.

Mom, she didn't want to let me go, but in the end she said it was my choice and I couldn't pass. Not after what Sabina showed me that first day, like something out of Jules Verne – a brass hummingbird she let hang in the air, its wings cutting a blur. I wasn't allowed to tell Mom about that. Part of the deal.

c   ⦿   c

I took my valise into the Castle Hotel on Front Street. I had plenty of cash, enough to stay at the Fairview, but I didn't want to make that sort of impression, like I was one of those well-kept proper ladies seeking a husband of suitable means.

Dawson City is a crooked place, buildings sinking and tilting like a jagged set of old men's teeth. The streets are all mud-churned so thick you can barely pull a cart through. It has about as much chaos as you'd expect from a place built in a year. Houses and shops hammered together from black spruce logs, false fronts doing nothing to hide the crude cabins behind them. Still, mixed in all that were places like the Fairview, two stories and even sporting a portico.

There isn't a lack of wealth in the place, that's plain, but it's the sort of wealth with foundations steady as permafrost. A constant bustle occupies the pilings by the river since the steamers come in regular, hauling in supplies or miners who'd spend a night watching Klondike Kate or sporting with the good-time gals. I wasn't ready for how noisy it was, and because it's light all night on account of the midnight sun, no one had reason to sleep. Not used to that after the quiet of the Yukon River, just the sound of the Indian pilot creaking the tiller and the slow sigh of the current. Dawson City, meanwhile, was like stepping into Calgary or Vancouver again. A ramshackle cobbled-up shadow of those places but wilder, so much wilder.

I had it in my head what to do, though, how to dress and where to go. I knew Lady Amery sent me here because I was the toughest of her girls, tough as Annabelle used to be. I could enter a tavern and stare down all the leering arses and make them turn away just like that, could swing a punch harder than Jem Mace, even made Soapy Smith break down crying back in Skagway. Meant I had no problem passing by the Dominion Saloon and Gambling Hall to more likely prospects. I started with the halfway respectable establishments and worked my way down till I came to Louse Town and a pub with no name, one of places that was just a shack with a few tables put in, some bottles of whiskey stuck behind the counter to keep company with the moonshine.

First I plunked down some gold but the bartender wasn't impressed. City was filled with it. Then I offered to blow him a kiss and that got me somewhere. He started me off on a chain of men and women, mostly shopkeepers and pilots and prospectors, mostly poor, not the good-time girls I'd expected. Wisps of rumour became more and more solid, like smoke out of an opium pipe the more you puffed.

I gathered soon enough that Jack Sheldon had gone on his last trip to some place called Ogden Creek – I reckon it won't have that name in a few years. Some of these places swap names three or four times a month. I found a spot on a flat-bottom going up the Klondike River and paid a Hän woman named Ruth to guide me.

c () c

We floated square in the middle of the river, away from the mosquitoes. It was almost pleasing just lounging there in the sun. On either side, broad shoals or cliffs topped with spruce passed us by. Camps sprang up where other rivers and creeks spilled in. Sometimes you'd see sluices and other machines set for separating ore or spilling stone. Plenty working, plenty broken and abandoned. Plenty of boat wrecks sticking up out of the water, too.

My guide took to whittling; she was short, broad, looked near ridiculous in her hat a size too big, brim so wide it stretched twice-length past her shoulders. Black hat, brown choker, vest rattling with beads. She sang in no language I knew, and normally that would get you dirty looks on a trip like this, but the tune fit so well with the water sounds that the others never told her to quit.

We kept on ploughing upstream, pulling alongside ragged docks or rocky spots to let others go. We turned up a tributary and then the tents started dwindling away. By the end, the boat was near empty, save for us and the boys at the oars. When most of the stampeders from the States hit the gold-fields the good claims were gone, so it took a special fool to go seeking this far up the North Fork.

What I'd gathered about Jack Sheldon, he'd come up in 1896, started even before news hit about gold in Bonanza Creek. Man out of Toronto, not much cut out for the Yukon. Abandoned his first claim, got in some squabble with Belinda Mulrooney over his second, had to give it up and went nos-ing around in unlikely places before he settled at Ogden. Something changed in him then; he wasn't bringing back gold but he'd lost that look of foolish fancy he'd had before and just plain clammed up, like he'd found something big. But what it was, no one said because he hadn't shown them. Then he'd just stopped coming to Dawson at all. Last time anyone checked on him they found his camp but no Jack. Not dead, though – fresh prints and cookery still around, and an Indian said he'd seen Jack hauling in scrap from down-river to some place in the hills. Old boilers, pistons and other things.

The pilot refused to go further, no matter how much I was paying him, and I had to head out off the bank with Ruth, on foot. The boat turned round and the pilot promised he'd be back this way in four days. Me, I had a pack slung over my shoulders and came wearing trousers and good solid boots for the walk. Ruth had a pack that looked maybe twice as heavy as mine did.

She looked round the hills before leading the way up alongside the North Fork. She didn't ask any more questions than she had on the boat.

c ⬭ c

I didn't see Lady Amery often after the meeting where she brought out the bird automaton. It was Annabelle, Pauline, Marguerite, and an older gentleman named Victor who did most of the teaching at a "special academy for young ladies." They didn't keep us together in some boarding house, though. We were mostly kept spread across the country, and there were only five of us. Not your typical class, not some typical classroom. I learned the usual geography and maths and history, learned some other things too: how to fight hand-to-hand, how to shoot, how to carry on in whatever part of society I found myself in.

I can act with proper manners if I have to, can talk like I'm from some rich family in London, only that's not truly me and I prefer speaking like this. Reminds me where I came from.

Lady Amery wasn't helping us from the pure goodness of her heart. Our benefactor provided our education and paid our families, and in return, when we finished up she expected us to work for her. Not that we minded that much. Me and the other girls all came from bad straits and preferred full bellies and soft beds to our hard-bitten lives before. Besides, we were the sort who'd crave adventure and never thought we'd have the chance to get it.

See, she wanted women like that because we could be invisible when we wanted, could survive tough scrapes and come out on top. Sabina wanted us because we'd already seen far more than any child should and there was precious little that could rattle us. We'd gone through hard times, we'd be grateful, we'd be *loyal* enough not to spill secrets.

Sabina had plenty of secrets.

Like that flying metal bird, or the glass eyeball that followed you round in its wire chassis, or the twelve-stack machine she kept in Kingston – you fed it a run of cards punched with tiny holes and it could draw you a picture of whatever you wanted. Saying that, you'd think Sabina was some genius inventor, but truth was she was just building them from plans out of old books and scrolls or reconstructing them from dug-up remains. We girls went out to get these for her, from dusty libraries or dank caverns or unlit tombs.

Any place something *odd* was going on, talk of ghosts or marvellous phenomena, we girls were there to steal whatever was at the bottom of it. Lady Amery was a collector, and she said she was keeping these things safe, that the world wasn't ready for them.

We believed her, more or less. That way we could see things no one else ever would, go places a lady wasn't allowed to go unless she was an archaeologist, *do* things most women weren't allowed to do.

That's how I ended up in the Klondike, a place running low on women, trying to find Jack Sheldon: to see if he'd found a bauble my lady wanted. Though I'd be lying if I said I didn't want to find out either. That's what drove us all on, another reason why Sabina chose us. Because we *wanted*.

c ⦿ c

We spent a long while walking under close-packed spruce till we came to the cascading trickle Ruth said was Ogden Creek. Took a bit longer following the path uphill, wading through beds of bruised fireweed, before we reached Jack Sheldon's camp. It wasn't in any condition for living. The wall tent was rent apart, canvas flapping loose, frame splayed over the dirt, dishes and cups spread all around.

"Bear?" I asked, as I walked round the fire pit. Ravens hopped away at our approach but didn't scatter, just gathered in a band to wait for us to clear off so they could go back to pecking through busted tins.

"No," Ruth answered, after a good look round. "No bear tracks. No bear shit. Bears have smelly shit. And look there – no bear would be able to open those boxes so neat."

The latches on chests were flipped open, locks broken clean off. I checked those: one filled with thick blankets, the other empty. The rough shed we'd checked before hadn't much in it worth investigating. Some dried meat, tough enough you could use it to drive in nails. "People did this?"

"If they did, they'd have come from across the creek." She shielded her eyes – late evening but the sun was still hanging above the horizon, bright and burning. "There's boot marks." Ruth pointed to the ground. "But there is no sense to them doing this."

She wasn't talking about them coming from the creek's right-hand side, she meant raiding the camp. People rarely killed each other up here – usually fever or the winter got them, or they starved, or they got in some accident while digging. Wasn't much in the ways of hospitals out in the wilderness. Sure people got in arguments, sabotaged each other's equipment or made nuisances of themselves, but the Mounties were sure to intervene before things got ugly.

This, though, wasn't usual. I reached into my pack from where I'd dropped it and pulled out my pistol, popped open the magazine. It took spirals of bullets that looked like Nautilus shells. Ruth raised her eyebrows seeing that. I shoved the loaded gun through the loop in my belt. Next, I drew out a contraption like a pocket watch, flipping it open and adjusting the dials round the edges till the needle starting shifting.

Ruth didn't ask what it was and I wouldn't have answered. No way to explain how it picked up decaying energies anyhow. Even I wasn't quite straight on how it worked.

We went further up the hillside to where Jack had burrowed down, sinking shafts into the earth by lighting fires to soften the permafrost, one layer at a time. Same people had searched through here too, looked like.

"Don't make no sense," Ruth said. "They didn't take a thing worth taking, and you'd have to be a special fool to come looking for gold around this place."

I nodded. Not even a trace of gold here. I looked down at what Victor called his "thaumaturgograph" (a damn mouthful that, we girls called it a "thaum"). The needle stayed steady at first, then shifted as I traced whatever veins Jack was following.

If there were other people after what I was after, you'd think I would've heard something about it in Dawson, some passing comment, but it looked like the locals thought no one was much interested in Jack. Jack London, now, at least he came down with a bad case of scurvy.

"You heard anything about him?" I asked Ruth, still keeping fixed on that needle creeping up and down with every step.

"He grew strange in the head, that's all I know. But that just happens to white men up here."

God knew Ruth was right. Men would go into the Klondike and go mad. I'd heard tales in saloons of men who stripped off and went into the forest to howl with the wolves, their broken corpses found later, stiff on the moss.

Only Lady Amery wouldn't have sent me here if Jack was just another man swallowed by the forest. And there were hints and mutterings about Jack, that for all his secrecy, he'd spilled when he got drunk about things he shouldn't have known – of shining metal monsters and creatures sailing from the stars and machines that could think.

Seemed he started off sinking one shaft, another, but then moved on to hollowing out trenches too, more like he was trying to dig up bones than find any gold in the bedrock. I was passing the freshest dig when the reading on the dial piqued up a few marks. I stooped down, saw the needle tremble some more, then hopped into the trench. My fingers felt at the ice-laced dirt. A trace here, but gone as soon as I moved the thaum away. Levels low but noticeable. Then I went down a bit further and saw he'd hollowed out a section, like he'd scraped something out. Something else shone there, glowing on its own accord. I pinched it up; didn't need to take it to the light because a bit of flame danced trapped inside. Some sliver of crystal or glass thinner than a thumbnail, surface patterned like a cross-stitch. The thaum's needle jumped when I held it closer. Not just residue, then, a bit more left behind. But it was just a fragment of whatever Jack found.

"How are you with tracking down a man, if he's still living? Or men, if he ain't?" I called to Ruth.

"That's what you brought me for." A pause, after. Then she said, "Might be you won't need those services anymore."

The way she said it… I scrambled up the slick frozen soil so I could see where she was staring.

The figure was a distance away, crouched on a rock. I straightened, let the thaum drop and let a hand stray to my gun. He wasn't pointing a rifle, though, just sitting silent. Even from there, even in his rough flannel and trousers caked with dirt and coming apart with rot, I could recognize him as the Toronto gentleman from the photograph Sabina gave me. Barely. Back then he was clean-cut, dapper even, suited up in black, and clean-shaven so you could see the smooth lines of his chin. Now he was gaunt, had a long and lanky beard to match his long and lanky form.

And he wasn't alone.

c (I) c

Working for Lady Amery, I was used to my share of strange sights, whether it was some priest sitting on a shield while hovering over the sand (Egypt, 1896, anti-gravity device) or a woman peeling free her face to reveal another one beneath (Colorado, 1897, special chemical compound that could mimic human skin). But Ruth wasn't, and I knew I'd chosen the right guide when she didn't collapse or run but pulled a big knife from her belt instead.

There were people hidden behind the various boulders along the slope, four folk rising up all at the same time and two of them *were* pointing rifles. People, I say, but their limbs and faces shone with wires wound tight around, points jabbed in like Christ's crown leaving dried blood streaking down their skin. The way their limbs jerked and swung and stuttered, it was clear it was those shining tendrils moving the flesh and bone and not any muscle beneath. Revenants, I thought at first, and I knew there was a bacteria that did that from one of Greta's missions last year. But no, these bodies weren't reanimated, they were more like puppets thrall to the whims of those fine prehensile cords they wore.

"You should have stopped," Jack shouted. "Stopped looking for me, stopped looking for us. You see what's happened to the last ones who tried their hand at searching." He indicated the four. "They tried thieving from me." He paused, I couldn't tell why. "Wanted to separate us. They came close, but they shouldn't have."

I clicked the tiny lever on my pistol over to the far right but didn't draw, not right then. Instead, I raised my hands over my head. "You mistake me," I called out. "I'm no thief. I came for you. I came to help you."

Neither he nor the four moved at all. "I can't be helped. You see what's waiting, why I didn't want any following. Who told you to come here?"

I racked my brains for a proper lie then, maybe about his sister sending me to come bring him home, but he'd been watching us that whole time. Something nearer the truth would have to do. "You're not right in the head, Jack. Whatever you found, it's changed you like it changed those dead men. You don't want to visit that on the world, do you?"

He said nothing.

I tried again. "You gotta *turn away*, Jack. Whatever you found is too big for just you. It'll eat you, maybe already has."

Jack took his time before answering. "Are you a nun, come to save my soul? Because I have already found God, and she is cold. She is pitiless. She was content just with me but you won't leave her in peace. You came and now we can't let you tell a soul. Why did you have to do that?"

He gave no signal, no fanfare, but I knew to spring aside just then.

The two with the rifles opened fire one after the other. I knocked Ruth down so a bullet only took her hat, made it soar. The dirt plumed up where I'd been standing and we both rolled down into the trench as Jack's dead men drew back bolts to feed in the next rounds. Me, I braced one hand on the lip of the trench and vaulted up, drawing my pistol while I did and letting the bullets unspool in a short burst. I was too far away to make much damage but the noise and patter made enough distraction to buy me a little time. I charged up that hill for the next bit of cover I could find, a toppled wheelbarrow, and the bullet meant for me went denting iron instead. They were clumsy with their aim, the frame-and-meat setup not suited for fine motor work. Fortunate, that.

Next time I ducked out, I took a half second to aim. A long shot, but I got it, blew through the one man's hand so the gun went fumbling out of his fingers, mangled flesh no good for the wire to manipulate after. I'd need a long sprint to get back to my pack, cursed myself for leaving it so far off.

The other two were running down with woodsman's hatchets free from the belts, following the one I'd just disarmed, while Jack was back behind the stone. From the angle, I could tell he was holding his hands over his eyes like he was weeping before he slid out of sight. Well, fuck him. I judged the distance, popped up to hit the remaining gunman, but got him in the arm instead. Meant I'd wasted the shot since I didn't bust open some bone. Opening holes in rotting meat wouldn't even slow them down.

"Make for the creek!" I told Ruth. I squared my shoulders and flicked out my knife with my left hand. The gunman aimed for her but this time my three bullets struck home, made his leg unstitch and sent him stumbling.

Already two were splitting off to run for my guide while she splashed through the water. Me, I still needed to conserve bullets and one of those bastards was too close for comfort. Thing is, hatchets like that are meant for cutting wood, not people. The heads aren't balanced for speed. You can see a swing coming from a mile off and I ducked as the axe went whistling over. I didn't want to get caught by the twitching wires moving the dead man about so I put a shot square in his chest. It sparked against metal criss-crossed like laces on a corset, but at a close range like that the force alone made the dead man stagger. I danced in, my knife plunging into his side and tearing through till the flat was resting against one of those cords. I hit the catch on the handle and yanked free the ripcord stashed inside. Didn't back off fast enough before the dead man gave me a good whack in the face with the axe's handle. Not hard enough to draw blood, but it still sent me sprawling.

Too late for him, though. He had the hatchet raised up for a strike but the dynamo in the knife was already engaged and on a two-second count sent a burst that crackled all through the metal holding him up. It didn't look nothing like when you used that knife on a person. No freezing and shaking as the shock fed electricity through the water running through you, no; instead those wires glowed red, blue, white, then stripped off in a bundle of coils. No burst of blood when the wires came free either. Just a slow ooze and the corpse dropping face-first. I rolled out of the way and ripped my knife out of him.

The other one coming up behind didn't seem so keen after seeing that, not after I shot him with my remaining rounds. I won't say he hollered for his buddies, because he didn't say a thing, but they were turning their attention. Another bullet from the hunting rifle sang by, though the one shooting it was balanced on one leg. I was all out of my own. Worst thing, the wires I'd freed were moving again.

The shock gave me enough time to get on my feet and make a run for it, just hoping that his aim wasn't steady enough. I was a few paces off from my pack before the other one reached me. He was acting different, the wires slithering out towards the ground like snakes. I tucked my gun back in my belt, barrel hot against my trousers, and dropped down to take up a rusty shovel. Just the end, I lifted it up one-handed and spun it for enough momentum to give that body a good solid whack without needing to drop my knife. He flew back. Space enough in there for me to flip open the side pocket of my pack where I'd stuffed the string of three ferocient canisters.

I let my knife drop, drew out one of those bundles of glass and brass and twisted the top to prime it. Closed my eyes, held my breath, and dashed it on the ground between me and the puppet corpse. A scream ripped through the air, so high it almost popped my eardrums, and through my eyelids I could see the flash of green. One big pulse of ferocient energy – it'd only work if I'd guessed right from the way the dynamo knife affected them, overload any electrical current, pack enough magnetic resonance to stop the smallest spark, fry them clear in a wave of heavy static.

The blast was wide-ranging too, which is why you had to be careful with them. Expensive as all hell. Lady Amery reserved them for the real nasty threats, when whatever technology your enemy had was far beyond the ken of humankind.

So after the few seconds where my vision cleared from white milky light, I saw the remaining three corpses were falling, the wires spread out around them like tree-roots from a precariously perched spruce. My knife's blade was twisted up into something useless because it still held a bit of charge. Couldn't hear nothing over the ringing in my ears and the air felt thick and smelled like ozone. I looked up the slope and saw that Jack was already gone.

"Shit," I said to no one in particular. Was then that I could hear Ruth's voice shouting, though I didn't know what. I sat down on the cold ground and fetched another spiral of bullets to feed into my gun.

She came over to me limping, though I couldn't see a wound on her. I said, "We need to chase him. Need you to track him."

Ruth's eyes couldn't hold more disbelief than she showed right then. She said, "I'm leaving."

"I'll double your pay."

"Nothing's gonna make me go up against...that."

"Triple." I said. No answer to that, so I said, "Five times. My benefactor can afford it."

She scratched her head, at the close-tied braids, and gave a worried look at the dead wires. "Okay."

I hefted my pack and we started after Jack.

c ⊕ c

I didn't need her for the tracking, not really. I was trained in that just as well as I was trained in anything else. Yet Ruth knew the land better than I did, not just where to step but how, the dips and fissures and too-faint game trails, the short-cuts that would save you time instead of landing you in brambles.

Pursuit went on well into the night and over to the morning; we only took an hour's sleep in between. Sunset came and went but a band of light kept shining bright enough to read by. Wind picked up under a starless sky, sending the spruce needles brushing together, whispering.

Jack wasn't careful about his flight. Truth is, we could have caught him a lot earlier, but I wanted a clear sense of where he was fleeing. Ruth ended up making a good guess. We clambered up onto a ridge above the trees, just hard rock and long grass beneath our boots, and followed to an outcrop of mottled grey stone. Spotted him for the third time since we started, just on the rough trail below us, and I fired a shot so he'd know we were there. Just like before, he tried running but the distance was too short for it to do him any good. I pattered some bullets on the ground in front of him and he stopped short. "There's nowhere left to run to, Jack," I shouted, while Ruth skidded down, holding a coil of rope.

Jack Sheldon stopped his wild glances and raised his hands, slow-like. He let Ruth shove him down to his knees; she trussed his hands together behind his back and divested him of his knife. I came skipping after.

"You can't follow," he croaked.

"I can go wherever I like, thank you kindly." I tapped the remaining two canisters looped to my belt where they should've been all along. "Now, we're gonna talk and you're gonna lead us good and proper to wherever you stashed this…thing of yours."

"I won't—"

I balled my hand up in a fist and gave him a hard smack. He cried out; spat a tooth and some blood after.

"If Ruth's got the right of it, you're headed for a cave a bit up north, not even an hour's walk more. She right?"

From the way he hung his head, I knew she was.

"You dragged it up this far. Why bother?"

First, Jack just swallowed and it was then I noticed how pale he'd gotten. Finally he whispered, "I didn't want others to hear her."

"Hear? No, stay there on your knees and speak up."

His body trembled just a bit. "Madam, I first came up this way to die. I couldn't face my family if I left the Yukon with even less than I came, so I staked everything on one last claim. If I failed, then I'd find someplace peaceful and hang myself. Only when I started digging, I heard something under that soil. Or not heard, there wasn't so much of a voice, but she was trying to speak, gave me waking dreams like I'd never had, pulled me like a current. I followed her, found bits and pieces of some red metal like I'd never seen, and then I found her in the dirt and hauled her up. After touching her, we – we bonded together. She got right in my brain. I was going to protect her. I was going to let her rest and feed until she was ready for the world. I hauled her where I thought no one else would come, where no one else would interfere."

"You fed her those men I fought back there?" I asked him.

He shook his head. "No, ma'am. We couldn't let them leave and spread the word. It was too early for that. What she wants is iron, copper, gold. She transmutes it. Builds...such pretty things. Such pretty, pretty things."

I could imagine those "pretty things."

"She'll leave me. The dreams aren't the same. They're angry. She'll do something to the world, something terrible, only, she wants to speak and tries so hard but I can't quite understand her. Maybe if I know what she truly means..." His voice choked at the end, like he was ready to weep.

Ruth looked at him like he was crazy. Me, I was more inclined to pity. He found something he shouldn't have, like so many people the girls met on Sabina's missions. But I wasn't going to let pity stop me.

"Show her to us," I said.

"I..." he finally looked up, looked me in the eyes. "Those other men, they found her. Tracked us all the way to the cave."

"Oh, I've seen things far worse than that," I said. "Come on."

c ⦿ c

I wasn't telling the truth, not then, probably not ever.

I heard her speaking when we came in sight of the cave cut in the hillside, though "hear" isn't the right word for it. More, a thickness to the air, a current of textures and colours. The relief that passed over Jack's face made me twice as wary. Coming closer, I saw in the darkness the gleam of platinum and amber, unknown alloys swaying slow like seaweed. I saw things flitting like Lady Amery's automata, only lacking solidness. Just frames of filament writhing into forms like dragonflies and bats. A glow, pure and white, suffused the tunnel's end, beckoning.

"Keep him still," I said to Ruth, and she tightened the ropes.

Me, I let fall my backpack and took hold of a canister, twisting the cap.

"Shouldn't go in there," Ruth warned.

The currents were stronger, snatches of memory invading my brain but nothing like the memories a person ever had. Hit your feelings, though, warm and seductive; hit your wants and desires and ambitions. I bit my lip.

No, I thought I'd be prepared for this and I was wrong, well and truly.

"You've been helping, this…" I didn't know what to call it and didn't bother coining a name, "build itself a form. But," – the strange voice was shifting towards frustration, hatred, a bit of anger – "there's something wrong. Incomplete. Lost.

"You were right," I said, the currents pushing from the cave growing stronger, making me weak-kneed, light-headed. "Whatever she brings to the world, it won't be good."

"What are you planning?" Jack asked, his voice catching.

"I'll disable it. Then I'll talk to it. Just talk," I said, so quiet I didn't even hear myself. I could barely move then, and all of me wanted to head forward, but I took a quaking step back instead. "You should have let it lie…" Whatever was there wasn't from Earth, and it wasn't whole. Everything about the thing in the cave raised the hair on my skin, made my stomach churn and bubble.

Something was moving out too, a skittering noise of barbed wire scraping stone.

I made ready to throw the canister. Only when my arm went back Jack leaped forward. I'd come too close to him, and somehow he got the strength to throw himself out of Ruth's grasp and sink his teeth into my wrist. The canister dropped to the dirt but didn't hit hard enough to break, and he was biting, drawing blood as he went. I jammed the barrel of my gun against his forehead and fired, spattering brains out the back of his skull, and that loosened his jaws well enough.

Not before a grasping hand caught me, not flesh but steel, life pulsing through it, the touch plunging me somewhere, elsewhere.

Shapes slick and graceful, moving between the stars, innards filled with thousands of seeds. At the heart of a great leviathan sat a crystal, throbbing and bright, patterned like the fragment I'd found at Jack's camp. I followed the one, steering the way, before something came crashing through, some blast of pink and purple dust. The crystal cracked and the leviathan broke and the seeds scattered in an expanding cloud and one piece of the vessel, the largest piece, came streaking down after a thousand years to the Klondike as a shooting star.

The visions shifted, taking me to mankind in those great black shapes. Ships, I realized, and the world beneath, crashing, clanking, suffused with tiny lights and moving pictures on a million screens of glass.

I drew in a deep breath, remembering I had a body again, saw how the wires tightened around my hand but not hard enough to cause pain. Jack's blood was still hot on my bodice, and then I knew – he said he'd bonded with it, with *her*. And she'd sensed that bond break when he died so she was drawing me in, trying to speak like he'd said. She had no voice but it was beautiful just as it was, beautiful and broken.

I hate to think what might have happened had I waited a moment longer. That thing was pointing a way, promising I could be a messenger, a prophet, trying to dig into my thoughts so it could adapt and use what I knew. The nearest thing that could think, because it needed a master just as much as it needed a slave.

I could have brought its plans to pass and I knew, even in that muddled space of time, I'd do a far better job of it than Jack, poor Jack, who just wasn't up to a secret like this.

Only I didn't wait. I lifted a foot and smashed my boot down on the ferocient canister and all the visions went dark.

c ⊕ c

It wasn't a thinking thing, not truly, else it would have survived the blast like me and Ruth did. The crystal was a machine of some sort with parts so small you couldn't see them move.

Commands fed in like a slip of paper in a golem, save this one only held echoes and fragments and its purpose was drifting dead between the stars.

I lay on my back with Jack's corpse beneath me and I sat up slow, rubbing my head and still sensing a faint pulse and rhythm shaking my innards. In front of me the cave was wilting, those fine metal meshes sloughing from the walls and chiming as they did.

I never felt such a headache before, all the blood squeezing away my brain.

Never felt so much sorrow before, either.

Not sure what someone else might have done, someone better than I am. A part of me still wanted to be with…well, Jack had called it *her*. Part of me still wants that, all she offered, all she promised if only you could *understand* and put her back together.

She'd reached for me as guide and saviour and I'd killed her.

Ruth was lying a few feet off uncurling from her ball, eyes wide and dazed. "You're not going in there, are you?" she asked in a high reedy voice when she saw me stumbling closer to the cave-mouth.

"Just…finishing the job," I said. My hands were shaking so bad I almost dropped the last canister while trying to make the twist. I limped closer and threw it hard as I could down the cave mouth, this time turning and ducking when the shock wave came screaming past.

The headache was still there after, but that floating sense of loss and sadness was gone. I bent down and hobbled into the cave, sharp metal biting at my boots, iron still hot from the surge. Their fading redness gave enough light to see by as I followed the slope into the hillside.

There it was, white crystal the size of two fists held to-gether, the last few pinpricks of light tracing slow lazy spirals like dandelion fluff over its rough surface before winking into nothing, leaving just a blank pale stone like uncut quartz with no life in it at all. It was only a piece of something greater, you could see the ragged edges where the rest had torn away. Around that, fine gold and silver mixed with black cast iron and dull copper carefully arranged in an emerging skeleton.

She'd been trying to make another body. One that looked halfway human.

c (I) c

I'm here in Dawson City waiting for a steamer after my letter went through to Lady Amery's agents arranging payment for Ruth. I'm not sure what I'll say when I get to Prince Rupert, if I get there at all. I have this dead crystal mind stowed in a dull grey sack and I don't know what to do with it.

I can disappear, I think. Abscond, if I really wanted to. Annabelle taught us how to do that, it wasn't even hard com-pared to the other things I'd done in my life.

Because there was one thing Lady Amery was right about, and mind it's just the one: The world wasn't ready for this. Maybe it didn't have to be. Maybe that intelligence had to be made ready for the world.

And if that was true, maybe I was the one to guide her.

BUFFALO GALS

COLLEEN ANDERSON

"Them buffalo gals stampede through at least one night a week. See there."

The prospector's voice came from behind Chex'ináx yaa wunagút[1] as she peered at the churned up moss and soft earth. She ran her fingers over the dentalium shell buttons that bordered her red serge jacket as she examined the ground's pattern. The harsh alcohol tang wafted on the man's breath and she wondered if it was another case of being alone for too long or too much drinking.

She debated dismissing his claim as hallucination. No crime was evident and she had more pressing matters. But it would be foolish to disregard anything unusual. "Why do you call them buffalo gals?" she asked the bearded prospector.

He smacked his lips and scratched at his unkempt hair, as if reluctant to reveal more. "Well, they's got these hoofs and steam comes outta their noses. Oh yeah, and horns of course."

"Of course," replied Chex'ináx yaa wunagút. "Then why do you think they're girls?"

If he'd been reluctant before, he now proceeded to tuck in his undershirt, walk back and forth, and flap his one hand as

---

[1] A note on English pronunciation: The letter "x̱" is a raspy h sound in the back of the throat, and "x̱'" is that sound, but cut short, thus "chay-kee-nah anah ya wun-a-goot." (The line under the letter is part of being rendered in English.)

he spoke. "Well, they's look like gals, despite them horns. They have girl shapes, you know." He looked at the ground as he motioned at his chest, with a rounding motion. "And legs, but with hoofs, and they's all buttery shiny, like brass or gold." Chex'ináx̱ yaa wunagút cocked her head, looking from the man back to the ground. There were a few circular imprints that could be hooves but spring runoff made the ground too soft to tell for certain. And his story was very elaborate even for a whiskey-fuelled imagining.

The North-West Mounted Police had only formed a year before and Chex'ináx̱ yaa wunagút was as experienced as anyone else on the force. One thing she had learned long before she left her northern village of Kadux̱x̱úká – after the trading post had been built and the *dleit Káa,* the white men, renamed it Tongass Island – was never to ignore her intuition. She didn't know what these "buffalo gals" were but it sounded like they were constructed. That meant someone had built them, and that took money.

"If you see anything else, please send for me. You will be able to find the office in Seńáḵw.[1] Your name is?"

"Umm, Ben McCready. And who should I ask for?"

"Constable Chex'ináx̱ yaa wunagút."

McCready tried but mangled it so badly she winced. She actually found it funny when the *dleit Káa* could not pronounce the Lingit language. "My name in your language is 'Walks Through Shadows.'"

He stammered and blushed. "Thank you, Miss Shadows – I mean, Constable Walks Through Shadows."

---

[1] Seńáḵw is to be read as Snawk, Snawq, Sneawq, or Snawkw – formally known as Kitsilano Indian Reserve 6, a site of the Indigenous Squamish band government, located near what is now the Kitsilano neighbourhood of Vancouver, British Columbia. Other words contain "ḵ" or "ʔ" as implied phonetic intention. Google for more.

Chex'ináx̱ yaa wunagút left the prospector and mounted her horse, returning north to the village of Seṅáḵw, but first she detoured to the Musqueam village west of her office.

A telegram from the North-West Mounted Police outpost in Fort Calgary had indicated that one Peter Stanton had robbed the Canadian Pacific train near the settlement. Chances were he was headed toward the *dleit Káa* townsite of Granville in the Musqueam community of Xwáʔxway, or Whoi Whoi, as the dispatch indicated. The nations of the people, including the *dleit Káa*, had worked hard to bring in the steam trains early, by 1866, and now, less than ten years later, there were those who thought the trains were great beasts to be gutted for their riches.

As she rode, she took in the sharp scent of cedar and fir trees. Pale pink bleeding hearts and the bright yellow petals of woolly sunflowers dotted the ground. Always observing, she gazed along the trail into the cool shade of the great trees.

As the villages came into sight, Chex'ináx̱ yaa wunagút saw a wisp of a wraith off to her right, lingering by a rough-trunked cedar. She pulled the reins and the horse stopped. Watching the spirit, Chex'ináx̱ yaa wunagút tried to sense its past. It was this unusual gift that had pulled her to travel, far from Kaduḵx̱úká. She would always be of the raven Taant'á Ḵwáan and proudly bear the clan crest of three eggs on a shell on her red serge. In the new townsites, she thought her skills could aid people, while in her village everyone had grown uncomfortable, earning her her current nickname. She had searched out the upholders of peace, always believing in a need for all peoples to live in harmony. A dream perhaps, but she would strive for it.

The spirit wavered between green and grey, solidifying, then turning to strands of mist. The other half of her skill was to disperse the ghosts to the world beyond. She urged the horse forward but the wraith spun up and away, and all she felt was an exuberant bubbling lightness as joy. Not a murdered soul then. She moved on.

The only member of the North-West Mounted Police stationed on the coast, her greatest concern was the murders of women from the townships of Granville, Hastings and Señákw. There had been six so far; Musqueam, *dleit Káa,* and Squamish. Another woman had gone missing three weeks before, and was presumed murdered as well.

The mossy ground held some imprints at this time of year and any change might give her a lead on the killer. She was but a half hour from the villages and the newly built Granville townsite. The Musqueam were worried about maintaining the rentals for Granville and Hastings as the areas grew with the *dleit Káa* hunger for lumber. The fact that women of both races had been murdered indicated that those crimes were probably not from racial tensions. After visiting the Musqueam, to no avail, she rode back to Señákw, smiling at the children running up and hoping to earn a coin for an errand. She dismounted, paying a penny to a boy to stable the horse as she entered the North-West Mounted Police office, a grey clapboard shack with one window. Two telegraphs had been dropped off by Yune's girl. Only the detachment, or distant villages sent anything of concern.

"Stanton last seen in Hope four months ago." A wanted poster followed.

The second telegram read: *"Cannot spare extra men to help with murder investigation. Do what you can."* Chex'ináx yaa wunagút's lips pressed together. She wondered, if it had been some rich banker would she have received more aid? She was one person handling three native villages, including the Capilano across the inlet, and two burgeoning *dleit Káa* townsites, trying to keep the peace when tensions or alcohol ran too high.

She had no leads on Stanton, where he might hole up or even where he would spend the stolen money. In order of importance, he came second. She couldn't dismiss that the buffalo apparitions came after the murders and train robbery, and she wondered if they were all connected.

It was time to start asking more questions, and the saloons, blacksmiths, dry goods store, and bank were the places to start. She poured a cup of the bitter coffee the *dleit Káa* had brought from their country. Sipping it, she winced at the first taste though she enjoyed the clarity of thought and burst of energy that shivered through her body.

Chex'ináx̱ yaa wunagút put the enamelled cup down, locked the important papers in the safe and left her one-room office with a poster of Peter Stanton in her hand. She pulled her long dark braid over her shoulder, its tip brushing against her brass buttons. As she walked through the village of Senákw, she greeted elders and women hauling fish to drying racks.

Moving between humps of grass and low brush, she approached Faro and George Wednesday carving out a new canoe at the water's edge. The water lapped sullenly at the small pebbles.

"What brings you here, Walks Through Shadows?" asked George Wednesday, his hair worn long in the traditional way. He sharpened an adze against a whetstone. They all kept to nicknames.

She showed them the poster, and Faro straightened from running his hand over the cedar prow. His hair came to just below the ears like many of the *dleit Káa* and he wore a blue cotton shirt but kept to deerskin leggings. "It's still too rough. We need to take down another inch of thickness or we may as well go out on a stone."

George Wednesday grunted, rubbing his wide nose. "Sorry, Walks Through Shadows, not seen his likes around but then I stay in Senákw most of the time. Have you checked in Whoi Whoi?"

"They haven't seen him," she replied.

Faro smiled. "Not seen him either, but then they all look alike."

She suppressed a sigh, knowing that Faro liked to joke. "You know that's not true. Still, if either of you see anything, please let me know." As she turned away, she stopped as if just remembering. "Oh, have you seen any unusual activity; men watching women for too long, following them, someone who just doesn't feel right?"

This time neither of them joked. They looked down at their feet in silence.

"One of those girls was my cousin's neighbour's wife. She never hurt anyone," Faro commented softly.

George Wednesday sighed. "Her husband spends too much time in the white man saloons now."

Which could be because of his guilt, but she doubted it. He would have had to kill the others as well, and anyone who took so many women was well past guilt. She thanked the canoe builders and walked over to the Granville townsite, which abutted on Senákw's eastern border, but the line was obvious, for the trees thinned noticeably. She dropped off the wanted poster at the newly minted printer and asked for ten copies to be printed and posted.

c ⦿ c

For three days, in between breaking up fights and investigating some minor thefts, she canvassed the villages of Senákw and Whoi Whoi, as well as the Granville and Hastings townsites. She took her horse to cover more area, and still the lack of information disturbed her. The women had been murdered over a span of six months. Who was this person? Some people had said it was a spirit, but Chex'ináx yaa wunagút had learned that more often than not, it was the flesh responsible for most crimes. The spirits that were left behind sometimes pointed to the perpetrators but they could not give her names.

At Gassy Jack Deighton's two-storey hotel the first clue came through. Jorgensen and Chu ran the local supply store for prospecting, mining, and building. Chu had helped lay the last railway ties and his tales of working the rail lines made Chex'ináx yaa wunagút realize that being the only viewer of spirits in her village had been a mild inconvenience compared to the hardships of those who had worked under such conditions.

They sat at a table drinking ale in the saloon. She sipped soda, for the North-West Mounted Police must always be vigilant.

Chu said, "Yes, young man-boy he come in and want brass. Why for brass?"

"Brass?" she asked. "And did you supply him with this brass? How did he pay?"

Jorgensen, a towering blond Swede with a moustache touching his chest, and a surprisingly soft voice, quaffed his beer and said, "Yah, ve are not stupid. Good money he pay. Good gold. Must be prospector. We sell – brass, wires, tools, coal, yah?"

She thought back to the prospector's description of buttery gold buffalo girls. Could it be? "Any idea where he is?"

Chu and Jorgensen shook their heads. "No," said Chu. "He come in. We take money. We give. Not question. Many different requests."

Jorgensen peered down at his friend, as round as Jorgensen was tall. He smacked him on the back. "Yah, ve like money and ve never question, only sell. Even ven man buy yards and yards of rope. Honest business, selling."

At this Chex'ináx yaa wunagút sat up straight and asked for a description. A man staking a claim might need a lot of rope but there was something... The bodies of the murdered women had shown burns or bruising around their wrists or necks. This could have been caused by rope. Unfortunately, the men's description was vague. A man of medium height with hair to his collar – brown they thought – brown eyes, average looking, maybe Indian, maybe white. They argued but neither had a name or any other information.

"Sorry, Constable Walks Through Shadows, ve see too many people."

"What you think of proposed name?" asked Chu, lifting his bleary gaze to his towering friend. "Granville, then maybe Vancouver. Why no stick with Gastown?"

c (I) c

While she knew a train robber and a murderer were in the vicinity, she could find no trail amongst the old thick cedars. She examined the areas where the women had been taken or found. Chex'ináx yaa wunagút needed to solve one of the cases before the North-West Mounted Police questioned her ability.

In the office, the pot-bellied stove built heat to stave off the spring chill. She pulled out a map and marked it in charcoal for every spot where the women had last been seen.

Then in ink, she marked the locations of where their bodies had been found. She wrote the dates beside each one.

The first woman, Marjorie McIntosh, was *dleit Káa* and had worked in the Hastings townsite's saloon as a prostitute. The second, a Squamish woman named T'óok', or Nettle, was taken at the southern outskirts of Senákw; the third, Mary Corn Woman had been of the Musqueam nation and working at Gassy Jack's saloon as a barmaid. A pattern began to emerge.

One *dleit Káa*, one Squamish, one Musqueam, and then they repeated. The woman still missing was *dleit Káa*. Whoever was murdering them was attacking each nation but always attacking women. With seven murdered or missing the next was sure to be Squamish, but what if the murderer couldn't tell the nation and only went for the area? Her map indicated the sites where they were abducted, but it wasn't clear. The concentration had been along the boundaries of the Granville-Senákw lands but that was only where each woman had been seen last.

It brought her no closer to finding the culprit, not at the moment.

Night had fallen already, with a slight mist rising, when she realized it was time to leave, eat, and stop thinking of crime. She folded the map and put it in her satchel, placed her cap on her head and closed the office.

"Ma'am! Constable Walks Through Shadows!"

Chex'ináx yaa wunagút finished locking the door and turned to the urgent summons.

McCready waved to her as his bowlegged gait brought him toward her. "You gots to hurry, ma'am. Them buffalo gals is active. I can show you where but we gotta go now or they'll be gone before you know it." He hitched up his suspenders, buttoning his worn jacket and shifted from foot to foot.

She grabbed a lantern from the porch, turned up the light, and asked, "You have a horse?"

He shook his head.

"We'll use mine. It will save time."

She handed him the lantern as she buttoned her jacket to the neck. The chill night puffed their breaths before them. Checking her pistol, Chex'ináx̱ yaa wunagút wondered if she would need more ammunition, but this was still not a crime.

Once mounted, she took the lantern from McCready, then had him hop up behind. "Hold the lantern but turn it low, just a glimmer. Now show me where." Her horse danced with her agitation, tossing its cedar-coloured mane.

Chex'ináx̱ yaa wunagút's skin tingled. Energy nearly pulled her forward as the sky turned from indigo to navy. The stars sprang out like shell buttons on night's blanket and the half moon added light, letting her eyes adjust.

They moved quickly but carefully south of the Granville townsite and then east. The forest thickened, weaving into patches of black shadows on navy.

"Right up here," he whispered. "We has to be quiet or they might spook."

She tossed the reins over a branch and leapt down, leaving the prospector to dismount. A barely discernible glow limned the trees and Chex'ináx̱ yaa wunagút motioned Mc-Cready to stay back. Tucking her braid in between the brass buttons of her jacket, she moved cautiously, finally peering between several cedar branches.

At first she saw just the shimmer of a shape but when her mind accepted what her eyes saw, her jaw dropped. There was only one – graceful, powerful, a brass and copper creature standing the height of a person. It bent a little forward at the waist but the shape was definitely that of a woman, ending in two legs with rounded hooves.

From head to toe, she glimmered gold, amber, oily in the faint light, small rivets marking seams up each leg, along the torso, suggestive in its feminine bareness. The arms ended in mitt-like hands and the head was a marvel. Large and round, it was more buffalo than woman, small golden horns curving upward, human-shaped eyes made from some sort of glinting green glass. Steam lazily rolled from the wide flat nostrils but the lips and hinged mouth were also reminiscent of a woman's. The construct shifted from hoof to hoof, lifting each leg high at the knee.

Then the buffalo woman pushed off, loping between the cedar trees and moving east. Chex'ináx yaa wunagút did not have time to mount her horse but ran after the creature. She had never stopped honing her skills and could pace most animals when hunting. Still, she barely kept up and cursed not bringing the lantern, but McCready was now far behind.

She lost sight of the metal being but continued, hoping to get a glimpse. Stopping, she listened, moving cautiously forward, pushing branches and sorrel aside. Her braid was tangled with bits of twigs and leaves, and her cap had fallen off somewhere along the way.

Chex'ináx yaa wunagút saw a brightening in the dark. Peering from the blackness that hid her against the contrast of light, she saw a small cabin, nestled in the surrounding trees. Rough tables nearly formed a square in front, with lanterns hanging from poles. A large oilskin covered something behind the cabin. The buffalo woman stood to the side, near Chex'ináx yaa wunagút. A man, in a black vest and shirtsleeves rolled up, bent over scraps of metal and coils.

Her mind jumbled the images, trying to assimilate everything. When she looked at the buffalo woman standing immobile like a gilded statue, steam trickled from the nostrils, and light flickered from the eyes. Was it alive, or a machine?

Then she saw a white and grey form shutter, as if someone opened and shut a shade, overlaying the brass figure. It rose and subsided, rose and subsided above the head. Features formed and wavered, a woman's face. As Chex'ináx yaa wunagút watched, stunned, she realized it was the face of one of the murdered women. The woman looked sad, staring at her and before Chex'ináx yaa wunagút knew it, she had drawn her gun and entered the clearing whispering a prayer, and reached up. Her fingers tingled as she sent the energy to disperse the spirit that had been tied to the machine.

A sigh, or a lightening of the air, moved through the glade.

The man turned, dropping the instrument he had been holding and ran toward her. "What did you do?"

She pointed her gun and stepped back. "Stop right there!"

His large brown eyes teared up and he fell to his knees. "What did you do?" he whispered, staring at his empty hands.

In the wavering light she saw his face. Nothing added up.

"You're Peter Stanton, wanted for armed robbery of the Canadian Pacific Railway."

He didn't seem to hear her, didn't even look up, still kneeling, head bowed as if he prayed. "You don't know what you did."

She frowned. "What I did?"

"You...dissipated her."

She narrowed her eyes. "You – you can see them? Their spirits?"

He nodded.

She had been going to ask how, but then she could not answer that question for herself. "What have you done to the women? Did you kill them all?"

Stanton frowned at her. "No, I didn't kill them."

"Then what are you doing with the spirit of a murdered woman?" She motioned with her gun for him to stand.

He did so slowly, as if he was realizing the severity of the situation.

"I didn't do anything with their spirits."

Their. "Where are the others?"

He motioned to the oil cloth and she made him pull it off. "Slowly."

There stood another four buffalo women in different stages of completion, like goddesses waiting. She could see two wraiths moving in and out of the constructs.

"The spirit was trapped by your machine."

"No." He clenched his fists. "No, she was not. She chose to inhabit it."

Chex'ináx yaa wunagút looked over to the buffalo woman. It still stood there, steam trailing from its nostrils. She gestured with her gun, for once feeling completely out of her depth. Murderers, she could track. Robbers she could arrest, but this, she had no idea what this all meant. "I don't understand."

Stanton ran his hands through his hair, shaking his head. "Of course not, how could you?" He moved toward his cabin, motioning her to follow. He opened the door to the modest room and went inside, lighting several lanterns, pulled out the single chair for her to sit, and grabbed a crate for himself.

He looked at her then, actually registering her red serge jacket and regalia. He sighed. "Oh. You're North-West

Mounted Police. Well, let me explain before you take me. And let me wrap up."

She sensed no threat, no subterfuge, but she kept her gun out. He was a man of average size, not overly muscled, but she remained alert, checking the room for guns or traps. She positioned herself so that she could see the door, in case he had partners. The lantern light left the corners in shadow but only a child could have hidden there.

He sat on the crate across from where she stood but stared out the open door.

She prodded him by saying, "You could see the spirit. I don't understand what you were doing with it."

He shook his head. "I wasn't doing anything. Well, not at first." He sighed. "I was coming out to get my sister. I didn't want her working...doing what she was doing in that saloon. But I was too late. She was murdered before I could get here."

"Marjorie McIntosh?"

"Her husband died. She came out here to work, to survive. I couldn't save my little sister. I robbed the train for her, to give her enough to start a new life. I didn't care if I went to jail. But I was too late."

Chex'ináx yaa wunagút's heart felt heavy. He had risked everything to no avail. *If* he was telling the truth. "But what is this construct you made?"

His eyes brightened for a moment. "They are my buffalo fighters. I heard of the other murders. The gold meant nothing after that. But I wanted people to remember my sister for more than what she had become. She'd been fierce and strong and independent and to see her..." He choked up and sat for a moment, breathing heavily. "To see her reduced to serving men to survive, it broke my heart. I'd been an engineer, and a bit of a sculptor before. I wanted to make something strong and beautiful, so I built the women. Better to create them than have the gold and money go to some rich baron who is getting fat caring little about people or land."

He stood abruptly and she brought her gun up, tensing, watching as he paced, running his hands through his hair. "I got more than I asked for. It's taken months but they're almost ready. I was initially building them to remember those missing women. But I wanted them to be more than sculptures, to be fierce and strong. Did you know the buffalo are being decimated?"

He whirled and really looked at Chex'ináx̱ yaa wunagút, walking around her, ignoring that she pivoted to keep the gun on him. "The crest on your jacket indicates you're from the north. You don't have buffalo there, or here, but that doesn't matter. The Plains People depend on them and they are wonderful wild beasts. These automatons I'm building are to protect the buffalo. I'm designing them to scare off those hunting for sport. The herds have to survive. My sister loved them."

With that last statement, Peter Stanton's fire dimmed. He just walked out the door and stood staring at the buffalo woman standing quiescent before the cabin.

Chex'ináx̱ yaa wunagút came out behind him. Conflicts warred in her. A madman might think it appropriate to kill women so their spirits would fuel his machine. There was a madness about Stanton. She was sworn to keep the peace but Stanton's cause captured her heart.

"You were going to build one for each murdered woman?"

"Yes, or until the money ran out."

She shook her head. "But I do not understand the use of their spirits."

He turned to her. Tears streaked his face. "I didn't use them. They started coming to me. Maybe they sensed my pur-

pose, maybe that's why I can see them. I never asked them –
they just came. Only two so far, now that you sent one away.
But I'm hoping Marjorie will show. They add something to the
machines. The automatons move more fluently. I think it's a
place for them to live."

Chex'ináx yaa wunagút replied, "Some spirits move on.
They do not stay. Your sister may already be gone."

Stanton closed his eyes, nodding ever so slightly.

"You know I must take you in. I must uphold the law and
you have to answer for your crime."

Peter Stanton turned to her, his brow creasing. "I know,
but I ask you, let me finish first and set them free. They'll
roam the prairies, protecting the buffalo, until they break
down, but those women's spirits will have a chance to live
for a while and do something for which they will be remembered."

Chex'ináx yaa wunagút knew the weight of spirits, of
deciding if she should send them on or let them be. Not all
wanted to go and she felt shame that she had reacted without
respecting that one spirit's wish. Yet, she had to also judge
whether Stanton was guilty and should atone for his crimes.
Her fingers ran over the shell buttons on her coat, back and
forth as she weighed her choices.

Stanton saw the resolve on her face. "Please, just let me
finish them. After that, I don't care what happens."

"I have a murderer on the loose. How do I know you
haven't been killing them?"

He closed his eyes. "I…could never murder anyone, least
of all Marjorie. Check the date of the robbery and you'll see it
was too close to her murder for me to be here."

That still didn't mean he wasn't responsible for the others,
but it just didn't add up.

"Please, Constable. Shackle me if you must, but let me stay here."

"I must take you in, but I will give you a month to finish. Do not try to escape."

"I give you my word."

She left the clearing, with Stanton and his buffalo woman watching her go.

c ◑ c

Chex'ináx̱ yaa wunagút had been staring out at the people moving around Señákw doing their daily business, laughing, shouting, children running to and fro. Gulls called out overhead and she shook herself. She was daydreaming and she still had a murderer to catch.

Before meeting Peter Stanton, she had seen ghosts from time to time. A few she had sent on to whatever place the dead inhabit after life. But she had given little thought to their lives beforehand. Now she had a link between the murdered women and at least some of their lingering wraiths. Could they tell her who the murderer was? They had not seemed angry with Stanton.

She knew Stanton wouldn't run. He was pierced by sorrow and would bleed out his efforts avenging his sister. The bizarre brass mannequins impressed her with the nobility of his desire. There was a sudden tugging pang for her people in the Whale house of the Raven clan.

The villages here lived closely beside each other; cultures and times were mixing. There was so much flux. Perhaps this unsettled feeling was only a time of change. She needed to move, release her restlessness.

She was just unsaddling her horse when several people approached. It was obvious from the grim faces that something had happened. One of the men from Granville said, "We found a woman by Hastings Mill."

Chex'ináx yaa wunagút thought of Stanton and for a minute wondered if he had needed another wraith, but he wore his grief like a cloak where each button was a deed he would take on to avenge the wrongs.

The unrelenting grey sky starkly revealed the white man's land thinned of trees, and laid out in rough grids with buildings on either side. At Hastings Mill, she approached the waterfront where reddish logs floated, waiting to be hauled in. By the water, the bloated corpse was nearly unrecognizable except for the long brown hair tangled about the face like seaweed, and the waterlogged clothing. They'd found her under a boom.

No spirit drifted about her, already having fled the horror of her murder. Chex'ináx yaa wunagút examined her neck and wrists where dark purple markings ringed the greying flesh. She had the men haul the body out so the woman could be given a decent burial. There were no other clues to the murderer's identity in the churned up earth, and the woman had been missing three weeks. She was definitely *dleit Káa*.

c ◑ c

Chex'ináx yaa wunagút revisited the sites where the bodies had been found again, and when nothing more came to light she stopped in several times to check up on Peter Stanton. His small clearing was littered with pieces of metal, and sucking mud required boots to navigate. A scarf wrapped his neck and a hat tilted crazily on his head but he worked tirelessly, moving back and forth from tables to the buffalo woman statuettes, tinkering and screwing on pieces of metal.

"How do they work?" she asked.

He looked up, not having noticed her arrival. "Constable Walks Through Shadows! They're steam engines. Much like trains."

He popped open a door in the torso. "Here is where I store the coal. They can run for three to five days before the reservoir needs refilling."

From a burlap sack under the leftmost table, he scooped up dusty coal chips and tossed them in, then shut the brass door under the bust. The buffalo woman's head swivelled toward Chex'in<u>á</u>x yaa wunagút and though the features weren't animated, she felt as if the machine watched her.

Stanton scratched his head, smiling at his creation. "They're a marvel really. The legs contain the pistons, and the buffalo-shaped head holds the water."

The mannequin raised its mitt-like hand and popped the door. Using her other hand, she scooped up coal chips and then dropped her jaw, adding the chips where a tiny orange flame danced in the back. Her mouth snapped shut and steam rolled from her wide nostrils.

The buffalo woman raised one knee and then the other and high-stepping, moved south. Just as she blended into the dappled forest cover, Chex'in<u>á</u>x yaa wunagút saw that she was moving faster.

"Where has she gone?"

"I've programmed them with punch cards for certain geographic areas. Eventually I'll add in the buffalo herds and a command to protect. But…" he stopped, his expression falling into sadness. "Since the spirits have attached themselves to some of the automatons, they don't always go where I want."

Leaning against a tree, Chex'in<u>á</u>x yaa wunagút watched him, trying to gauge his mad genius. The machines were more efficient and elegant than any train she had seen.

"Do you think they could find the murderer?"

Peter stopped and frowned, his finger idly spinning a loose screw on the table. "I…don't know. They haven't seemed to do so yet… Maybe I can send one to you, see if it can do anything. But let me finish them first. It might take a week."

In the meantime, she asked more questions. Each murder had been closer and closer to the border between the *dleit Káa* land rented from the Musqueam and the villages, or along the shoreline. That still left her no closer to finding the killer, nor on how to protect anyone.

All she could do was patrol in the evenings and hope to see something that would give her a lead. The abductions had not been spaced evenly but as the days tumbled past the villagers grew nervous, knowing another killing could happen anytime. Many women didn't want to go out in the evenings, while others retorted that they refused to live in fear.

Chex'ináx̱ yaa wunagút chose the township of Seńáḵw, knowing the next victim would be Squamish or Musqueam. While the area was too large to cover entirely, it was obvious that the murderer would be where women were likely to walk, and at night the few open establishments were the hotels and the saloons. This night she chose the Deighton Hotel in the area the locals still stubbornly called Gastown. Hours passed walking in the light chill, and Chex'ináx̱ yaa wunagút found herself staring into the inlet, seeing the ghost outline of a few ships. Straggly trees poked into the dark skyline.

She shook her head, wondering what the future would look like with the land shaved, and shivered. A small splash reached her, no doubt some night bird dipping for fish but she moved forward quietly, and unholstered her gun. The scatter of stars and the waning moon gave minimal light, and stumps or logs hunkered as darker shadows.

Nearly at the water's edge, with the light reflecting back, she saw movement, heard the half-strangled whimper of a woman, and knew. She aimed at the back of the man she could see fighting with someone. She fired and the figure spun as the bullet hit.

The man turned and ran straight at Chex'ináx̱ yaa wunagút. She must have hit the arm. Her reflexes were good but she couldn't move fast enough and he was on her, slugging her as her other arm came up. He wrenched the gun from her hand, and as she kicked out he grabbed her braid, pulling her head back and dropping her. She couldn't see who it was but she wasted no time, going for the knife in her boot. Slashing up, she caught a sleeve but the knife didn't hit flesh.

The next thing she knew he had wrapped her braid around her neck and was twisting. Chex'ináx̱ yaa wunagút slashed out again, hitting the leg, but a hard wrench of her hand and she was without her knife, pulling at her own braid as he strangled her. She would be the next victim. As her vision reddened and turned grey, she felt only sadness that she wouldn't be able to aid the people.

Suddenly, the pressure released on her throat and Chex'ináx̱ yaa wunagút rolled over onto her side, coughing, blinking back tears. Something metallic glinted. Sitting back, her head spinning, she looked up as her lungs struggled for air.

The thin moonlight silhouetted a buffalo woman. The automaton smashed the man high into the air with one arm. He flopped down like a rag doll across a stump, a grunt escaping as he collapsed.

Chex'ináx̱ yaa wunagút patted around and found her gun. Grasping it, she pushed herself up and staggered forward, swallowing past the burning in her throat.

The woman first attacked was kneeling and weeping but seemed okay. The buffalo woman stood like justice staring down at the man. Chex'ináx yaa wunagút moved in and looked at him. His eyes shone bright, staring up at the stars, blood trickling black from his mouth. She didn't recognize him.

"Why," she rasped, moving close to peer at his face. "Why kill them?"

His hair was dark and he might have been part native, part white but it was hard to tell. His mouth moved wordlessly. She leaned in.

"Sacrifice," he said, then expired.

Chex'ináx yaa wunagút stared for another minute, puzzling what his one word could have meant. But no words would have appeased her anger at his monstrous treatment of the women. She faced the buffalo woman, who turned toward her. A golden mitt touched her shoulder as gently as a feather. Then a wisp of ethereal fog rose from the head, hovering above, and a woman's features, definitely Squamish, smiled at her and nodded. The wraith didn't disperse as she thought it would but settled back into the construct.

The buffalo woman turned and walked away, raising each knee high as her pistons brought her back to the grove where Stanton worked.

c   ◌   c

Peter Stanton had cleaned up and wore his coat and hat. For once his hair was combed and his shirt tucked in.

Summer had moved in, bringing with it the soft warm air and a hum of bees. South of the Granville townsite and the villages, the trees were still thick, towering close and keeping the day lively with moving shadows. A clear scar moved off to their left where the railway had come through years before.

Five buffalo gals, as the prospector had called them, lined up facing east. Peter sighed.

"I wish I could have created more. But I hope this will do. I can only send them with the directives and hope that they can save the buffalo."

For once, Chex'ináx yaa wunagút wore her people's dress. She had left the red serge and the pistol behind. She looked over at Stanton, then back to the brass automatons. "You could sell the information of your creation to the railways. It would save them money with the efficiencies you have created. Probably save you a sentence."

"I'm not interested in making them more money."

About each bison-shaped head, between the horns, an image formed as the ghosts of the murdered women rose up out of the automatons.

Chex'ináx yaa wunagút raised her hand to them. She would not be sending these spirits on their way. They each raised their hands back and waved to Peter and her.

"Your sister?"

Peter swallowed, still looking at his inventions. "No, she never appeared. I can only hope she is at peace with the others. These five are the ones who have stayed."

The buffalo women popped open their compartments and shovelled some coal chips into their mouths. Shutting the doors with their hands, steam billowed from their noses, and the machines raised a hand, then turned east. Raising their knees high, they built speed and began running beside the rail line, following it to the prairies, golden avenging angels on their way to save the bison.

Peter Stanton sighed. "There they go." He turned to Chex'ináx yaa wunagút. "I'm ready to go now."

She asked, "Do you think they will protect the buffalo?"

"I hope so, but they have their own wills. It's up to them now." He turned toward her. "Constable Walks Through Shadows, where do you plan to send me?"

She looked at him, tilting her head to the side. "I took an oath to uphold the law and I won't forswear it. But there is right and wrong. You have tried to right your wrongs and what I see here is that you have already paid for your crimes. I imagine the buffalo might still need your help."

It was her turn to raise her hand to Peter. Chex'ináx yaa wunagút mounted her horse and rode back into the teeming world of people and the borders they would brush against every day.

OUR CHYMICAL SÉANCE

TONY PI

To thoroughly inspect the spacious Silverbirch Room before the séance would take more time than we had, but I did what I could. No clockwork cheats lay hidden between the wall of books and the arched windows, and no mystical runes had been etched onto the crystals of the chandelier or cut into the fossil calygreyhound skeleton on display on the mantelpiece. All that remained was the grand salon harmonium, also the most troublesome. Madame Skilling could have hidden a charlatan's trick anywhere among the instrument's countless parts, from its mahogany upper casework to the hundreds of pipes at its heart.

Cesar De Bruin rolled the key to the room between his palms as he stood watch, peering through the slightly ajar door. "Anything yet, Tremaine?" he asked. "Too many so-called spirit mediums have preyed upon my family's grief, but they were charlatans with parlour tricks, all. I would rid myself of this one quickly as well. We haven't got much time."

I couldn't fault my friend's dander. His only son Poul had shot himself with a palmcannon last summer, a year to the day. Cesar had this lounge closed to the guests at Château Banffshyre ever since. Had his wife not insisted on the séance, he would have been content to leave the Silverbirch Room sealed. "Laroux said he'd stall her, and he will. He's nothing if not resourceful."

"Let's hope. This Skilling woman's convinced my wife that her 'chymical' method will not fail to contact the other side. I know too little of alchemy to prove her and her Ektoptikon device false, and Fay will not see sense. Have you nothing?"

"In all likelihood Madame Skilling hasn't breached this room, Cesar, judging by the dust." I gave the lion's-head handle on my new walking stick a quarter-turn clockwise, revealing a clever compartment in the shaft beneath the collar. Freed from its cherrywood cocoon, the foxfire-in-amber within shone brightly from its silver setting. I ran the illumination along the pedal keys, but they showed no signs of tampering.

Discrediting a medium had not been my intent when I came to visit Sir Cesar De Bruin at Château Banffshyre. My team would always visit his château before and after a dig in the badlands east of here. What better way to bid adieu to civilized comforts than to indulge in them? Or afterward, to wash away the patina of antediluvian dust in the thermal springs? The grand hotel had much to recommend it, thanks to Cesar's vision: scenery, hospitality, and luxury unparalleled. The railway baron had built a formidable chain of grand hotels across the Canadas and ensured that tourists would choose his line when they travelled across the continent by train. The Banffshyre was the jewel of his endeavours.

Cesar and I had become friends on my first foray to the fossil valleys of Canada Northwest nearly a decade ago, when rumours of newly unearthed Leolithic skeletons had lured me across the Atlantean Ocean. Though my doctorate was in

Aigyptian archaeology, my research into sphinx cults had led me to fossilized specimens of countless leonine hybrids worldwide. By chance I had boarded the same empyreumatic train from Montraal to Calygrey as the De Bruins. I was surprised the President of Pacifica Railway of the Canadas was onboard and that he had heard of me. He had invited me to talk fossils over dinner with his wife and son in his parlour car. At journey's end, Cesar wouldn't let me continue to the badlands without a stay at Banffshyre at his expense.

The palatial mountain hotel among the pines was Sir Cesar De Bruin's dream rendered real with unparalleled workmanship. During that first unforgettable stay, I walked Cesar and Poul through the hotel, teaching them about the fossils embedded in its limestone blocks. In the evenings, Cesar regaled me with tales of the Canadian rail over brandy.

I hadn't heard about his son's death until I arrived this morning with my team, when Cesar had met me in the foyer, a husk of his once exuberant self. I had gone through the same depth of grief when I lost my wife years ago, and asked if I could help. I could, he said, come to the séance.

"This spiritualist from Huronto has bewitched my wife with promises of contacting Poul on the other side through her Ektoptikon. If only we could, truly could!" His voice shook. "Fay and I were in Calygrey, only seventy-five miles away. We should have been here. He had such a wondrous talent for music, one that should have taken the world by storm! What pain would possess him to take his own life? We saw no signs, and he left no note. The question of *why* wakes me in the dead of night, every night, and it too is killing Fay. A séance might bring answers, but only if it's not a scam."

Hence, my scrutiny of the Silverbirch Room.

Jules Laroux nudged the oaken door open from outside and slipped in. "You've two minutes before they arrive, Professeur." The stout man unslung his hand-crank cinetoscope and tripod from his shoulder, leaned them against the bar, and poured himself a shot of whiskey. "I tipped the porter well to take extreme care with Madame Skilling's Ektoptikon device, and the lift man to stop on every floor on their way down."

"Thank you, Laroux."

"Will it be enough time, Tremaine?" Cesar asked.

I raised my walking stick to the pipes above the keyboard and stops so that they'd catch the light of the foxfire amber. "Only to clear the most obvious components of tampering, I'm afraid. But I suspect that whatever trick she has, if indeed there is one, would be part of her Ektoptikon."

"Trick?" said a disdainful voice. A fawn-like woman invaded the Silverbirch Room fleetly and soundlessly. Dressed in a deep purple silk satin dress with a white tulle jabot, Madame Skilling regarded us in turn, first Cesar, then Laroux, then me. "A chymical séance may be a novel technique for channelling the spirits, but it is no trick. Do not mistake the new alchemy for chicanery. Skeptics are welcome at my sittings, and become believers soon enough. Mister…?"

"Professor Tremaine Voss, archaeologist." I twisted my walking stick to re-seal the amber in its hidden compartment. "I never said I didn't believe in spirits. Quite the contrary. I've roused spectres in Aigyptian tombs, fled from phantom tigers in the Orient, and faced down the ghost of a riddling sphinx. Put some to rest. Left others undisturbed."

"It's me you need to convince. Jules Laroux, truth-reelist." Laroux set his shot glass down. "Didn't you take the lift with Madame De Bruin and your Ektoptikon?"

Skilling smirked. "I sensed the stairs would be quicker."

"Nothing thrills me more than unmasking a fraud. You won't deceive us with mere clockwork poltergeists or magic lantern shows." Laroux patted his cinetoscope. "Mind if I film?"

"You may not, Mister Laroux," Skilling replied. "If you're staying for the sitting, I require your full participation. Even the dead demand respect."

Laroux began to protest, but I calmed him. "Perhaps it's for the best, my friend. If our efforts succeed in summoning Poul's ghost, it'd be considerate to pay heed to the moment. But if you could explain the workings of the Ektoptikon, Madame, it will help dispel our doubts."

A chime from the mezzanine heralded the arrival of the limbeck lift on this level. Skilling smiled. "Ah, the Ektoptikon arrives. All will be clear soon, Professor. Gentlemen, if you could kindly draw the curtains?"

I made my way towards one of the round-headed windows, relying only slightly on my walking stick for support. In the past, the thermal springs here have had a miraculous effect on the old injury to my left leg, and each time I bathed in these waters I felt as spry as a man half my age. I hadn't time to partake in a soak as yet, but it was a comfort I looked forward to.

As we pulled the red velvet curtains closed, a porter carried a sturdy metal trunk into the lounge with languid steps. Lady Fay De Bruin, clad in mourning black, trailed in behind him clutching a leather handbag to her bosom. I hadn't seen Fay as yet this visit, and what I saw broke my heart. She was Grief herself, gaunt from fasting and pale from seclusion. Had her joy and pride died with her only son?

I crossed the room to take her hand. "Fay, I'm so sorry for your loss. How are you?"

"Adrift, Tremaine." Fay brushed aside a stray lock of hair from my forehead. "I curse myself for being blind to Poul's inner demons, for choosing to believe all was well when it wasn't. A mother should know. A mother should have better instincts."

Her words made me question my own fatherly duty. If my son took his own life as Poul did, could I say I knew him well enough to guess at his heart?

No, no parent could. We had to trust our children to tread their own path in life, for good or for ill. Fay would have agreed with that sentiment, once. Now she wallowed in a flood of *what ifs* and *if onlys*. The only glimmer of hope I saw in Fay was when she looked towards the spirit medium for support, who in turn nodded.

Skilling raised her hands and wandered through the room, whispering an indecipherable incantation under her breath.

Laroux watched the show with growing mirth. "I do that too, but only when drunk on absinthe."

The medium ignored him. She stopped halfway between the unlit fireplace and the harmonium, where she was struck by a fit of shudders. "The chill's here. Porter, please put the trunk on the seat of the harmonium, then bring that table to this exact spot. Five chairs as well."

When that was done, Skilling unlocked the trunk. "May I have your assistance with the Ektoptikon, Mister Laroux?"

"With pleasure. Let's have a look at this thing."

Together, Laroux and Skilling lifted a magnificent device the size of a large pumpkin out of the cushioned box and placed it on the table, dead centre.

Imagine a krakenesque chandelier gilded with red gold, its mantle an alchemical show globe sloshing with a cobalt fluid. Its eight tube-like articulated arms extruded from the symbol-laden pyramidal base, and for the nonce they lay curled against the crystal core as though in defence of the filigreed automaton.

Madame Skilling flipped the symbol for *tin* to reveal a hidden keyhole in the base. She produced a slender silver key seemingly out of the air, and inserted it and turned it.

The arms of the Ektoptikon unfolded like a blossom greeting the sun. The limbs didn't snap flat against the table, but retained their signature curl. At the terminus of each was an intricate silver iris valve.

"It's less machine than work of art," I said, appreciating the workmanship that went into the Ektoptikon. Like my walking stick, it was an exemplar of the new philosophy called Finesse Oblige: *subtle gearwork, supernal grace.* This design made alembic engines and other chymical devices resemble flailing, gutted automata. "But what does it do?"

Skilling offered an oaken chair to Fay, so that she would be seated directly in front of an Ektoptikon arm. "Do you know the theory of *ectenic force*, Professor?"

"Only vaguely. I read somewhere that it has to do with a hypothetical fluid in the human body."

"Hypothetical? I think not. During a trance it can be coaxed forth as ectoplasm, a phantasmal vapour that manifests under certain conditions and aids in the manifestation of spirits and their power," Skilling explained.

Laroux snorted. "I've seen frauds with their ectoplasm, always in the dark. In the light they're just regurgitated butter muslin, or gauze rubbed with goose fat. Which is your hoax of choice, Madame?"

The medium gave Laroux an icy stare. "Obviously advanced alchemy is beyond your ken, cameraman. The Ektoptikon uses a newly discovered chymical reaction to create

ectenic effluvium. Breathing the vapours induces the ema-
nation of ectoplasm from the participants at the sitting,
which greatly magnifies our chances of contacting the other
side. All we need is the catalyst. Do you have it, Lady De
Bruin?"

"Yes." Fay took from her handbag a pink silk pouch con-
taining something the size of a large goose egg, leaking a deep
red light from within. I knew then, even before she revealed
what the object was, that it was the rare amber that I had discovered in the badlands and gifted to Poul De Bruin ten years
ago.

Unlike the yellow foxfire-in-ambers of the Old World or
the blues from Antilla, this piece had the characteristic car-
nelian colour of ambers with *Ignisfatuus* inclusions found in
Canada Northwest. I had donated all the ones I found to
museums across the Atlantean, but had saved this sample for
a wide-eyed, eleven-year-old boy who had promised to keep it
safe for life.

Cesar caught his wife's wrist before she could hand the
glowing amber to Madame Skilling. "That's our son's."

"Which makes this better than any other *because* it was
dear to Poul, my love. She needs it for the séance and she shall
have it."

"You said *reaction* and *catalyst*, Madame," I said. "Is the
amber destroyed to produce the effluvium?"

"Of course it's consumed by the process," Skilling replied.
"That's the touchstone of my New Alchemy."

"Technically, the creature in that amber is genus
Ignisfatuus, not the Europan foxfire species, but what the pale-
ontological societies are calling fellstars," I told her.

She didn't seem impressed. "You quibble over small details, Professor."

While Cesar and Fay argued over the stone, Laroux pulled me to the bar to pour me a whiskey on the rocks. "Is that gem worth a lot?" he whispered.

"To some collectors and museums, yes. Not many fellstars-in-amber have been found."

Laroux smiled. "Then I think I know her scam. Drop that rock into the blue drink, bubble it up to give a good show, but drop it through a hidden hatch in the machine and claim it had dissolved."

"I had the same thought. Stir in some fumes to make our heads spin, and who's to say that we didn't see a phantom or two?" I furrowed my brow. "And yet I wonder. Such a unique piece would be too easily identified. It could very well be that she really does need the amber for her alchemical reaction. Likely she intends to fleece the De Bruins with a series of costly séances, leeching their fortunes while living in luxury."

The shouting match suddenly came to a halt. Though the amber was still in her left hand, Fay had worked her wedding ring to the tip of her finger.

At last, in defeat, Cesar released Fay's wrist.

Madame Skilling took the fellstar-in-amber. "Dim the lights and take your seats. We are ready to begin."

The porter extinguished the magnesian lanthorns in the salon and left us five to begin the séance in earnest. The only illumination remaining came from the amber and the dregs of light creeping around the curtains, beneath the door and through its keyhole.

Skilling claimed the eastmost seat and bade us to sit according to her plan. Clockwise from her, it'd be Cesar, then Laroux, then me, and finally Fay. As I was close to the fireplace, I rested my walking stick in the fire irons stand before sitting directly in front of a raised Ektoptikon arm.

The spirit medium unscrewed the lid to the show globe and dropped the amber into the blue liquid. The reddish light became a cerulean glow as the fellstar shone from within the concoction. I thought I saw a fleeting frown, but she reclaimed the air of confidence and replaced the lid. "Excellent. Join hands and listen carefully."

I took Fay's hand. It was cold.

Laroux set his shot glass aside and grabbed my right hand. His palm was sweaty.

"This will be unlike any other séance because of the Ektoptikon," Skilling continued. "Once I activate the machine, it will generate ectenic effluvium through the duct in front of you. Effluvium has no pleasant smell but you must steel yourself and breathe it in. Within a few breaths you will feel ectoplasm flow like warm smoke out of your mouth and nostrils, but don't be afraid if it turns viscous as it leaves you. Merely focus and do not break the circle under any circumstance. Once enough ectoplasm has materialized, I will enter a trance and guide Poul's spirit to us. Any questions?"

I felt Laroux's grip tighten. Knowing him, he was biting back a snide remark in deference to the De Bruins.

"What if nothing happens?" Cesar asked.

"Cast aside your doubts, Sir De Bruin." Skilling took Fay's hand, and with the other turned the little key in the base another full revolution.

The Ektoptikon whirred and hummed. Bubbles percolated through the glowing fluid in the show globe, changing the sapphire hue to emerald. The fellstar-in-amber was turning in the churn, bathing us in its eerie, mesmerizing light. Skilling took Cesar's hand, closed her eyes, and began to chant and sway.

Eight sounds like sharpened knives ran clockwise around the Ektoptikon arms in rapid succession. A foul gas hissed forth from the valves, assailing us with a stench that reminded me of frankincense laced with rotting cod and sheep milk gone sour. My face must share the same snarled disgust as the others around the table, but for the sake of the séance I had to endure the stink and inhale.

On my fifth exhale, I felt it: a tasteless phlegm that coated my tongue, my teeth, and my lips. A white mist, not unlike a warm breath on a wintry day, escaped from my mouth in a constant stream. Yet instead of dissipating, it became semi-solid and gathered in a snakelike tendril that angled for the Ektoptikon orb.

Fay gasped as the same thing happened to her. I almost thought she'd let go of my hand, but instead she inhaled even deeper. One by one, tendrils from the rest of the participants merged with the swirling cloud of ectoplasm around the glass sphere.

I half-marvelled and half-questioned this phenomenon. What *was* this ectoplasm, I wondered? If it came from somewhere within us, what was its true function? Did we need it to live, and would something untoward happen to us if we forced it out our bodies like so?

"Damn, I need to film this," said Laroux, his words slurred by the mucosal ectoplasm in his mouth and nose.

Madame Skilling's incomprehensible incantation grew louder, and the Ektoptikon began to shake. The show globe, coated in ectoplasm, now held a roiling green tempest. The caged fellstar-in-amber rattled against the glass like hailstones in a storm. In the midst of the noise I heard a muted cracking sound, but it wasn't the show globe breaking. The amber within had broken into shards.

The light in the Ektoptikon didn't abate with the destruction of the amber. In amazement we watched a ball of golden light pass upward through the glass and into the ectoplasmic tangle.

No, that was wrong. The luminous object didn't so much as find the plasm, but rather drew the substance to it. The pseudopods of ectoplasm seemed to vanish *into* the fellstar. At this, the ectoplasm in my throat suddenly thickened so much that I couldn't breathe, and I felt stabs of pain in my lungs. I tried to call out to warn the others but found no voice.

I didn't have to. They too were afflicted, same as I.

Skilling opened her eyes and seemed startled by the appearance of the unknown light. She used her last breath to spit out a spell, likely one to quell the spirits, but her words did nothing.

The séance had gone terribly awry.

I broke the circle of hands, as did Laroux, but Skilling held on to the De Bruins. I tried to look away from the hypnotic fellstar but found I couldn't. It forced us to keep our eyes open and focus upon it.

Laroux flung his shot glass at the fellstar, but it only sailed through the creature to smash into against the floor.

I groped around the base for the silver key in front of Skilling, hoping to shut off the Ektoptikon before we all suffocated. But even as I turned the key and wound down the machine, I feared we'd already breathed in too much effluvium to make a difference.

Cesar had the good sense to cover his own eyes with his left hand, which seemed to free him from the fellstar's mesmeric effect. However, it didn't stop the ectoplasm thickening around his nostrils and mouth.

I could do the same, covering my eyes, but I didn't. I had to understand what this fellstar was doing, which meant I had to keep observing.

Laroux stood and grabbed his chair from under him. Lifting it with both hands, he swung it at the fellstar. For some reason the chair managed to catch the creature of light this time, though I didn't know why. Unfortunately, Laroux's attack also smashed the Ektoptikon globe, sending broken glass and blue liquid flying into Madame Skilling's face. She fell backward, her mouth open to scream, but only a squeal escaped.

Knocking the fellstar away from the mass of ectoplasm somehow caused the ectoplasm in our mouths to thin. I gasped for air, while the first words out of Laroux was an apology to Skilling. But though most of us regained our ability to breathe, the fellstar fixated on Fay, coiling up the ectoplasm still issuing from her mouth. Even as it was asphyxiating Fay, it lured her out of her seat, made her lurch towards the door.

That creature of light had been trapped in amber for untold millennia, and it *hungered*.

Cesar chased after his wife while I made my way to Skilling's side. She was moaning. There were some cuts to her face but I was more concerned with her eyes. I didn't know what that liquid was in the Ektoptikon but it might be caustic. "Don't rub your eyes. I'll get something to flush them clean."

Laroux dropped the broken chair. With one hand he grabbed a poker from the fire irons stand, and with the other he tossed me my walking stick. I recalled that there was a bucket with half-melted ice for the whiskey on the bar, and pushed to my feet.

When Cesar caught up to Fay he stumbled to the floor, pulling her down with his weight but cushioning her fall with his thickset body. But the fellstar continued to drink in Fay's ectoplasm, and she was on the edge of fainting from lack of air.

Laroux swung the fire poker at the fellstar, but again it passed straight through the ball of light.

My mind raced. Why did the chair work but not the shot glass or the poker?

Wood versus glass and iron. Was it as simple as that?

"Laroux, only wood will work!"

He dropped the poker but there wasn't much in reach except the bookshelves. He grabbed a thick volume and swatted at the fellstar. His strike connected, sending the ball of light flying erratically away from Fay. The ectoplasm choking Fay suddenly regained smoke-like consistency, allowing her to take a giant breath.

Cesar lifted Fay in his bearish arms and carried her towards the chaise lounge. "Breathe, my love, breathe."

The fellstar fled the room through the iron keyhole in the door.

"Don't let it hurt the other guests, Laroux," I said. "I'll follow as soon as I can." I knelt beside Madame Skilling and pulled out my handkerchief to soak in the cold water.

"D'accord, Professeur." Laroux threw open the door and raced through with an atlas in hand.

As I washed away the alchemical brew from Skilling's face and eyes, I started formulating a hypothesis as to what the fellstar was and what threat it posed.

Foxfires and fellstars both belonged to the genus *Ignisfatuus*, colloquially known as will-o'-the-wisps. Amber was fossilized plant resin from ancient trees, and the theory was that these prehistoric creatures of light had been trapped and died in the sticky secretion before the resin became amber. The foxfires-in-amber had been in use since early civilization as fireless illumination, and it was known that wood blocked their light. Like resin, paper and wood also came from trees.

"Madame Skilling, does your chymical reaction only work with foxfires-in-amber? And does ectoplasm only manifest when you use one?"

"Yes, and yes." She sat up, taking the wet kerchief from me. "Thank you, Professor. Go help your friend. I'll care for myself."

"Your effluvium might not be the reason ectoplasm's drawn forth." I stood. "I suspect the foxfires and fellstars feed on animal ectoplasm, using their hypnotic effect to hold them. When you used the Ektoptikon, it likely revived the *Ignisfatuus* in the destroyed amber. The creature then coaxed ectoplasm from us to devour it. Maybe the ones you used before died or escaped in the process, but this specimen is hungrier and more predatory." I called to Cesar. "Are you two all right?"

"She's weak, Tremaine. I can't leave her." Cesar touched Fay's face. "Take care of that monster for me."

I hobbled out of the Silverbirch Room onto the mezzanine, finished in native fir. No sign of Laroux or the fellstar on this level or in the open lift ahead.

"Laroux, where are you?" I shouted.

The burly uniformed operator in the lift heard me but shrugged. "Who are you looking for?"

"A droll man in a rumpled suit, wielding an atlas, chasing a deadly ball of light." I stepped onto the balcony overlooking the main lobby of the hotel and looked down at the crowd of glamorous guests below. Neither Laroux nor the fellstar were among them.

"Er, can't say I've seen them."

I looked up instead. The Banffshyre's octagonal central rotunda rose nine stories up, topped by a glass dome.

There! On the fifth-floor gallery, above and to my left. Laroux was leaning over the balcony, his hands locked around the legs of a young bellhop who had gone over the railing headfirst. The fellstar floated near them over the open area, devouring ectoplasm from their mouths and noses. The creature must have hypnotized the boy and lured him over the edge. The only thing saving the bellhop was Laroux, but who knew how long he could hold on when he couldn't even breathe?

The people on the main floor were oblivious to the death scene about to play out.

Even if I could get to Laroux and the boy in time, what could I do against a flying creature of light? It was too far away. If only—

The damned creature was made of light.

Film captured light.

Laroux had left his cinetoscope by the bar. I couldn't run, but the lift man could. "You, sir, fetch the camera from the Silverbirch Room. Now!" I shouted.

He ran.

I entered the limbeck lift. Made of steel and glass, I could see out into the rotunda from the lift cage and keep the two in sight. I prayed that Laroux could hang on just a bit longer.

The lift man raced back with the cinetoscope. I hung my walking stick on the lift rail and took it from him. The pancake-shaped camera and tripod unit weighed fifty pounds, at least. How could Laroux call this portable?

"Fifth floor, please," I said, as I unscrewed the lens cap to the camera.

On the long train journey here, Laroux had told me about the alchemy of filmstock. "Film's made of nitrocellulose, which is just cotton exposed to an alchemical process," he had said.

Cotton was plant matter. If I had extrapolated the nature of the fellstar correctly, then it might be possible to use Laroux's film reel to trap the creature of light.

As the lift doors closed, I pointed the camera up and through the glass at the fellstar and the handle, keeping to the rhythm that I had become so accustomed to whenever Laroux was filming.

Chymical cylinders above and under us burbled and impelled the limbeck lift slowly upward.

From this distance, I couldn't tell if my filming it was having an effect.

A bell chimed. "Five," croaked the lift man.

"Thank you." Now that I was at the same level as the fellstar, I thought could see it flickering. "Go help them!"

He nodded and hastened out while I kept cranking the handle. It'd be better if I could get closer. I used the cinetoscope tripod as an improvised walking stick, and hobbled as fast as I could towards Laroux and the fellstar while continuing to film.

The lift man had his arms around Laroux's waist, anchoring him.

The closer I got, the more the creature flickered and dimmed. I was slicing the fellstar with every new frame, binding it bit by bit to the celluloid. The ectoplasm choking its current victims was thinning, allowing Laroux and the boy to draw breath again.

At last, the fellstar winked out.

Laroux mustered his strength and pulled the bellhop to safety, then fell on his back on the marble floor, his chest heaving. "That was a close one. *Merci, Professeur.*"

I breathed a sigh of relief and replaced the lens cap. "You're the hero, Laroux." I turned to the lift man. "You too, my good man. Your name?"

"Willem, sir."

"Thank you, Willem." I tipped him generously. "I will put in a good word with Sir De Bruin."

Laroux and I returned to the Silverbirch Room.

Both Fay and Madame Skilling were recovering well from their ordeals, it seemed.

"What was it? Is it gone?" Cesar asked.

Laroux put his cinetoscope down. "Let's just say we've captured it all on film." He stretched his arms over his head and yawned. "I need a good, long soak in a sulphur bath after this."

Cesar smiled. "Please do, Mister Laroux, and take advantage any other services of the château, on the house."

I explained to them my theory as to what the creature was, and recounted how we had defeated it. "Like the legends of the will-o'-wisps, the fellstar would lure its victims to their deaths so that it could feed on the ectoplasm from their bodies. Madame Skilling, your chymical séance revives these deadly creatures from their amber prisons. You must never use the Ektoptikon again."

Skilling traced her finger over the remains of her machine. Her eyes were still red from contact with the alchemical substances, but we had washed them clean quickly enough. "Perhaps, Professor. Or perhaps you've shown me what's missing from its current design." She glanced at the cinetoscope.

Then, with a flourish, she made the silver key in the lock seemingly vanish. "You cannot stop the progress of magic and technology."

"That may well be," I admitted. "But now that they march in step, in the wrong combination they also unwittingly cause senseless deaths. I've seen it first-hand many times."

Fay stood. "Madame Skilling, I thank you for coming to Banffshyre, but my husband and I no longer require your services."

Cesar nodded. "My porters will see you safe to the train station in the morning."

"We could still contact your son, Lady De Bruin," Skilling said. "I sense his spirit is near—"

Eerily, the harmonium played four mournful notes, startling us.

Fay's eyes teared up. Did she recognize the music?

"It seems Poul will always be near, even without your trances," Fay said, taking Cesar's hand. "Good night, Madame."

THE SEVEN O'CLOCK MAN

KATE HEARTFIELD

Jacques did not throw up his hands to protect himself from the eggs. He did not duck the cabbage-core. He let the piss from overhead pots trickle through his hair; this was why he never wore a hat when it was time to wind the Clock.

Having long since sloughed off the capacity to flinch, he walked the narrow streets of Lagarenne like an automaton, carrying his lantern although the sun had not yet set. It would have been kinder if he were an automaton, if it were made evident, to everyone, that he had no choice.

The town square opened before him like a surprise, as it did every evening.

It was some small relief to walk out of range of the town's windows. Jacques rounded the bricked corner of the bakeshop and there it was, its dirt trampled as hard as stone. Lagarenne liked to think of itself as a second Montréal but the truth was, there was half a day's hard ride and a half-century of progress between Lagarenne and Montréal, between Lagarenne and anywhere.

The square was very nearly empty now, at eighteen minutes before seven. Jacques did not usually come this late. He liked to wind the Clock in plenty of time. But his wife, Marie-Claire, was in one of her bleak moods, bleaker than most, and he had feared to leave her with a pot on the fire. Feared to leave her with only little Felix to help her.

The only people left in the square at this hour, so close to seven o'clock, were those with no children at home, mendicants frocked and otherwise. A few people with faces as wilted as his own watched him as they watched all the works of God, as if they expected nothing better.

The Clock had grown in the five years since its appearance, spread like a black fungus on the face of the squat grey tower. When it appeared, the year Jacques was sixteen, it had been nothing but a great round clock face, brass wheels and arms clicking against the grey stone, with a man-sized archway on either side of it, and in each archway a black painted door. In the years since, as the children had been taken one by one, new doors opened up, above and below, off to one side or the other.

At a quarter of the hour, the little black doors opened. The Clock kept angry time.

In each open door, a statue of a child appeared.

Jacques watched, speaking their names in his mind as a penance. There was little Augustin, with his stick and wheel. His chubby wooden face looked off to the right, as if a horse and cart were about to run him down. There was Louise, who was perfectly still, always, until she spun her little pirouette. On the other side, Marie-Claude with her cat, and Jérome, nearly twenty-one, a man grown, smoking his pipe. And in the middle, gliding across from one door to the other almost before he could see them and mark them: Pierre, Jacques, Marie-Marguerite, and Anne.

Eight children in five years. A bleak harvest. Most of the children were Mohawk like him, had been born with other names, like him. Little Louise was blonde; her father had been a wealthy merchant. The Seven O'Clock Man did not make exceptions. The Governor had said, when he first built the Clock, "All children who act like savages will be treated as savages. And all children who keep order, who say their prayers and get into their beds at seven o'clock, will be good French children in my eyes, and the eyes of the Intendant of New France, and the eyes of God."

The chimes rang out tunelessly and Jacques bent his head. He trudged to the door on the ground and opened it with his little iron key. He had fifteen minutes for his work.

He climbed the short ladder, up through the trap door, up through a second to the top floor of the tower, and set the lantern on its hook.

There were six wheels to wind. The first four were the big ones: two-handed handles that took all his breath and left him puffing. Each one pulled a weight to the top of the tower, weights that would slowly drop over the next two days and power the gears of the Clock.

The first weight was for the Clock itself.

Click click click click click.

The second was for the chimes of the quarter-hours.

Click click click click click.

The third was for the bells of the hour.

Click click click click click.

The fourth wheel, the wheel that drove the automata, stuck and would not turn. The weight was nearly all the way down to the bottom. Jacques pushed until he could feel the veins in his temple pulsing. He cursed and forgave himself. He took off his gloves and spat on his hands. No good. There was something in the gears. With a groan, Jacques leaned forward, stretching his hand into the works, scraping the gummy oil and grime out of the wheel.

Damn Marie-Claire and her broken mind.

It took him several long minutes but he got the gear clear and the wheel moved.

Click click click click click.

This fourth wheel was for the stolen children and for the two other automata, the ones in the big doors on either side of the Clock face. They rolled in and out of their doors using the same gear train as the children.

But there remained two more wheels to turn, because soon the Seven O'Clock Man and his dog would walk out of the Clock.

Down he went to the middle level, carrying his lantern, setting it on the nail.

Jacques checked the watch the Governor, always cruel in his kindnesses, had left him in his will. Mother of God, two minutes left. He was a fool, had always been a fool. He took too many risks, even now. Left too many openings in his life for the Devil to come in.

If the Seven O'Clock Man did not walk, his Félix, his darling boy, would die, his heart winding down to a stop. Jacques should have left earlier. He should have trusted that Marie-Claire would be fine. There was always something keeping him at home: some pot burning on the fire, some scrape on little Félix's knee, some reminder that his boy was still soft brown flesh despite the wheel in his back, but that if Jacques ever failed, even once, Félix would be up here in the Clock, wooden like all the rest. Some hope that the sorrow would clear from his beloved Marie-Claire's dark eyes and she would look at him just for a moment as she used to.

In the first year of his task, the Governor used to come with him, to watch him wind the wheels, watch the weights rise. "You have done well, Jacques," he would say. "In rectitude there is strength. You are learning to regulate yourself. And in bringing order to yourself you bring order to Lagarenne. The town is grateful."

A few weeks later, the Governor had caught fever and died. How astonishing that a sorcerer could die of fever. Now the old man was rotting in his tomb while his decrees still staggered on in relentless motion, while the town showered its gratitude upon Jacques' head every second night.

And what did they do about it? They could have burned the Clock down, set fire to the Seven O'Clock Man. Jacques had to be grateful they did not, for the sake of his own boy. But the town hated him while praising the Clock, praising the old Governor's rules, saying that yes, order was necessary. The new Governor was no sorcerer but he was a weak-willed man who was afraid of what might happen if the rules relaxed, if the Clock were no longer there to keep the people in their place. The priests said the Clock was a miracle, God's will. And the people believed that. Yet still they cursed Jacques.

Jacques stepped out onto the beam beside the Seven O'Clock Man, reached over the brass wheel on its back. His last and most despicable task was to wind it and the dog. Jacques put his gloves back on, and not only because of the stink of oil and metal that got onto his hands and kept him awake on Clock-winding nights.

One day, he felt sure, the Seven O'Clock Man would turn around and look at him, here inside the tower. Jacques feared the face that had belonged to his former owner, Monsieur Martin. It had frightened him in life but in the way of living things, a fright that sped the heart, not a fright that chilled the blood.

It was not mere fancy, this fear Jacques held that the Seven O'Clock Man might turn to stare at him, even before the thing was wound. Who among the living could understand the decaying sorcery that made the Seven O'Clock Man leave the Clock and walk abroad, the sorcery that made him see the children who were out of bed and turn them into wood? Why, God, couldn't that sorcery work without wheels and gears, and leave Jacques out of it?

"You must not think of this as punishment but as a blessing, as penance is not punishment but expiation," the Governor had said. "You were born a savage, but now you have a chance to redeem that condition."

And sometimes Jacques would nod and think: *Yes, Governor. I am trying.*

And at times Jacques would think: *My father was a warrior.*

He finished winding the Seven O'Clock Man and scrambled over on the slippery, worn beams to the dog. In here, in the workings of the machine, the light from the lantern was mutilated and strange. He had barely finished winding the dog when there was a loud clack and the gears overhead groaned and whirred. The doors flung outward and let the grey light of a summer evening in.

Jacques nearly wept with relief. He held onto a beam and panted for a moment. For two more nights, Félix was safe, because Jacques had done his awful duty.

Somewhere, someone cried the alarm, as if the bells were not warning enough. *"Bonhomme, sept heures!"*

Out the Seven O'Clock Man slid, never turning to look at Jacques but performing his task as he always did. He flipped his right hand, in time with the great hour-bells of the Clock, as if he were ringing a handbell. In his left hand he held a cane.

Jacques could see the near-empty square below. If it were not a sin, he might leap out into that void. If Félix would not suffer for it. The bells boomed seven times in his ears as he scrambled back onto the platform, took his lantern and climbed down the ladder.

As he emerged, the Seven O'Clock Man and the dog were just finishing their hourly ritual. The hand had flipped seven times. The black dog had turned his head right, left, right, left, right, left, right, until he was looking expectantly at his master. Then they both slid out into the air and floated down. They hit the ground and slid forward, the dog still looking from side to side as they went.

The evening's hunt had begun. All children in Lagarenne must be in bed, or the Seven O'Clock Man would take them.

c   ◊   c

Félix ran through the streets, looking for his father. He was used to Maman's moods but he had never seen Maman's face so still, as if she were dead. She blinked. She even closed her eyes and sighed, and opened them again. She answered him with a muttered word or two. But she wouldn't talk to him.

His legs were so tired. But as he rounded the corner by the bakery, he felt the wheel in his back slip and catch and turn. Papa was winding the Clock. That meant Félix had another two days of life, and a little more life in his legs, as if he'd taken a big breath.

It also meant the Seven O'Clock Man was abroad. Félix had always been curious about what the Seven O'Clock Man looked like when he was alive. He had been a rich man, Maman told him. A rich man named Monsieur Martin, with a beautiful African slave named Marie-Claire. That was Maman.

Were you happy in those days? Félix would ask. Sometimes, Maman would say. In the same house there was a Mohawk boy of just the same age, not a slave but a ward. Taken from a village in battle. That was Papa. And what was

Papa like? Jacques was just like any other boy except he was bright and sharp as a knife, and he made Marie-Claire laugh, and when he looked at her she loved him with her whole heart. She knew she always would.

Marie-Claire's tummy grew big, with Félix inside it.

Monsieur Martin had been angry. It was all right for slaves to have children but they had to wait for instructions first about who the father should be.

The Governor was angrier still at Monsieur Martin. He said he had had great hopes for his Mohawk boy Jacques, that he could rise above his race and show the world what came of Christian education. And now what?

Then came the uprising, *"l'émeute des sauvages,"* people called it, although there were a few French boys involved too. The Governor had sent troops to destroy five Mohawk villages, the same villages where his soldiers had taken the children a few years before. They burned the crops and slaughtered the people. These were Félix's grandparents, Maman explained. That's why Papa was so angry.

Is he still angry? Félix would ask.

Of course not, Maman would say, as if she was afraid someone had heard. They signed a peace treaty, the Mohawks and the French, not long after that. But that was after Papa and the other boys set fire to the Governor's mansion. The Governor was able to escape; some said, even then, he must have been a sorcerer.

The following Sunday after mass, the Governor spoke in Lagarenne's town square. He said the children were running wild. There must be order. There must be virtue. There would be punishments. There would be a curfew, for anyone younger than twenty-one.

That was when the Clock appeared.

It was a very lazy man who would let his slave get a baby in her belly without permission, the Governor said. Laxity! Disorder! Vice! So Monsieur Martin became the Seven O'Clock Man, as an example, and Papa had to wind the Clock, as another example, and Félix had a magic wheel put into his back. As an example, he asked Maman? No, she said. To make sure that Papa would do his duty.

That was what Maman told Félix, on one of the days when Maman would talk.

That old Governor was dead now. He had given Maman and Papa their little house, near where they used to live with Monsieur Martin. Father had told him that. But the Clock, and the Seven O'Clock Man, still wound down every two days, just like Félix.

Félix had peeped out of the window once, and his mother had yelled at him, said he was acting like a savage, out of control. Then she cried.

Today when Papa left she said nothing. When Félix asked her if it was time to get into bed, if it was seven o'clock yet, she only stared, as if she were turning into a statue too.

Félix had cried out, screaming out the open window. No one came, whether because it was almost seven o'clock, or because it was his voice calling out, he did not know. To his face they called him *p'tit bonhomme*, unkindly. He could only guess what they called him when he could not hear. Félix had given up on trying to understand; he only wished someone had come when he had called out, "My mother is ill, I need help."

He had gone first to Madame Bourget's house, near his own. Madame Bourget was kind. She did not stare at the wheel in his back or call him names or throw things at his father, and sometimes she brought them extra food, when Maman was at her worst and it was Clock-winding night for

Papa. But she had not come today, and when he pounded on her door there was no answer.

He skidded around a corner and ran into Papa.

Papa looked stunned. His hair was matted. He blinked as if he had something in his eyes; probably something nasty, because it was a Clock night.

"Félix, what in the name of God?"

Papa picked him up under one arm, although Félix was nearly six and so big that his feet dragged on the ground as his father walked. Into the narrowest alley Papa ducked, his breath coming fast. He carried his lantern in the other hand. Félix wished there were a wheel on his father's back that he could wind, to give his father the strength he needed to get home quickly.

"Félix, for God's sake, don't you know what will happen if the Seven O'Clock Man catches you?"

Of course Félix knew. All the children of Lagarenne knew. He would turn into wood, like the Seven O'Clock Man and his black dog. He would live inside a little painted doorway in the Clock. He supposed he would keep the wheel he already had in his back.

He knew because on those nights when Papa did not have to wind the Clock, he put Félix into bed at six-thirty and held him close, and would not let him out, not even to use the pot. And once, when Félix had been little and crying about something and would not stay in the bed, Papa had held him down and screamed, "Just go to sleep, for God's sake!" Félix did not like Papa at bedtime. He preferred Maman, when Maman was herself.

"It's Maman," Félix said. "She is bad tonight. She frightens me."

"She let you out?"

"She couldn't stop me."

"Wouldn't, you mean. One of her moods, that's all it is. I wish she would snap out of it."

Félix did not want to defend his mother. He wanted Papa to make her talk again. "It's bad, Papa. I think she is very sick." To Félix's surprise, tears ran down his own face and his nose bubbled.

Papa let out a heavy sigh, hoisted his son higher in his arm and ran. Félix's feet banged against Papa's knees. Papa's arm pressed against Félix's back-wheel just a little uncomfortably. The world jounced and Félix could not watch it any more. Nothing would stay in one place. He buried his face in Papa's filthy wet shirt. Papa had him.

"You must not take such risks, my boy," said Papa. "Not for anyone."

"But Papa, don't we love Maman?"

"Yes, we love her," said Papa. "That's how the Devil gets in."

Félix said nothing, because he might sob, and make too much noise. But he wanted to know: gets into where? Into Lagarenne? Into Félix? Into Maman?

Around a corner and they came into a thin alley, almost home. Papa's lantern lit the houses on either side of the alley with orange light, like a giant's fire lighting the walls of a cave. The alley smelled of old piss. There was the door of their little house at the end of the alley.

And as it crossed in front of their front door, a dog turned its head and looked at them.

A black dog. A wooden dog. Félix saw the wheel in its back, the sorcery in the sweep of its head toward him, away from him, toward him.

The dog turned its whole body to match the direction of its head and slid toward them.

Jacques stumbled backward a few steps then swung around. One of Félix's shoes fell to the street.

Behind them, the Seven O'Clock Man stood with his hand out as if he were waiting for alms. In the other he held his cane. His motionless face was wooden like the dog's. But he wore real wool and silk, and his hair was a real wig, like a rich girl's doll. Had Monsieur Martin worn that very shirt, that yellowed cravat, that same long brown wig, in his natural life?

"You can't have him," said Papa.

The Seven O'Clock Man slid toward him, his empty right hand turning up and down as if he were ringing a handbell. Félix peeked over Papa's arm. The dog was still sliding toward them, his head turning again, left, right. A pigeon fluttered out of the church tower. A window shutter opened above.

"You cannot take him!" Papa screamed. "I have done as I was told!"

His voice echoed. Somewhere, not far, the bark of a real dog ended in a stifled yelp.

If only Maman had not let her face get so still. If only she would have looked at Félix as if she were looking out of her own eyes, just once. He would like that better than a bedtime story. He would get into bed every night well before seven o'clock if only he knew Maman was well.

"Maman!" the cry bubbled out of him wet with tears. He sounded like a baby, he knew, but he couldn't help it. If only Maman knew that he and Papa were coming for her. If only she knew that they loved her.

Their door opened and Maman came out, like a figure in a clock.

"Maman," he said again, reaching out his arms over Papa's shoulder.

The dog leaped up, as if it thought Félix were trying to pat its wooden head. The jaws clamped down and the metal teeth bit into his hand. He screamed.

Maman screamed too. Her face moved again and she was there, she was his Maman again. She ran toward him and pulled the dog off but his hand only hurt more as the teeth tore into his flesh. The dog did not growl or snarl. It made no sound at all.

Papa eased him down to the ground and began to pound upon the dog's head with his fist. He squatted and tried to pull the jaws open.

"Behind you, Jacques!" Maman cried.

Jacques turned.

The hands of the Seven O'Clock Man were gloved in soft kid leather that had been white. These were the hands that held the punishment in them, the long wooden cane that reached out toward Félix, hook first.

It would not take his boy.

Jacques picked up the lantern and if he hesitated a moment it was because he wondered what was left of Monsieur Martin in this abomination. Monsieur Martin had not been a particularly good man but he had been a man. When the lantern smashed against the wooden head, the wig went up like corn silk, each curled strand glowing crimson until the Seven O'Clock Man was a walking torch, its gloved hands still reaching for them, the cane not yet on fire, protected by distance and the leather of the gloves.

Jacques kicked the dog but it did not yelp or loosen its grip. So he reached around its body, lighter than a real one's would have been, and picked it up.

"Carry Félix," he gasped to Marie-Claire. "Let's get him away from here."

Marie-Claire was herself again. For the moment. She had always been a mystery to him. She was a mystery to herself; she was born in Portugal, Monsieur Martin had said, a slave born of slaves, but she did not remember her own parents. Neither of them ever spoke of their parents, of anything in the past.

Jacques and Marie-Claire ran, or rather lumbered, as Félix's body shook with pain and sobs, the pudgy little arm dangling from those horrible teeth, the dog's legs moving patiently as clockwork. Behind them the orange light grew brighter and hotter as if the door to Hell was coming for them, ready to swallow them up.

As the Man's cane knocked against his shoulders Jacques pushed Félix away, pushed him into the doorway, into the house. Jacques turned and grabbed the cane out of the Man's arms but the cane came too easily; it hit Félix behind him. He saw the dog open its maw to let go of his boy's bleeding hand. He felt all the aches disappear and heard his heart stop, the way one can almost hear a clock stop, if one is listening very carefully at just the right moment. The way the world stopped the moment he first saw the face of his beautiful boy.

Félix's face was turning to wood, too, in front of him. Jacques tried to reach for Félix again but his muscles were inert. He could not open his hand to drop the cane. Some force was pulling him down the length of the alley. The little house and the door and Marie-Claire and the dog grew smaller as Jacques and Félix slid backward, away from them, and away from the burning wreck as it fell to the cobbles.

C   ʘ   C

The morning was grey and wet. Jacques could see it through the crack of the Clock door. He could smell the damp and fear in the air, and the fire that still lingered in his own scorched and filthy shirt. All his senses survived, like phantoms of life.

He took some comfort in how quiet it was, here where he could almost hear his son breathing across the gears and beams. Félix was there with him. Jacques tried not to be grateful for that; perhaps death would have been better for the boy. But at least now Jacques knew that his son's mind, his loving little heart, was still in the world. He knew he might even see Félix, catch a glimpse of that face, now motionless.

A door banged. Someone was coming up the stairs.

"My dears," he heard.

He would have turned around if he could, for it was Marie-Claire's voice.

"I am sorry," she said, and he knew that timbre, the sound her voice made when she was not allowing herself to cry. He had never seen her cry.

And Jacques wanted to say: You are blameless. But what did his wooden mind understand of blame? What could he comprehend of the condition of even his own soul in that moment of flame and anger? What of all the moments of cold decision that came before?

"My dear, I do not think they can hear you," said a second person. Madame Bourget.

"Whether they can hear me or not I must tell them. I must tell them that I will come to wind the Clock for as long as I live. And if they hang me for setting the fire, then you will come, won't you, Madame Bourget? And you will come even if I live, on those nights when I cannot. If... if I cannot. You will. Say you will."

"I will. Of course I will, child. Now let's get on with it and be gone."

Jacques listened as his darling Marie-Claire wound the cranks that pulled the weights, listened to the sound of her sobs that finally came, the sound he had never heard before.

"But what shall we do," he heard Madame Bourget whisper, "if they walk, as the Seven O'Clock Man and that dog did? What shall we do if he hunts the children?"

"I shall never wind them," said Marie-Claire. "I wind the Clock only. They will move on its track but they cannot move on their own. I hope."

"And if you are wrong? If there is some sorcery stronger than gears and wheels?"

"Then I will bring a torch and watch him burn as I watched the other, and I will know that it is for the good of his soul."

Then his wife stood before him and kissed his wooden lips, while Jacques could not move, could only feel the dryness of her lips and the wetness of her tears.

C (l) C

The Clock loses time, now. The gears lock and skip. The old Governor's sorcery is aging, cracking. Jacques has found that at seven o'clock, at the very moment when the gears turn his body toward the clock face, he can through his own will reach out his hands toward the figure on the other side of it. He does this every day like clockwork although he can never reach far enough.

Every evening when he is out over the square, Jacques can hear the murmurs. They call him Jacques of the Clock now, with affection, or sometimes *le jacquemart*. They call his boy *p'tit bonhomme*. They say, Jacques Martin saved the town from a monster. They swear to visitors that the story is true.

He is glad at least that he never leaves the Clock, that his punishment is not Monsieur Martin's punishment.

He is also grateful for the cowardly clockwinders of Lagarenne, for the men and women who take turns winding now that Marie-Claire and Madame Bourget are long dead, now that there is no danger and no sin in it.

He cannot but be grateful, for though the clockwinders keep him in this purgatory of stillness for most of every day, while the rats run over his body and the bats swoop and he can hear the sighs of the ghosts of children all up and down the Clock tower, though the clockwinders give him this torture of perpetual inaction, they also give him the daily hope of one more glimpse of his son.

THE TUNNELS
OF MADNESS

HAROLD R. THOMPSON

I would not have gone to the Exchange Coffee House, a three-storey Georgian structure of red brick that dominated one end of Market Square, if not for the mysterious note I had received that morning, a note telling me to meet a man named Jacob Dorian, who would be sitting alone in the northwest corner of the second floor. When I came to the table in question, I'm afraid that I stopped and gaped like a fool. I had not expected Mister Dorian to be a black man, though I suppose I should not have been surprised, given that Halifax, capital of Nova Scotia, was a navy town, the very seat of British naval power in North America, and the coffee house was a haunt of sailors and merchants involved in the West Indian trade. Dorian could have been either. He was also a very large fellow, and apparently prosperous, for when he stood at my approach, I· noted the fine quality of both his frock coat and his waistcoat of deep mauve silk.

"Captain Frame?" he said, his gentle tone at odds with his expression of stern command. Petty officer, I decided, or former petty officer now in business for himself.

"Yes," I said, adding, "Though I'm retired," for my career in the British Army had ended four years before. "You sent me a note, on behalf of my old comrade, Major Edward Black-burn?"

"Aye, sir," he said. "I am in the Major's employ."

I sat and placed my hat and stick on the table. My right hand, the one with the scars, I held out of sight, a silly habit.

"You were a navy man, Mister Dorian?" I asked.

Dorian's smile was grim.

"I have been many things, sir, including a slave in the Carolinas from which I escaped in a row boat to join the crew of H.M.S. *Terrible*, which had been lying off the coast. In that capacity I was given an opportunity to strike a blow against the slave trade, for a time."

"I see," I said. "I suppose that must have brought you some satisfaction. But tell me, why did Major Blackburn send you in his stead? I had no idea he was in Halifax. He didn't so much as send me a letter!"

"I am instructed to take you to him, sir. He is involved in matters of a delicate nature. In fact, he is rather in a bind, and wishes your help."

This was very mysterious, and not altogether welcome, but I could not refuse to help an old friend who had suffered alongside me through the trenches before Sevastopol. Though he had been in the Royal Engineers and I in the infantry, our paths had crossed many times in the course of our duties, and we had become fast friends. Since then, I had visited his home in Hampshire on two occasions, but had not seen him since resigning my commission in the wake of the terrible events in India that we call the Great Mutiny.

"You'd best lead on, then," I said, standing. "I'm curious to see what all this is about."

Dorian nodded, and soon we were making our way through the crowd and down the stairs to the front doors.

Outside, we found Market Square filled with vendors and potential buyers. The sun was high and bright, and from the harbour, on my left, a steamer gave a great blast of its whistle.

"Do you mind if I ask you a question, sir?" Dorian said as we headed south along Bedford Row.

"Of course not," I replied. "Ask away."

"I've heard it said, sir, that you have been an outspoken supporter of independence for the Southern States."

I believe I must have smiled. Given that Dorian had been a slave in those Southern States, this was a potentially awkward question, but I do not shirk from awkward.

"I am not certain what you may mean as 'outspoken,' but I have made my views on the subject known, Mister Dorian. And I suppose you wish to know why?"

Dorian looked straight ahead as he walked.

"There are many Nova Scotians fighting in the armies of the North," he said.

"That is true, but there is also a great deal of support for the Confederacy here, since an independent South means a weakened United States, and some think a weakened United States is good for the British Empire. However, that is not the basis for my opinion. You see, after the rebellion in India, I decided that men must rule themselves. It is as simple as that. They must rule themselves and be permitted to make their own mistakes."

Dorian fixed me with a hard stare.

"And what of slavery, sir?"

I met his eye.

"Slavery is a great wrong, perhaps the greatest wrong of our age, but solutions to great problems cannot be imposed upon nations by other nations or powers. We tried that in

India. No, a nation, like an individual, must first recognize its errors, then find solutions itself."

Dorian was silent for a moment.

"And how many men, women, and children must suffer, sir," he said at length, "before the Southern States realize the error of their ways?"

I am afraid that I had no satisfactory answer.

"There is much suffering in the world, Mister Dorian," I said. "I have seen it and been the cause of it. I wish I knew the solution."

After that we walked in silence.

c   ⊕   c

We turned west onto Prince Street, climbing the steep slope toward Citadel Hill from the harbour, at last halting at a three-storey house of wooden clapboards painted a dark brown, as so many residences in the city seem to be. I expected Dorian to go to the main door, but instead he entered the alley to one side and stopped at a pair of cellar trap doors.

"What's this?" I said in surprise.

"You have to trust me, sir," Dorian said. "As I said, the Major is involved in some delicate matters. Secret matters, you might say. This route will take you to him."

I had my stout ash cane and was confident that I could best Dorian in a fight, man to man despite his size, but I reasoned that if he wanted to rob me, there were simpler ways of doing so than concocting such an elaborate tale.

"Very well," I said.

A short flight of stone steps led to a dark chamber smelling of damp and must. From a shelf, Dorian produced an oil lamp, which he lit, the bright flame illuminating the brick walls around us. On the far side of the chamber was a dark doorway about seven feet tall and three feet wide. Beyond was a tunnel, lined with brick and with an arched brick ceiling. The earthen floor was covered in dry wooden planks.

"Smugglers," I said. "This is the work of smugglers!"

Dorian glanced back at me.

"No, sir," he said. "I believe it's the work of the British Army."

The tunnel terminated at a second passage that ran at right angles to the first. Dorian led the way to the left, and as we walked I noticed that every so often there was an alcove in the wall, or the gaping entrance to another tunnel, or a flight of steps leading down.

"These must go on for miles," I said. "You say the army built them?"

"Perhaps, sir. At least they built some of them. There are tunnels running under the streets that lead down from the Citadel, and many branching tunnels. They come up in the cellars of houses throughout the town, sir."

The Citadel was a massive stone fort built on top of Citadel Hill, the strategic high ground in Halifax. Its purpose was to defend the Royal Navy station, so I supposed these tunnels were some adjunct to the many fortifications surrounding the harbour, perhaps to move troops and material from fort to fort under cover, or to spring up in the enemy's rear were the town to be overrun.

Whatever their purpose, the tunnels were extensive, and we seemed to walk for over half an hour before we came to another doorway of sorts, this one perfectly circular and made of steel. It appeared to be the beginning of a massive steel pipe.

"We're going in there?" I said, for the first time feeling a little oppressed by my close surroundings.

"Yes, sir. Watch your step, sir."

Dorian entered the pipe, and I had no choice but to go after him. I could not see very far ahead in the lantern light, but the passage seemed perfectly straight, and after only a few minutes, we came to another pipe, this one vertical and housing a steel ladder. Dorian began to climb. Gripping my stick in my left hand, I followed, going slowly, rung after rung, gazing upward at the bobbing light of my companion's lantern.

The ladder ended at a very tiny chamber lined with red brick. In one wall was an ordinary wooden door.

Dorian rapped on the door three times with his knuckles.

The door creaked open on damp hinges, and light spilled out. I followed Dorian into a large circular room with mortared stone walls. In the centre of the room was a spiral staircase made of wrought iron, and all around this central feature were work benches covered in glass beakers, burners, rubber tubes, what looked like jewellers' tools, and tools of a more mundane sort, the sort found in carpentry or machine shops. In essence, it looked exactly like the sort of laboratory or workshop where I would expect to find Edward Blackburn, for he had built such a workshop for himself in his Hampshire home. And indeed, sitting amidst all of this scientific paraphernalia, was my old friend.

"John," he cried, rising from his stool and approaching. "You've come!"

"Of course I've come," I said, both relieved to see him but somewhat shocked by his appearance: his cheeks were sunken, his eyes red and ringed with dark circles. "How are you, old fellow? What's all this about?"

He did not answer me at once, but shook my hand, jaw working.

"I was going to tell you, as soon I was able," he said. "And now that time has come. I need help, John. You see, my daughter Alice – you remember Alice?"

Of course I remembered Alice from my visits to Hampshire – a dark-haired girl with a quick wit and a glint in her eye, who was always tinkering with small machines and devices, clockwork devices, animals and toys. Not the sort of things a lady was supposed to get up to, but given that her father was an engineer and an inventor, I supposed it was not so very strange. She would have been about eighteen years old by now.

"Yes," I said, "I remember her. Is she well?"

Edward squeezed his eyes shut, and when he opened them again, he said, "No, John. You see, she's been kidnapped."

c ⊙ c

Dorian hovered near the door as I sat on a tall wooden stool to listen to Edward's story.

"I've been working on several secret projects," he explained, "in co-operation with the Artillery. Do you know where we are?"

I shrugged. "No idea, I'm afraid. What was that enormous pipe?"

Edward managed a nervous smirk. "That was a unique element of the Halifax tunnel network, a submarine conduit running under the harbour, suspended by chains from floats just under the surface. It leads from the shore to Georges Island. That's where we are, on the ground floor of the Martello Tower in Fort Charlotte."

Georges Island was a small rounded island in the middle of Halifax harbour and the key to the inner harbour defences.

Fort Charlotte sat square in the middle of the island, an oval stone wall bristling with cannon, with a single stone Martello Tower at its heart.

"You're saying we passed under water?" I said, quite amazed.

"Yes. Forgive me for resorting to this secret route, but I've been specially tasked with developing new weapons for the army and navy, including pneumatic and electrical guns, and other things." He indicated a glass beaker of pale yellow liquid resting on the bench beside him. "For instance, this is a distillation from the flower of the Bohon tree of Java. Do you know of it? The legendary poison tree?"

I shook my head. "A myth, I thought."

"No, it's real, I assure you, and the sap and nectar are particularly obnoxious when it comes to men, for they at first cause madness and rage, followed by a breakdown of the basic faculties, then death. What I've done is create what I call a gas bomb, a device that releases a mist made from the essence of the Bohon flower. This gas will kill anything living in a fifty-foot radius, but leave all inanimate material intact."

This sounded horrible, another awful method for men to kill each other, and I was not pleased that my friend had been involved in creating such a thing. As a soldier I had seen plenty of killing and did not wish to see any more but, of course, killing other men is what the army does, and Edward was still a serving officer with a job to do. Such is duty.

"You know, of course," he went on, "that the United States is engaged in a civil war, and that Halifax, as a neutral port, is swarming with both Union and Confederate agents?"

"I would expect that to be the case."

"It is! Somehow a group of Confederate agents, a parcel of rascals, learned of my gas bomb. They took my Alice and are holding her for ransom. The ransom is a completed gas bomb. I must deliver it to them tonight!"

I jumped from my stool.

"This is outrageous! Why don't you go to the police? Or inform your commanding officer, tell General Hastings-Doyle!"

Edward rocked in his seat and tears sprang to his eyes.

"I can't do that, John! They'd kill her if I showed up with a file of troops! No, I need a friend, someone I can trust. I have Dorian, of course, but two men against these villains are not enough. I intend to give them the bomb – I have no choice – but I'm not confident that they will release Alice unharmed."

So, I thought, we were essentially going into battle. This was a bad business, bad all around, and though I believed in the Confederate cause, their desire for independence, I did not like these methods. I struggled to think of some clever suggestion, a way to save Alice without delivering the bomb, but could not. The situation seemed off somehow, but Edward was my friend, and there was no time for reflection.

I glanced at Dorian, then at Edward.

"Very well," I said. "How do you propose we proceed?"

c ⊕ c

We would use the tunnel system to travel to where the Confederate agents were waiting, and we would have to carry the prepared Bohon Bomb by hand.

"Take these," Edward said, thrusting a bundle of white cloth at me and passing another to Dorian. "They're gas hoods of my own design, which will protect us in case we accidentally stumble in the dark and break one of the vials."

I unwrapped my bundle and saw that I had two hoods.
They were made of a dense canvas, painted white, and fitted
with two circular glass lenses to allow one to see.

"How do they work," I asked, "and why do I have two?"

"The paint on the fabric neutralizes the poison," Edward
said. "And one of them is for Alice. Just in case."

He rummaged in a box on one of his work benches and
produced three pistols, Colt revolvers, and passed one to
myself and one to Dorian.

"Keep these concealed," he advised. "We don't wish to
provoke our tormentors."

I saw that my pistol was loaded, so removed the percussion caps and placed them in my pocket. An accidental firing
was a danger I believed we could do without.

Finally, Edward pulled a canvas cover from a square
object that rested on one of the benches, revealing a wooden
and copper frame, about twenty inches a side, supporting several glass vials of the yellow Bohon extraction, each connected to what looked like the bell of a small trumpet.
Edward explained that the detonator was another vial of acid.
When broken, the acid would leak out slowly, corroding a
strip of iron which, when parted, would release a spring-
loaded clapper which, in turn, would smash through the yellow vials, releasing the gas.

The contraption was heavy but had brass handles on
either side. Our first order of business was to get it safely into
the tunnels by lowering it down the vertical pipe with ropes.
For this purpose, Edward had prepared a block and tackle,
fixed to a ring in the floor of the lab. Dorian took hold of the
falls and eased the bomb down while Edward and myself
waited at the bottom of the ladder to guide it safely to the
floor. It was a moment of extreme tension, but a success.

After that we shared the burden of carrying the bomb, two men at a time, with the third walking in front, holding aloft a small brass oil lamp to illuminate our way.

I was the lantern bearer when we reached the end of the steel pipe and entered the first brick-lined passageway on shore.

"Turn right at the next divide," Edward told me.

We walked for some time. Edward was the only one who spoke, giving directions to myself, though not to Dorian, who must have also known the way. Once we climbed a short flight of steps, and another time we passed through a large underground chamber, but our tiny lantern was not bright enough to show its extent.

At last we entered a narrow passage that ended at a rough wooden door with a rusted latch.

"This is it, gentlemen," Edward announced. "There will be a sentry behind that door."

c   ⑩   c

Dorian knocked three times, and the door opened. A young man, bright-eyed and handsome, ushered us into a dirty little room lit by a single lantern. When he called out, a door in the far side of the room opened and four more young men and one woman entered. The woman was no doubt Alice. The men, I believed, were all members of the Confederate army, out of uniform and so spies.

"There you are at last," said the tallest of the men, a thin fellow with lank blond hair, dressed in a long dark frock coat. "And I see you've delivered our goods."

"It's there, Major Butler," Edward said, pointing to the gas bomb where it now rested on the dirt floor. "Now release my daughter!"

"Very well," said Butler, and he gave Alice a little nudge. She was dark haired and pretty and wearing a deep blue dress with the skirts pinned up, revealing tight-fitting trousers underneath. It was the sort of rig a labouring woman would wear, save for the quality of the cut and cloth. Over one shoulder she carried a small leather bag like a haversack. She threw Butler a look of hatred as she went to her father's side.

"I apologize for this unpleasantness," Butler said. "We would not have harmed her. She simply would have had to come with us."

Edward was trembling. "You damned villain! I don't believe you."

Butler's features darkened. "You call us villains now? I'm surprised and disappointed, but at least you've fulfilled your promise at last."

"I made no promise," Edward said, a little too forcefully. "You have your bomb, now let's go."

He took his daughter's hand.

"No promise?" said Major Butler. "Of course you made us a promise, sir. An offer and a promise!"

I stole a glance at Dorian, but he was just watching Butler with a similar expression to Alice's. I turned to Edward. That nagging sense of something off had returned.

"What exactly does he mean?" I asked. "What promise?"

Butler looked at me. "And who are you, sir?"

"Captain John Frame," I told him, "late of the Royal Hampshire Fusiliers."

"Well, Captain Frame, did your friend the Major here tell you how we came to this predicament?"

"Let us go now!" Edward almost shouted, making for the door.

Butler produced a pistol, its long black barrel glinting in the dim light. "Stop right there."

My own pistol was in my pocket and without fitted percussion caps. Dorian's and Edward's were similarly inaccessible. We all stood still.

"Major Edwards came to us, sir," Butler continued. "He offered us the help of his experimental gas bomb. He wished to test it in a battle situation, but then he reneged on his deal, and refused to deliver."

Edward raised a fist. "I learned your plan and it's monstrous!"

Butler cocked his head and looked confused. "In what way, Major? Our situation is desperate. General Grant's forces almost have our capital of Richmond surrounded. Our ports are blockaded and we require supplies. We must resort to extraordinary measures to secure our freedom, sir. You understand?"

"I understand perfectly," Edward said. "The Federal steamer U.S.S. *Castine* is in port, and under the laws of neutrality she must depart in twenty-four hours after re-coaling and resupplying at the dockyard. You intend to slip the gas bomb aboard with those supplies. Am I correct?"

Butler's stony silence seemed to confirm Edward's suspicions, and I saw it all as clear as crystal. Once the Yankee man-of-war was under way, the bomb would detonate, the gas disposing of the crew so that Butler and his fellows could take possession of the empty vessel. A new addition to the Confederate Navy! Then there was the added chance that the Union would blame Britain for the loss and so declare war, which would, in turn, bring the Royal Navy in on the side of the South.

It was a diabolical plan, and Edward had been a part of it. I looked at him, but he would not meet my eye. Why had he felt the need to hide this from me? Shame, I suppose, but I still would have helped, for I believe a man may admit to his mistakes and make up for them. Instead, I felt my heart sink. At least now I understood why all the secrecy, all this creeping through tunnels.

"You had a change of heart, Edward?" I said.

"I persuaded him to give up on it," Alice said, pulling away from her father and rounding on Butler. "The plan, the gas bomb, what does it matter? It's all wrong, every bit of it! Despite all your talk of freedom and fighting for your rights, there is only one right in question, and that is the right of rich men to hold other men in bondage and live off their sweat and toil!"

I found myself nodding. With her words I felt myself, perhaps for the first time, tugged in the other direction regarding the Confederate cause. That brought a moment of dismay at my fickle nature. How could I change my mind so easily? Perhaps it was the experience of being held at gunpoint and having both my life and that of my friends threatened, which had eroded my sympathies for these people on some primal level.

"Enough!" Butler shouted. "I am no cold-blooded murderer and have no wish to shoot any of you, but neither I nor my colleagues will hesitate to do so if any one of you tries to run. I'm afraid you all must remain our prisoners until our scheme is complete."

Keeping his pistol levelled on us, he looked at Dorian and said, "You there, boy!"

I saw Dorian's shoulders stiffen. It was absurd to refer to a man his age and size as "boy," but I knew that this was how some Southerners spoke to all black men.

"Pick up the gas bomb and bring it here," Butler continued. "You will carry it to its next destination."

Dorian did not hesitate. Stooping, he grasped and lifted the bomb by its handles. It was then that he looked at me, just a flick of the eyes, and I understood his intentions at once, and also that I had to act quickly.

Dorian took one pace forward, and I fell back, stepping close to Alice, at the same time pulling the gas hoods from my right pocket and saying, with as much composure as I could muster in order to not alarm our enemies, "Put this on, please, at once!"

I think she knew what it was, for her eyes widened and she pulled the hood over her head. I glanced at Edward, and saw that he also understood, for his hood was in his hand.

Dorian dashed the Bohon Bomb against the floor of the cellar. The glass vials exploded, filling the room with a dense cloud of yellow mist. I heard Butler shout, his pistol roaring, and I ducked as I fumbled with my gas hood, at last bringing the twin lenses in line with my eyes. I glimpsed Dorian, his face a mask of anguish, struggling to fit his hood over his head, and then he was gone, into the mist. The room was full of men screaming, a strange and beastly sound. I had a firm grip on Alice's hand, but could not see Edward in the mist. I hoped that he had also managed to don his hood.

"Edward!" I shouted, my voice muffled by the hood. "Edward!"

Hands suddenly appeared in front of me, hands like claws, reaching for my throat. One of the Confederate agents, his eyes those of a madman, no doubt from the gas, was attempting to tear off my hood and perhaps rip out my throat in the bargain. Finding my pistol in my left pocket, I managed to pull it free and strike the man twice in the forehead. He let go, and I whirled around, saw Alice still there, so grabbed her hand again and pulled her toward the door.

In the tunnel, I ran, not caring in what direction. Voices followed us, screams and maniacal laughter. Before us was nothing but darkness, for I had left our lantern behind.

"Wait," Alice said, tugging at my arm. I stopped and heard her rummaging in her leather bag. A second later I heard the strike of a match and the tunnel filled with light from a device in her hand, a sort of miniature lantern, made of brass and blazing with a bright white flame. "Did you see my father?"

I shook my head and raised my hood, reasoning that the gas had not followed us. "We'll have to go back!"

Laughter echoed in the tunnel to our left, and I once again reached into my pocket, finding a few of the percussion caps I had placed there, and fitted them in place at the back of my revolver's cylinder. Pulling my hood down, I retraced my steps, pistol at the ready, until we came to the passage that led to the Confederate lair.

"Edward!" I shouted as loud as I could. The flimsy door stood open, and Alice thrust her little light inside, the beam illuminating the remnants of yellow gas. Not a soul was in sight. The room was empty.

I dashed for the door on the other side of the room and tried to open it. It swung inward. I had expected to see stairs, perhaps leading to the lower floor of a house, but instead I found another chamber, another cellar, outfitted with rough tables and a few dirty cots. In the far wall was the entrance to still another arched tunnel.

"Through here," I said to Alice.

She held her lantern aloft and we went ahead slowly, carefully. Laughter and shouting still echoed around us, but I could not pinpoint the direction from which it was coming. My hand on the grip of my pistol was becoming slick with sweat, and I could barely see through the lenses of my hood.

My heart was racing. I had lost Edward and I had lost Dorian, and the best thing to do, the only sensible thing, was to get Alice to safety, but I also wanted to find Butler, find him and take him into custody. That is, if he had survived the gas.

A scream close by sent a shock through my spine, and a figure rushed toward me from out of the darkness. I recognized the handsome young sentry, his face twisted and his skin a horrible yellow. I raised my pistol and fired. The poor fellow dropped at my feet and lay still.

I pulled off my hood and bade Alice do the same.

"There's no gas here," I said. "Do you know these tunnels? How do we get back to the surface?"

She shook her head. "I don't recognize where we are, but they all lead to houses and public buildings."

"I don't fancy popping up in some chap's parlour," I said, "though I suppose it can't be helped."

We carried on, past the body of the dead lad, and after a few yards came to a flight of steps, unfortunately leading down. Laughter sounded from just ahead, and I saw a glimmer of light, so we carried on, emerging into the largest underground chamber I had yet seen, too large to be an ordinary cellar, and illuminated by a lantern resting on the floor. Racks of muskets, old 1842 smoothbores and rifles of the Brunswick pattern, lined the lower walls, and crates and boxes were stacked in the corners, while a wooden platform or gallery ran along the upper level.

Edward and Butler were on the gallery, locked in a fierce struggle. It was Edward who was laughing as he attempted to throttle his opponent.

Alice and I rushed forward, and I nearly tripped on a dark shape on the floor. Looking down, I saw Dorian lying with his back to a stack of barrels.

"Mister Dorian!" Alice cried, kneeling at his side. Dorian was not wearing his gas hood and was clutching his arm. There were two pistols in the dirt next to him.

"Miss Alice," he grunted, and I was pleased to see that the gas had not harmed him. "I have a bullet in my arm, but I'm alright. You have to help your father."

As he spoke, there was a shriek from above, and Edward came tumbling back, down the flight of steps that led to the gallery.

"Butler!" I shouted, aiming my pistol and thumbing back the hammer.

Butler saw me and reached into an inner pocket of his coat. Reflexively, I squeezed my revolver's trigger, but the percussion cap misfired. Cursing, I dashed for the staircase, stepping over Edward's sprawled and sputtering form, and gained the gallery in three bounds.

Butler had produced a large knife, which he held in front of him like a sword.

"You tried to poison me," he said. "Now I'll finish you, sir!"

I did not bother to reply to this threat, but made my attack, quickly getting inside his guard, grasping his arm and twisting it around while propelling him toward the gallery railing. The old wood split, and with a cry, Butler plunged to the floor below, where he landed with a crash on top of one of the crates.

Edward, apparently uninjured from his fall, leapt upon Butler and encircled his neck with his hands.

"Edward, stop!" I shouted. I ran back down the stairs.

He turned to face me, but I saw at once that he was no longer my old friend. His face was a ghastly yellow, his eyes those of a lunatic. He had been unable to don his gas hood in time. Letting go of Butler, he began walking toward me with shuffling steps, all the while laughing.

A shot rang out, thunderous in the enclosed space of the underground store room. Edward pitched backwards to fall across Butler's prone form. I turned to see Alice, a pistol in her hand and powder smoke wreathing her head.

"There's no antidote," she wailed. "No cure for the poison flower! I had to save him from a terrible death!"

I knelt at Edward's side, but he was already gone from this world. So was Butler, killed, I believe, by the fall. I let out a deep sigh. In the war in the Crimea and in India, I had developed the ability to detach myself from moments of sudden tragedy. I had retained that ability, and so remained calm in the face of what had just happened to my friend. However, I knew that I would feel the full force of it later.

"He paid the price," Alice continued, choking out the words, not suppressing her horror and sorrow. "My father paid the price for his terrible weapon."

"They are all terrible," I said, going to her and gently taking the pistol from her fingers. "Every one of them."

c ⑪ c

Having stopped the flow of blood from his wound with a strip of cloth torn from his fine silk shirt, Dorian was able to lead us out of the tunnels. We emerged into the coolness of the evening, finding ourselves on a cobble beach. The harbour lay before us. A large steamer with a full ship rig, sails furled, was chugging its way past, perhaps a Royal Navy frigate or the U.S.S. *Castine*. It was difficult to say in the twilight.

LET SLIP THE SLUICEGATES OF WAR, HYDRO-GIRL

TERRI FAVRO

Audience with Lady Laura Filomena De Marco, Patroness of the Royal Niagara Hydraulic Fusiliers and Defendress of the Realm, on the occasion of the fiftieth anniversary of Victory Day. At the personal request of H.R.H. Edward VIII, Lady Laura graciously agreed to provide her first-hand account of the deciding battle to restore the United States of America to the Crown, with a transcription of her words to be entered into the royal archives.

In attendance was His Excellency the Right Honourable Bruce Duncan Campbell, Governor General of the Kingdom of the United States, accompanied by Vice-Regal Transcriptionist James Hansom.

All statements attributable to Governor General Campbell have been redacted at his request, in compliance with the Privacy of Dignitaries Statute 45X224(a).

Lady Laura waived all rights and requirements under the Statute and is quoted here in full and without prejudice.

c ⊕ c

I heard you coming up the stairs. Tramp tramp tramp, like you was dragging a goddamn hydraulic cannon. Hope you never need to sneak up on an enemy, Excellency. I'm an old woman and even I could do a better job in the stealth department.

You armed? No? You're a fool then. I never go out no more without a sizzler in my apron pocket. See here? I call this little beauty Lola.

Hands up!

Just joking, Excellency. I can't hit the side of a turbine barn no more 'cause of the glaucoma. Price you pay for overstaying your welcome on earth. Let me plug Lola back in her charge-stand. Named her after a lady friend I met in the Diggings. Got to flush the valves and give her a rubdown, or she seizes up in the cold. Kinda like me. (*Laughter.*)

Yes, I know why you and your scribe are here, Excellency. Same reason as every so-called dignitary who pays their respects on Vic-Day. To swarm me with quizzicals about how the revolutionaries was punished for their insolence to the Crown. They call me the Ultimate Heroine of that battle, the Defendress of the Royal Hydroelectric Commission. The one who brung a conclusion to a war that started in 1812 and seemed set to carry on long after Father Time had turned his wheel from the nineteenth century to the twentieth. Thank the Lord, we adapted the Alternating Current instead of the inferior Direct Current the Staters preferred. Not to mention, we had the bigger Falls, the great Horseshoe.

Still, it took more'n eight decades of skirmishes and bombardments to capture the peace. Poor Isaac never lived to see the treaty signed with those filthy buggers in Buffalo, excuse my French.

I'm going to do something I never done before in one of these bullshit Vic-Day audiences. Since the King compels me to tell the unvarnished truth, I'll compel you to hear it, Excellency, and your scribe Mr. Hansom to write down every word just as I say it.

One thing though. His Majesty might not like what I got to say. You, neither, Excellency.

c　ɸ　c

I met Isaac a few months after Destiny Day, May 24th, 1899. The day we girls officially turned sixteen and learned our futures. Boys, too, maybe; I don't know much about the rites and passages for Her Majesty's Loyal Sons. (We worshipped a Queen then, you'll recall.) I had a brother, but he took off for the canal boats before they could press-gang him to the municipal turbine station crew. You can't blame him for wanting something better than digging and drilling and pumping 'til his heart burst and his arms give out. Most of those boys didn't live past thirty, thirty-five at the outside. Old men in young bodies. All of them deaf as posts from the din of the turbines. Smart ones learned to fingerspell, so's they could talk to one another, trimming sentences to a letter or two – W for *What the hell?* and the like. I'm glad I never had to comfort a pumper. It would have felt like screwing a dead man, pardon my French.

Where was I now? Oh yes: Destiny Day.

I was marshalled with the rest of Her Majesty's Sweet Sixteens in an abandoned tunnel behind the Falls. When the examiner barked out your name, you went through the white curtains, lay on the slab, put your feet up, spread your legs and tried to breathe in through your nose, out through your mouth. That way you hardly felt nothing.

The examiner said, That's a good girl, as if I didn't know already.

While he did his job, I listened to the pumps inside the walls, whoosh, crunk, whoosh, crunk, to keep the lamps going. Sometimes you'd hear a voice yelling for more light, then the thunder of sluices opening in the turbine room. It were the brightest, loudest room I ever been in.

I heard the examiner make a clicking noise with his tongue – chuk, chuk, chuk – like he didn't like what he seen. Tipped womb, he said. You're only good for one thing, sweetheart.

He handed me a card with CF on it, for Camp Follower. What I expected. Momma was one, though she started off a Respectable Wife And Mother. 'Course by 1899 there warn't no camps left to follow. The troops was put up at Fort George but most of us younger CFs comforted the workers digging the longest tunnel in history, the one that would amp up the voltage of hydroelectric weaponry high enough to fry those miserable bastards on the other side of the gorge, no offence.

When the exam was done, I met up with the other girls, weeping in the mist. Turned out all of them had CF cards, too. Boo hoo hoo.

Over the river, all we could see was the great big black hot air balloons, bumping against one another to block our view of the enemy. The sniper posts near the rapids on Goat Island were probably manned that day but they got no aim at that distance.

On our side, a few troops in their red serge uniforms were lined up at the Table Rock canteen for coffee and doughnuts. They sniggered and stared at us, knowing full well what the cards in our hands meant.

SMOS, one of them fingerspelled, meaning: *Suck me off, sluts.*

YSYS, I fingerspelled back. Short for: *You shame yourself, sir.*

c   ◍   c

I got to admit, it was strange that all us girls who got CF cards
that day come from Voltagetown, home to Wops, Frogs, Wogs,
Chinks, Polacks, Bohunks, Darks and other outsiders who
clung to the edge of the British Empire by their dirty fingernails. We didn't count for much, so the Hydro Commission
made us the first to suck surplus power from the Falls' mighty
teat. After they wired up our shacks, some of us just got
shocks or burns; others were flat-out electrocuted. The electricians said the Voltagetown deaths warn't in vain, 'cause they
helped them understand the dangers of over-amping and
made things safe for the better sorts of folks.

c   ◍   c

When I got home, the place were quiet except for creaky bed-
spring sounds from Momma's room. By then, she warn't
working much. She was old, thirty-five or so, and losing her
looks. She only had one regular client left, an old vet of the
Battle of Peachtree Lane, who'd come by with a bottle of
sparkly wine. He got his bits blasted off, so the infantry
medics give him a prosthetic cock. Momma was the only CF
who'd put up with him. Because of the wine, I guess.

I lay down on the daybed and turned on the Marconi wireless. It could take twenty minutes or better to bring in the
scratchy voices of someone singing an aria or reciting a poem.
Though Disloyal, I liked Stater stations best. You could get
a notion of what their heathen rebel cities were like, the
houses always burning to the ground at night, Buffalo especially.

While I waited for the Marconi to warm up, the door of
Momma's room opened and her old soldier boy, Guy, shuffled

out with his pants off, one hand cupped over the hole in his groin, the other holding his prosthesis. He went to the sink and stuck it under the pump. A little door at the tip flipped open so he could fill it.

Water's tainted, less you boil it, I told him. You don't want to be dribbling dirty water into Momma.

He smiled at me all toothless and said, It's okay, it's a closed system, turns into cool steam when I 'jaculate.

Guy sat down on the couch next to me. The wireless had gone to static. Off in the distance we could hear the zinging of the cannons sending electric charges over the gorge. Guy put his hand on my knee.

If my father was alive he'd slit your throat, I warned, and Guy took his hand away.

Vince should have stayed safe in Dago Land 'stead of joining a fight that warn't his own, observed Guy.

He didn't mean to join no fight. He was a chef, I said, which Guy already knew full well. My father, Vincenzo De Marco, came to the colonies on a cook's contract but got pressed into battle when the troops was shorthanded. He got shot off the side of the gorge in the Third Battle of Lundy's Lane. They never found his body. Not that they looked so hard. After a few months, soldiers started turning up at our door with food and condolences. Pretty clear what they expected. Momma become a Camp Follower before she were a widow for one year.

c   ⊙   c

My marching orders come by post. Report to the Diggings of the new tunnel, they said. A red and purple dress come too, marking me as belonging to the Tesla Brigade, Digger Division. I shed a few tears over that! Not a few Camp Followers at the new tunnel didn't live much longer than the Diggers themselves. I'd even heard stories of girls who threw themselves over the Falls in despair 'cause they'd fallen in love with some dirt-faced boy who'd died in a rock fall.

On my first shift I had to see Sir Manager for *jus primae noctis*. His private secretary, Miss Lola, showed me into his office, her sad eyes looking me up and down. I got scared by the ragged scar running down one check. Like someone had taken a fish knife to her. Soon as I went through the door, Miss Lola closed it behind me, fast.

Inside, I saw Sir Manager waiting for me in a big leather desk chair: a fat, old man with his pants off, legs spread wide to expose his bits. Right off, he says, Remove your frock and underthings. After I done that, he pats his lap and says, Sit here, Laura. I had to straddle his puddingy thighs 'til he was stiff as a post, then he hoisted me up by the hips and pulled me down, hard, 'til I wailed with pain.

(*Pause.*)

Pardon me, but that's what *jus primae noctis* means in English, Excellency – a man's right to have a girl on her first shift. Wouldn't want to cheat the King by leaving anything out that were done to me in the name of the Crown.

Satisfied by the sight of blood on my thighs, he ordered me to clean myself up in his washbasin. Then he showed me what the boys would expect me to do for them in the Diggings, none of it pleasant.

He said he made it a rule never to be gentle with girls on *jus primae noctis*, as it only raised false hopes. Best to break us in rough, he said, as we would continue to be handled in that vein. He said the Diggers were not gentlemen and I would get no caresses or loving kindness from them, nor would their deaf ears hear my cries for mercy. When I said I could fingerspell at them, he laughed. Just try to make your-self understood when you got two boys holding you down while another stuffs his filthy bits in your mouth. Sir Manager smiled as he said this. He enjoyed filling my brain with such nightmares. Yet, he never sent me down to the Diggings. He said I was something special and kept me to himself.

Truth be told, I was a pretty thing in those days – what they called fetching: long black hair, full mouth, slim, but full in the bosoms. In the Camp Followers' tight-bodice dress, I'd catch anyone's eye, so no wonder the boss took me as his pet, though it was clear enough that he liked to cause me pain, pummelling and penetrating me every which way he could think of. The only mercy was that he let me go back home to Momma twice a week to have my bruises soothed and wounds staunched. Wouldn't want you to die too fast, girl, he liked to joke.

(*Pause.*)

True enough, Excellency. I reckon the King don't need to hear all the awful bits.

The other Camp Followers resented me getting what they called special treatment. Why, you hardly have to work at all, it ain't fair, they griped. I just shrugged, not wanting to admit that I'd rather've been with the Diggers, many of them famil-iar faces from Voltagetown. I never believed those boys capa-ble of the horrors visited on me by Sir Manager.

The private secretary, Miss Lola, warned me he always took the youngest, prettiest girl for his special pet, until an even younger and prettier one come along.

I was his favourite up 'til a year ago, she said, which shocked me. Miss Lola looked about fifty. Turns out, she was eighteen. The ugly scar on her face come from Sir Manager lashing out at her with the spur of his boot while he was in his cups. That's what being Sir Manager's favourite meant. Ruined, crushed, tired-out and old before your time.

(*Sound of Lady Laura sobbing.*)

Yes, thank you, Excellency. I'll take a moment to collect myself. Could I trouble you for your pocket hanky? Been fifty years, but I still recall the torments that fat bugger visited on me like it were yesterday. I still wake at night sometimes, thinking his belt's round my neck again.

(*Sound of Lady Laura voiding her glands.*)

One day, we were warned a high ranker was coming, a general with the Princess Priscillas. Isaac, of course. He showed up looking all splendid in his redcoat uniform to inspect the workers. The Digger boys stood in a raggedly line in their shit-brown overalls, fingerspelling *W* for *What the hell?* over and over again, so scared they wanted to burrow back into the protection of the tunnel. Like worms.

I stood at attention beside Sir Manager, who I could tell was nervous. He squired Isaac around, showed him the new tunnel the boys were digging and explained about how we needed a longer vertical slope to boost what's called the head. The farther the water falls, the bigger the head, the more force to the turbines, the bigger the electrical charge, and the more miles they could send it. He explained to Isaac about how the tunnel would harness power for the Ring of Death, a line of high-voltage electric cannons set up along the gorge, linked to the turbine room by a wire that run from Niagara Falls all the way to Queenston.

And how many fusiliers would be required in the field to man these cannons? Isaac wanted to know.

Sir Manager puffed himself up. None at all, General. The transmission line carries the firepower. Once the tunnel's dug deep enough for the turbines to give enough amperage, why,

I just flick a switch and the cannons will discharge electric volleys across the river. The Staters' revolutionary brains will boil inside their skulls before they can even think of skedaddling.

Sir Manager ordered the Diggers to give a demonstration, lighting up the sky with cannon fire from guns a half-mile along the gorge. When one of the boys didn't skip lively enough to his post, Sir Manager smacked him to the ground. Tell him what he's to do in that lingo of yours, Sir Manager ordered me. I fingerspelled to the boy: *Open the sluice gates on the eastern side.* The boy nodded and scampered away.

How did the girl make herself understood to the lad? Isaac asked Sir Manager.

Sir Manager grabbed me by the arm and jerked me back in line beside him. It's a dumb show the deaf ones use among themselves, he said. A language for girls and idiots, which comes to the same thing in my experience. Laura seems to have a knack for it, even though she can speak well enough when she's a mind to.

I noticed Isaac looking at me with an expression I couldn't quite figure. Maybe he was curious about a young Camp Follower who could talk with her hands.

Afterwards, Isaac give us a little pep talk about what a brilliant job we was all doing for Her Majesty, etcetera, etcetera. At the end of it, Sir Assistant Manager got up with a pitch pipe and led the few of the boys who could still hear in a rousing chorus of "For He's a Jolly Good Fellow." Isaac looked embarrassed.

Isaac was tall, way over six feet, with pink skin and blond curly hair. Good-looking by anyone's standards. Before he left the station, he asked Sir Manager if he could have a private word with me. Sir Manager looked dismayed but told me to be a good girl and go with the General.

I thought Isaac wanted a quick push but once we was alone together in the office, he touched the front of his tall black hat to me. Ma'am, he called me, which sounded funny since I were only sixteen years old. This sign language you used with the boy, where did you learn it?

I always knowed it, I told him. Everyone in Voltagetown does, 'cause so many men are deaf from the machines.

Isaac sat down in Sir Manager's big leather office chair, and motioned me into one next to him.

Show me, he said, adding: If you please.

Surprised that anyone this grand would want to finger-spell, I went slowly through each letter. For A, make a fist with your thumb pressed on the knuckle of your pointer finger. For B, put your hand flat up with your thumb in your palm. And so forth.

Spell my Christian name, he asked.

Pinky finger up for I, clenched fist for S, two A's like I showed you, and a cupped hand for C. Isaac tried it after me.

You must know your letters well to use this language, observed Isaac.

Yessir, I agreed.

So you have schooling, then?

I shrugged. My momma taught me my letters by reading the Good Book.

Isaac smiled and said: The Staters are wily. They intercept our messages as quickly as we can send them by wireless. This finger language could be useful. Soldiers could pass information from a distance with nothing but one hand and a telescope. I would like to master this silent language and I can think of no abler teacher, nor no prettier one, than you, ma'am. If I may be so bold, are you dedicated to Sir Manager?

I cast my eyes down at the floor, trying not to make a show of my eagerness to leave my monstrous master.

I'm sure you outrank Sir Manager, General, I said.

True enough. It's settled, then. You'll come to my headquarters in Queenston for a week or two and teach me the finger language. Where shall I fetch you from?

When I told Isaac where Momma and I lived, he wrote it down with a silver pencil in a little book.

c   (i)   c

Back at home, Momma had rationed enough power to pull in *Red Ensign* on the Marconi, her favourite patriotic-religious show. The preacher, a Loyalist named the Royal Reverend Nigel St. James, sang "Jerusalem" in a shaky tenor voice and explained how lucky we was to be living in an empire where the sun never set, even though I'd noticed it setting just the day before.

After the hymn, the Reverend started in on the prayers, Momma reciting along with her eyes squoze shut, fingering her rosary beads, strung together from old musket-shot:

St. Michael Faraday. (Pray for us.)

St. James Prescott Joule. (Pray for us.)

St. Heinrich Hertz. (Pray for us.)

Lord William Thomson Kelvin. (Pray for us.)

Sir Alexander Graham Bell. (Pray for us.)

Marquis William Marconi. (Pray for us.)

The Most Reverend Nikola Tesla. (Pray for us.)

Maid of the Mist. (Pray for us.)

All the saints and martyrs of Her Majesty's Royal Electrical Corps of electricians, engineers and journeymen,

*who lay down their lives to boost the voltage of hydraulic
armaments in the Lord's name. (Pray for us.)*

*Shower your blessings upon Niagara, O Lord, the great
engine of Loyalist civilization, powered by the turbines of
the Royal Hydroelectric Commission, praise be to Her
Majesty, May She Reign Forever. Without thy Divine Right,
there would be no divine light by which to smite the revolutionary Staters for their heretical war on our beloved
Kings George III and IV, King William IV, and Queen
Victoria. Thou hast graced us with thy holy mystery, the
Alternating Current, in this most holy place, Niagara Falls,
to create a perfect circuit of hydropower and fry the brains
of our enemies in their heads. O Lord, we beseech thee.*

After she'd finished hearing prayers, Momma kissed her
musket-shot rosary and closed the wireless. Then she had me
read aloud to her from the Good Book: *Hawkins Electrical
Guide, A Progressive Course of Study for Engineers, Electricians and Those Desiring to Acquire a Working Knowledge of
Electricity and Its Applications.* Momma took comfort from
hearing of conductors and insulators, resistance and conduc-
tivity, magnetism, electromagnetic induction, basic principles
of the dynamo and other holy mysteries. When she started to
snore in her chair as I read about armature construction, I
closed the book and tiptoed off to bundle up my few things
for the trip to Isaac's headquarters.

c   ⓞ   c

Isaac come to get me before supper hour. At first, I thought
his asking me to teach him the finger language was just a
dodge, that he really wanted to open those red breeches of his
and get down to business on the daybed. Instead, he present-
ed himself politely to Momma and said I was to be his helper

for a fortnight, so he was riding me out to his Queenston quarters on his electric horse, Alfred. I never seen the like. Alfred's head and body was made of caramel-coloured leather and his steel legs could gallop as fast as a real horse, without ever tiring or needing hay. Isaac pulled a cord from Alfred's tail and plugged him into the socket-pump in our cabin so he'd have enough juice to carry us the ten miles to Queenston. Momma was too awed of Isaac to tell him he'd sucked enough electricity to keep us out of rations for a week. She watched him put his hands around my waist and lift me into Alfred's saddle, then jump up behind, wrapping his arms around me to take the reins. We must've cut quite the figure, Excellency. Before we galloped off, Momma scraped up her nerve to press the *Hawkins Electrical Guide* into my hand, along with a pair of asbestos gloves she got from an electrician in trade for a quick push. When I leaned low in the saddle to kiss her farewell, she whispered in my ear: Read the Good Book every day and you'll have power, no matter who your master may be. And remember to put on the gloves before you touch any live wires.

c   (1)   c

We rode the trail through the bush along the gorge, following the transmission line the Commission strung to charge the hydroelectric cannons positioned every quarter-mile or so – the Ring of Death. At Queenston, Isaac took me through a field to a ten-room stone house, which were his and his alone: such was the privilege of being an officer of Her Majesty in that never-ending war against the Staters.

He hitched Alfred to a charging post connected to a transmission wire slung off the Ring of Death. He smiled and said, I don't think anyone will begrudge a few volts to nourish my steed, do you?

I shook my head, shy to be taken into his confidence. Feeding off a power line warn't legal, strictly speaking; you had to ask the Queen's Own Electricians to ground them, a perilous job. But people done it anyway.

In the sitting room, he had a sweet cake and a bottle of sparkly wine set out. We ate and drank, then sat facing one another and I repeated the alphabet, slow, letting Isaac mirror me. We went from letters to words – easy enough, I thought, but when we started talking back and forth, Isaac sounded like a baby.

You got to go fast enough for letters to blur into words, General. That made him laugh, but I didn't know how to say it better. Fingerspelling isn't just a bunch of letters, it's a language.

True enough, Isaac allowed.

c ⦿ c

After our lesson, he showed me a room with an actual feather bed, first I ever seen, warmed by another wonder – an electric fireplace. To my surprise, he made no move to poke me, just bowed low and wished me a good night. I got the whole room to myself.

Next morning, he showed me the wood stove and the larder. I was surprised when he brought the eggs in from the hen coop with his own hands, putting them on the table in a bowl, something I never seen a man of his rank do before. Momma had said he'd no doubt have a house full of servants but so far, there warn't no one there but him and me.

Ain't you got no girl to do for you, General? I asked.

He looked sad and shook his head. The last cook and scullery maid proved Disloyal so I've been seeing to my own needs.

You mean your help turned traitor? What happened to them?

Escaped to the other side of the gorge with my battle maps sewn into their corsets, unless they drowned in the river crossing, said Isaac.

I tightened the apron strings around my middle. Good thing I'm here, I said. Which was when I took on the job of being Isaac's housekeeper as well as his teacher. I was determined to make it worth his while to keep me around for longer than a fortnight.

c ◑ c

Fast enough, we fell into a routine, like an old married couple. I'd rise before Isaac to stoke the fire, clean the ashes and lay out his breakfast. After that, we had an hour of lessons. I made him talk to me using only his hand.

Pass the salt, if you please.

Would you care for more coffee, sir?

Thank you kindly, Miss Laura.

He fingerspelled that one so often, we shortened it to *TYKML.*

c ◑ c

Middle of the day, Isaac was mostly away soldiering on Alfred but sometimes he took guests at the stone house, like a certain Lieutenant Barnfather, who Isaac called the finest military officer in British North America. Despite his qualities, Barnfather warn't never going to make Colonel, Isaac said, as he'd adopted the company and habits of Her Majesty's Indian allies, the Mohawks, himself being Mohawk on his mother's side. Instead of red wool breeches and leather boots, he wore deerskin leggings and moccasins, growed his hair long and daubed on face paint to go to battle. On account of his native ways, not to mention his blood, Barnfather warn't considered fit company for British gentlemen of a certain rank. Time and again, he'd ride into Queenston with a splendid retinue of Mohawk warriors on horseback. Much as Alfred was a mechanical wonder, the smell of manure and real horseflesh made me homesick for Voltagetown. Barnfather was the most agreeable of Isaac's acquaintances, the only officer who didn't gape and leer at me as if to suggest that I was just hanging around to satisfy Isaac's fleshly needs. When he observed me fingerspelling, he cottoned to its usefulness right off, saying the Mohawks had their own sign language to communicate silently, a boon when you never knowed who'd be behind the next tree, friend or foe.

I am late to learning this silent tongue, but my teacher is making up for lost time, Isaac told Barnfather. Woe betide me if I miss a single lesson.

c ⁕ c

One night, Isaac come home looking weary and thoughtful. At lessons, he was forgetful and clumsy, the letters slipping out of his memory like sand off a beach at low tide. He finally stilled his fingers and took my hands in his.

I must declare myself, dear Miss Laura, he said. Since your arrival here, I find myself consumed by thoughts of you. It's all I can do to keep my mind on my guns and maps. Do you care for me, at least a little bit?

When I confessed that my feelings for him matched his affection for me, he kissed me long and hard, caressing me like no one ever done to me before. Finally, he took me to his four-poster bed and asked permission to take all my clothes off, which I granted, then 'scused himself and come back naked, 'cept for a leather harness buckled low on his skinny hips. A pouch at the front held a prosthesis, like that of Momma's client, Guy, but made of creamy porcelain with masculine curves and bulges and a wreath of shamrock, thistle, rose and maple leaf painted daintily around its head.

I guess I were gape-mouthed 'cause Isaac asked: Are you frightened of Old Toby, Laura?

I shook my head. I seen one like that before, just not so pretty. Did you get your bits shot off?

No, said Isaac, real quiet. Then he added softly: Old Toby is actually a cleverly engineered device, of French design and British manufacture, for the release of feminine tension. It is said our own dear Queen Victoria has taken comfort in such a device, ever since the death of her beloved Prince Albert. It works by electrical stimulation – shall we try it together?

After what I'd gone through with Sir Manager, you'd think I'd've hemmed and hawed and tried to put Isaac off. But I figured if the Queen liked it, why not?

Excellency, I don't know how to describe the lush pleasure Isaac give me. When he put Old Toby between my legs and made him hum, I spasmed for the first time ever. In my ignorance, I thought I'd been electrocuted! When I thrust up my hips, offering myself to the machine, Isaac obliged, all the while moaning and crying out my name, so I knowed he liked it too. Old Toby's vibrations tickled Isaac's nerves and mine, that was the science in it. But more than that, Isaac took pleasure in my pleasure. Even started calling me by a pet name, Hydro-Girl.

(*Laughter.*)

I ain't trying to embarrass you or myself, Excellency. As the poet wrote, the grave's a fine and private place but none do there embrace. If I don't say my piece now, I'll be dead 'fore I get the chance. If his Majesty wants the story of my life, can't I get the joyful bits in, along with the horrors?

Prudishness don't suit a man of your rank, Excellency. All you need do is listen, and let that Hansom scribe of yours write it all down exactly as I say.

Now, then. Being with Isaac were different from being with Sir Manager, and not just because of Old Toby. Sir Manager were hairy and fleshy, but you could feel the muscle under all that flab, the way you'd expect with a man, even one gone soft. Isaac, on t'other hand, were smooth and hairless and pink as a baby and though he was tall, his body under the red serge tunic were slender and delicate as a bird's. Round his chest he wore a tight band, like a corset – at first, I thought to hold in his guts 'cause of a war wound. But one morning I watched him through slitty eyes and seen him unstrap Old Toby's harness and unwind the corset from his chest. Isaac had no bits at all, but a cleft like mine between his legs, and his chest showed swellings same as mine, too, if not as big. Light dawned, as they say.

Isaac warn't a man.

How a woman come to be a soldier, then a general, was a puzzler and a question that I never got any answer to. You probably heard stories like this before, Excellency – I learned they ain't rare, especially in times of war. Isaac – or whatever his woman name was – had height, looks, learning and courage. I've known natural-born men who got less going for them, no offence.

I stayed that night and every night thereafter. Isaac sent a post to Sir Manager and to Momma, letting them know that I'd been seconded to be the General's Aide-de-Camp. I liked the sound of that a lot more than Camp Follower. At least in French it sounded good.

Days, Isaac would take me into a field and show me how to shoot a hydroelectric gun, sizzling crows straight off the farmer's fence. At night, he'd caress me with Old Toby. Good thing there warn't any neighbours, account of our screams of passion would've waked the dead.

Once, after we were both spent and Old Toby set aside to re-charge, Isaac asked: Did you enjoy being a Camp Follower, Laura?

I told Isaac life was hard and short for us CF girls. Even told him some of the abuses Sir Manager had visited upon me.

Isaac started to weep and pulled me into his arms: Laura, you are no longer a Camp Follower, but my own true sweetheart. Then he went down on his knee before me and said, When this war is over, will you do me the honour of marrying me?

Well, I was struck right dumb at the thought of it: me, the ruined daughter of a cook from Dago-land, getting proposed to on bended knee by a General of the Realm. I thought he must be pulling my leg. Only when I saw the tragedy on his face, did I understand he were serious. I searched for the proper words but could not speak them, so overwhelmed I was with emotion. Instead, I fingerspelled my acceptance: *Isaac I wish to wed you with all my heart.*

He kissed me and took off his regimental ring, placing it on my hand – so big, I had to wear it on my middle finger like a knuckleduster. He asked me to accept it as a symbol of his promise.

Sadly, that were the only promise Isaac made me that he didn't keep.

c   ⊙   c

One night, while I waited for Isaac, the lights all went off at once, something that never happened before at the stone house, the generals being the last to get their power rationed. Off in the distance, I could hear the zinging sound of an electrical bombardment and smell the scorch of battle. I knew right away my Isaac were in trouble. While I rooted in the kitchen for matches and candles, a knock come at the door – I should've been suspicious but I throwed it open to three Staters, ugly as sin, on the stoop.

Where's your master? the leader of the thugs demanded, seizing my wrists.

Don't know and wouldn't say if I did, I answered – 'twas God's truth, but as soon as the words was out of my mouth, they set upon me, holding me to the floor by my arms and legs. The leader unbuttoned his trousers and shook his bits at me. I'll give you this 'til you bleed information, girl, he said, but before he could make good, his body jerked in the sizzling blue light of an electrical gun and he fell to the ground in a death-seizure. Isaac stood over the thug's still-jerking body, pointing the muzzle of his gun straight at the head of the man holding my arms.

Let the girl go or you shall meet the same fate as your dog of a master, he said.

Even though they outnumbered him two to one, they run off, leaving me on the floor. Isaac give chase, shooting volts into their traitorous asses until one of them turned and got a lucky shot off; fortunately for me, they didn't see Isaac fall. I pulled him into my arms and could see by the smoking hole in his chest that he warn't long for this world.

Laura, it's an ambush, he gasped. Take Alfred. Warn Sir Manager. Tell him the time has come to turn the Ring of

Death against our enemies, ready or no. Let slip the sluice gates of war, my Hydro-Girl.

I was crying and begging Isaac not to leave me when he died in my arms. I were just a child in many ways, Excellency, but I knowed my duty.

Stupid with grief, I ran to get Alfred and found him out of power: the wily Staters had cut his electrical feeding line. I went back to the house to fetch the Good Book, a wooden stepladder and Momma's asbestos gloves, trying not to look at my poor dead Isaac on the stoop. Dashing tears from my eyes, I made myself think about how to fix the wire and get Alfred charged up. The Good Book explained the steps clear enough, although I could barely see for weeping. Before I got the horse charged halfway, I grew nervous that the Staters would return and mounted Alfred too soon, taking off at a gallop. Alfred ran out of juice a couple of miles into my journey, his mechanical legs collapsing beneath him into a heap of metal. I had to follow the transmission line on foot, through the bush and the swamps, all ten rugged miles to the Falls.

Every schoolchild in Upper Canada knows the rest of the story, Excellency. How I came upon a lost cow that give me cover as a wandering milkmaid. How the Mohawk scouts found me, almost fainting from my exertions, and kept me going, protecting me from bloodthirsty Staters creeping in the darkness, whilst Lieutenant Barnfather tracked the scoundrels who murdered Isaac and meted out swift justice in the silence of the forest, cutting them ear to ear. The Indian troops were as big a part of the victory as me and Isaac, yet they never got their due. Thanks to those good men, I reached the Falls and stumbled into the Diggings, shouting to rouse Sir Manager from bed but finding him in his cups, insensate. Miss Lola and I had to alert the Diggers by fingerspelling WABA, for *We Are Being Attacked*, the alarm to get them to man the turbines and trigger the Ring of Death. The Camp Followers worked alongside their boys. That day the Diggers became Royal Fusiliers and the Camp Followers, Loyalist Defendresses of the Empire.

When we flooded the tunnel and charged the turbines to transmit power, the volley of cannon fire could be heard all the way to York, the screams of the Staters across the gorge louder than the transformers exploding over their heads. The surrender of the Staters to the rule of Her Majesty that day was absolute and unconditional.

Sir Manager were clapped in irons for dereliction of duty. At his trial, it come out that he was the two-faced traitor who'd bribed Isaac's housekeepers and sent the Staters to the stone house to kill Isaac and do with me whatever vile things they seen fit. I watched him swing by his neck, and took no small pleasure in the justice of it.

c   ◑   c

Today, when I stare at the pounding cataract, I see thousands of lost Loyalist souls, none more dear than my Isaac. They built a statue of him raising his sword in one gallant hand as he looks toward the Kingdom of the United States.

Now, here you are, Excellency, a Stater yourself. I hear King Edward married himself a common Stater lady – the woman he loves, my foot, he took up with her to buttress the loyalty of his realm to the south. The King's grandmamma would be rolling in her grave, if she knowed that skinny American bitch was calling herself Queen of the United States and British North America.

After the war, the last real queen, Victoria, honoured me with a title, as well a hundred fertile acres and this very stone house of Isaac's where we're taking tea. I shared these rooms 'til recently with my dear companion and comradess-in-arms, Lady Lola, as she was so designated. We lived like sisters, 'til I took her to Isaac's big bed and introduced her to the touch of Sir Toby. For fifty years we slept in one another's arms. Losing her was as bad as losing my Isaac, only Lola were killed by Father Time, not the Staters.

My only other true friend, Lieutenant Barnfather, were offered a title and land, too, but he turned them down to live with his mother's people, the Mohawks. No offence to Isaac, but I couldn't stomach turning myself into a British gentleman, he told me. He's gone now, sad to say, but not before reaching the ripe old age of ninety-four.

Oh yes, Excellency, and the Queen made good on the promise of a Letter of Thanks from her heirs and successors at Buckingham Palace every Victory Day, personally delivered by whatever codswallup had been recently installed by our government as Vice-Regal Representative of the King. I may be half-blind but I'm guessing you have this year's letter in your pocket, Excellency. Hand it over, if you please.

Thank you.

Now, if you don't mind, I'm done in. Time for my afternoon nap with Old Toby. Kindly show yourself and your vice-regal scribe out of my house.

END TRANSCRIPTION.

c ⏀ c

The above is classified "eyes only" and will be sealed as part of the historical record for 200 years, by order of H.R.H. King

Edward VIII, King of the United British American Empire, May He Reign Forever.

I swear all statements set down here by my hand to be accurate and true, so help me God.

JAMES HANSOM, ESQ.

Transcriptionist to the office of the Governor General

October 12, 1949

EQUUS

KATE STORY

At dawn, the woods fall silent. Birds, wind, even the bright murmur of the river seem to falter.

"When's she coming in, sir?" asks Albert, one of the three St. John's boys assisting the survey.

"Soon, I think." Sandford Fleming gets to his feet, eyes fixed on the east. "If I am not mistaken, very soon."

First Albert then the other boys, Edward and Andrew, let their breakfast dishes fall around the campfire with a clatter. Conne River Joe comes to stand next to Fleming, shading his eyes with his hand. "Do you hear it?"

Fleming shakes his head, but he feels a smile spreading across his face. "Not yet. You?"

Joe nods. "A…" He searches. "A sound from your Empire."

A great *clang* makes them all jump. Jack, the cook and campmaster, a Scotsman like Fleming himself, has dropped a cast-iron pan into the fire. He does not apologize. He stands, eyes fixed eastward, arms stiff at his sides.

Then Fleming hears it: a mechanical noise, cutting through the silence of the ancient boreal forest. It grows louder; they can hear the rhythm of it now, and the hissing. Unconsciously, the boys draw together. Fleming scrubs his hands through his mane of red hair and his thick ruddy beard, and moves in front of the group, straightening his jacket, pulling himself up to his full height. His skin prickles, his heart beats faster. He feels a laugh bubbling up inside as he notes his desire to tidy himself for the encounter.

He's not seen the Theodolite for almost five years. Not seen Emmanuel Smith since that time either, the wee quick English mechanic hired by the East India Company when he was sixteen, no older than these boys here now, to drive the first prototype of the Ramsden Steam-Propelled Theodolite commissioned in the 1830s to complete the Indian Survey.

Closer still. A grinding noise, then the sound of dragging chains, like an approaching visitation of ghosts from that fellow Dickens's imagination, burdened with all their past sins – good! With a touch of theatricality, Manny has released the measurement chains! The first railroad surveying team in the history of Newfoundland will see how this thing works in its entirety.

The creature comes lurching into view, then, along the rough trail the team has cut – a long and gentle, railroad-friendly curve. Surely the entire vast island holds its breath in astonishment, for who has seen such a sight?

Manny rides the Theodolite, or rather, controls it the way a marionetteer controls a puppet. Straps on his hands and feet enable him to walk-ride the creature. It strides along on clever jointed legs, brass and mahogany gleaming. There's a spring to it for, of course, the carriage must be level and the precious mechanism on top must be preserved from the worst of the jolting. The boiler clanks and hisses, releasing a gentle steam, tinged shell-pink in the morning light.

"Lord, she's beautiful!" breathes Albert, at the same time as Edward and Andrew utter religious oaths, quickly suppressed. Joe says nothing.

Jack – dark-haired, handsome Jack, who had the St. John's girls hanging off him the entire time the team was being

assembled in the city – steps backward, away, into the shelter-
ing shadow of the trees. When they'd met in the city, Fleming
had instantly recognized Jack's accent, from his own region of
Scotland. "You're from Fife?" he'd asked.

"Aye," Jack had answered. From Fife almost instantly, too,
if Fleming can judge the edge of the accent, for he mourns the
loss of his own, so many years now in this new country. Fellow
Scotsmen barely recognize him as their own, but Jack had.
"You'd be from there yourself."

"What is it, man?" Fleming asks him now. "That's no way
to greet our lady!"

But Jack's eyes are wide, his feet in his big boots shuffle
from side to side, and with two, three, four trembling steps he
disappears into the cool shadows of the dawn forest.

Fleming, concealing his irritation, turns back. He raises
his hand in greeting as Manny clanks up to the party, exe-
cutes a saucy turn, and comes to a halt. He releases a valve,
and the Theodolite settles down with a mechanical sigh, its
legs bending so that Manny can slide out of the saddle onto
the ground.

Fleming senses the boys trying not to back away.

"Manny, Emmanuel Smith!" he yells, and embraces the
small Englishman in a bear hug.

Manny pounds Fleming on the back. "Good to see you,
sir." He steps back and looks searchingly at Fleming's face.
"You look fine, just fine, sir."

"I *am* fine." Fleming puts a touch of asperity into his voice.
Manny will have heard the gossip of course; it is a topic of
interest from London to the west coast of new Canada. "I am
glad I merit your approval."

"That you do, sir!"

"How was the trip out from the city?"

"Took me almost an hour to lose the entourage." The two men laugh; the gossip, the weakness, are banished. The Theodolite is a magnet for children of a certain age and, of course, men – and women – of a mechanical mindset. Any time it has appeared in public it has garnered a following; in Truro they'd had to control the crowds with the help of the police.

Fleming introduces Manny to the others. Manny hesitates to shake hands with Conne River Joe, until Fleming coughs meaningfully and the Englishman takes the Micmac guide's hand. "And there's Jack, but he seems to have disappeared entirely."

"Can I touch her, sir?" young Albert asks, hands twitching at his sides.

"Certainly," says Fleming, adding rather unnecessarily, "Watch the boiler," for these boys will know not to touch the scalding thing, cradled underneath and to the rear of the gorgeous telescope and frame. Joe has already given the mechanism a circuit, making a particular survey of the leather reinforcements and brass-and-steel jointing. The woodwork is ornate, carved with artistic exuberance by the unnamed craftsmen who constructed it back in England; the East India Company can afford the best, paid for with plunder. Horses – some with wings, some with tails scaled like fishes, some centaur-like with human faces – adorn the Theodolite; and suns, radiating light and heat and power.

"What is it like to ride?" asks Joe.

"Smoother than you'd expect," Manny says.

Albert points. "And on top, there, it's just like a regular theodolite. Only, does that frame rotate, sir?"

"Indeed. One hundred and eighty degrees," Fleming approves. Albert is an unusually bright youngster; he reminds Fleming of his own son, Frank Andrew.

Fleming encourages the youngsters to climb the creature, and soon they are scrambling over her like magpies. They immediately grasp the utility of the retractable measurement chains that run between the middle and back sets of legs. The Theodolite's stride pulls the chains taut with every step, with mechanical precision, even on a mountain slope. It is a far cry from the usual way of measuring distance, where the survey chief sets the end point, then the chainmen set the chain, and the crew inchworms along the ground.

"The inchworm has been transformed into... well, if not a butterfly then at least a six-legged twelve-foot-tall spider," Fleming sums it up.

"Caw!" squawks Edward, overcome.

"How much does it weigh?" Joe asks.

"About a thousand pounds," Manny says proudly.

"Caw!" Edward squawks again.

"That's less than her predecessor, a Great Theodolite of the non-self-propelling kind. That one weighed almost fifteen hundred pounds in its travelling cases. They wanted it to survey the Himalayan mountains. Imagine."

"*They*, meaning your East India Company?" Joe asks.

"The very same," Manny confirms.

"They needed one they could ride," Joe muses.

"Yes, and isn't she a beauty?"

Everyone agrees that she is.

"And she can climb a mountain like a monkey." Manny looks a bit uncertain. "If monkeys climb mountains."

"Never mind. If they do, they'd be left in the dust by our lovely girl here." Fleming pounds Manny on the shoulder. "Wish I'd had her last year in the Rockies."

He wishes – as soon as the words leave his mouth – that he'd not evoked last year. His weakness, pain, the opium.

Doubt, intolerable hesitation, morbid introspection. He turns, bellowing into the woods to banish the memory. "Jack! Jack of Fife! Where are ye? Come and have a look at this, will you, man?"

c   ◑   c

Fleming, pedagogically committed to instilling traditional surveying methods despite the arrival of the Theodolite, has all the boys counting strides as well as cutting the trail. And Albert, so intent on numbers that he failed to gauge the terrain, has walked straight into a bog.

"Hold on tight, now, I'm going to give you a heave." Fleming braces his feet and hauls Albert out of the sucking quicksand by brute force.

"Thank you, sir!" gasps Albert. "Lord, this mud stinks."

"Indeed it does. Wash yourself off in the creek."

"Thank you, sir."

Fleming laughs as the tall, gangly boy, ears red with embarrassment, scampers off. His strides are so long that he always comes up with a smaller number than the other boys. Fleming remembers his own apprenticeship with John Sang, back in Scotland, when he'd been fourteen. "Ye great lummox, yer strides are too long!" the man would yell at him, not without affection.

Sang and his sons had had to sell their surveying equipment, Fleming heard from his father, some years ago. To have stayed in Scotland would have meant that same fate for Fleming: financial and professional stagnation, and ruin. In coming to this New World, he'd made his fortune.

True, there are doubts now. In Ottawa he is no longer the hero. Millions of dollars spent on the survey West, then a sudden shift in government policy that stripped him of his

Canadian Pacific Railway commission; and now they want a private company to complete the project. Fleming was taking too long to reach British Columbia, they said; a reckless election promise, impossible to keep. The injustice is almost a physical pain. The larger picture, though, the expansion of the Empire – no one can take that from him. He is here, now, in this beautiful, improbable country that calls itself always in perpetuity a New Founde Lande; what better place to be?

Fleming remounts the Theodolite. The instant his weight settles into the saddle, she rises up on the tips of her clever legs. He settles his feet into the stirrups, hooks his left elbow through the bridle.

Riding her is not easy. Manny surrendered the honour to Fleming with visible reluctance. Her plumb line indicates she is level; he checks the spirit levels, makes some minute adjustments of the thumbscrews on the centring plate. He peers through the eyepiece, takes his measurement, and calls out to the others that he is done. Then he urges his steed forward, on to the next triangulation.

It cuts surveying time in half, or better, this machine. On uneven terrain she needs to walk slowly, making sure the measurement chains go taut with each stride. A meter keeps count; Fleming glances at the numbers as they tick over, and keeps his own tally. But the joy and sheer muscular work of guiding the steed on her thaumaturgical legs almost carries him away from the gravity of what he is doing. There is something marvellous about working one's way through territory, about being the first of the Empire to put a mark upon a place. He has tried to analyze the phenomenon in himself. It is a passion, a mingling of protectiveness, ownership, and an almost violent desire to crack open the land's secret life.

Fleming sees the flash of a bird's wing; a raven takes off with a knowing croak. High above, three young bald eagles wheel.

This island will make a beautiful landing for European passengers on their way to New York and beyond...

His peripheral vision picks up movement, off to his right. A shape, a great black shape, slips in and out of dark spaces, sliding between spruce trees. He cannot hear it above the noise of the Theodolite. It shadows him. A bear? No, it's too tall—

Suddenly, his hand burns. Fleming snatches it to his chest. How could he have been so careless as to touch the boiler?

He grinds the Theodolite to a halt.

But it's impossible. The boiler is behind and beneath him.

The shadow, the creature, if it was ever there, has vanished.

He looks at his hand. It is the same palm that inexplicably wracked him with pain last year, after the collapse of the CPR project. His weakness, pain, the amnesiac opium dreams: Jeanie had almost worried herself sick over this unexplainable illness. Nothing had ever felled Fleming until last year. Until then, he had conducted surveys and driven spikes for railroads from Halifax to British Columbia, carving virgin territory, accomplishing the impossible. And then that intolerable weakness, dreams, crying out in his sleep that boys were drowning, that his hand was burning, that he heard his own mother's voice. *Sandford, stay away from the water!*

There is nothing – no mark, no redness, nothing.

As Fleming stares at his hand, the pain radiates up his arm, almost forcing a cry from between his teeth.

And then, it fades, draining away into the ether.

c ⏀ c

Days go by, a week.

"We are making great progress," Fleming says around that night's campfire. Dark-haired Jack has cooked them a fine dinner, and set up a comfortable camp. He has kept his distance from the Theodolite, Fleming notes, as if he wants nothing to do with it. Or is he, possibly, afraid of it?

Fleming doles out tots of rum to all, and toasts, "To the Theodolite!"

They down the rum. Jack snorts and shakes his head from side to side, a strange series of actions he always repeats when consuming alcohol.

"So, Mr. Fleming," Joe asks, "is it true that you rode that thing through the Aroostook River territory, and dazzled the Americans out of almost ten thousand square miles of land?"

Fleming laughs. "This very one," he says. "And I wouldn't say I *dazzled* the Americans, so much as—

"Showed them reason!" Edward crows.

The Pork and Beans War, as it was known, had been dragging on for decades at that point – no real war but a series of skirmishes, with neither Great Britain nor America wanting to step in and alienate the other. But when the Americans threatened violence over the contested area and started stealing Acadian lumber equipment, the Acadian lumbermen actually took a Maine land agent and his assistants hostage. Then the diplomats were, finally, summoned. "It wasn't just the territory…an extensive census of the inhabitants was conducted as well. But since the Americans didn't even seem to be able to find the 45th Parallel—"

The others explode into laughter. "Fort Blunder!" shouts Andrew, referring to the fort the Americans built just after the

War of 1812, south of what they'd surveyed as the parallel. The fort had turned out to be three-quarters of a mile inside Canada.

"Yes. So we were able to prove Great Britain's superior surveying abilities. Quite simply, the American maps were in error."

"Imagine if they'd kept that big chunk of New Brunswick," Albert muses. "When you built that Intercolonial Railroad from Quebec City to Halifax, you'd have had to go all the way around."

"Indeed. That final survey of the U.S.–Canadian border saved the new Canadian government hundreds of miles of track, and millions of dollars. But beyond that, it was a decisive moment. Great Britain signalled to the Americans that they'd not stand for petty wrangling. If two countries are to share the longest undefended border on earth, they'd better become adept at communicating. And if Great Britain had let the Americans walk over them during the Maine incident… Well, they didn't, and a great deal of that was due to our technological superiority."

Fleming remembers riding the Theodolite into Washington. He'd hated to take such a theatrical approach, but he'd had to clearly demonstrate its sheer awesome technological capability, and then compare the rude surveys the Americans had done versus the near-perfect results he was able to achieve.

"I am an Empire man," he says into the silence. "We have a common history, culture, *instruments*. And beyond that, I am a Commonwealth man. If I espouse any political position at all, it is the cause of colonial unification." His voice gains power. "Through technology, we can and will create a global network of the Commonwealth states. The creation of a greater Canada is only part of the picture. This railroad across Newfoundland will connect Europe to the North American rail system, and thus to the world."

"You aim to make Newfoundland part of Canada? My father might have a word with you about that, sir. Me mudder, too," Edward jokes.

"It would diminish the length of a voyage from Europe to New York by half, lad," Manny points out, "if a proper land communication existed between the eastern coast of Newfoundland and the railways of America."

The last of the sun's light has leached from the sky, and the night has become a circle described by firelight, surrounded by great primeval darkness. A log shifts and falls with a soft crackling sound. An owl hoots, to be answered within seconds by another: mates, hunting.

Fleming takes from his pocket his beautiful, scratched old watch, and, leaning into the firelight, flips it open. "My father gave this to me." The boys, Joe, Manny, and even silent Jack lean in to look. "Gave it to me when I was eighteen, the day I left Kirkcaldy to sail across the Atlantic and seek my fortune." He remembers that passage: the many weeks it took to cross the ocean; the vast storm that almost swallowed them up. Remembers the sound of that storm, an awful roaring as the waves hovered and fell, hovered and fell, implacable, terrible. Fleming leans again into the firelight and indicates the watch. "It has, you see, a built-in sundial, as well as a clockface. I carry it with me to remind me of where we have come from, and where we are going. We have come from a world of sail and horse power. We have been using the sun to measure time. My own homeland, Scotland, is built upon a horse-powered industrial heritage."

"Aye," spits Jack, the first word he has uttered this night. He stands just outside the circle of light. Everyone turns to stare at him.

"At the beginning of this century," Fleming continues, "the annual cost of maintaining a horse was four times the wage paid to a labourer. Our very prosperity, based on the horse, has become dependent upon transcending the horse. We have left the horse and the sun behind."

Jack blurts, "The railroad, it's madness. A disorientation that leads to madness!"

Conne River Joe, his eyes fixed on Jack, begins to speak, then silences himself.

"What is it, Joe?" Fleming is curious.

"There is a price," the guide says softly, "for change."

"For progress, you mean," Manny puts in. "Surely you aren't against progress? You're employed by this surveying expedition, same as the rest of us. Your people use guns, sure enough."

Joe meets Manny's eyes; it is the Englishman whose gaze drops.

"This progress leaves a mark. On the land." Joe looks at Fleming. "On you."

"Aye. And so our land is blackened with smoke, and cut through with railroads!" Jack's voice rings through the forest.

Fleming's throat dries; he forces himself to smile. "Change does come at a price, it is true."

Joe nods. "Great change has come, from across the water, as was foretold."

"Foretold? By whom?" Manny asks.

"We have a Creator, we have a world of the spirits, just as you do. They foretold the coming of great change and hardship. And more change will come with this railroad."

"This very place was my first glimpse of the New World," Fleming remembers. "Twenty-one days after a terrible storm, I was just appearing on deck to put some handkerchiefs out to dry, when I was agreeably surprised to see hills on the horizon. Immediately everyone came on deck, some nearly dancing for joy. This was the south coast of Newfoundland."

"Yes. I remember," Jack mutters. And then the man turns and disappears into the darkness, into the woods, his feet clopping inside his great old boots.

Remembers that? How? The thought runs through Fleming like cold water.

The others watch Jack go. Edward whistles softly between his teeth and rolls his eyes; Andrew and Albert suppress a laugh.

Manny seems unaware of the tension. "We'll make a proper park out of all this," he gestures grandly at the boreal night, "just like back home."

Fleming shakes off his uneasiness. "I hope not! I love the wildness of this place. And I want others to see it. I picture a near future, a future where the North Atlantic is virtually bridged by a system of steam-propelled floating hotels."

"Caw!" Edward breathes. "Imagine that!"

They all fall silent. Through Fleming's mind runs a vision of a vast fleet of gorgeous mahogany and brass ship-buildings, run on steam and clockwork. With ballrooms and chapels, with private rooms that rival a palace for luxury. There are stained-glass windows and turrets. And from the turrets flutter stalwart Union Jacks. Vast ships, towering over the waves, sailing serenely in an endless procession, across an Atlantic forever tamed by steam.

c   ◑   c

It rains in the night. The pattering on his tent awakes Fleming; he emerges to make sure the Theodolite is covered, only to find Manny already there with a lantern. "Sir! Look at this," Manny whispers.

Fleming hastens to the little Englishman's side. "What is it?"

In answer, Manny swings the lantern in a gentle circle about the foot of the Theodolite. He has already thrown its waxed covering over it, and at first the brightness of the canvas confuses Fleming's eyes, creating blurs and traces in the darkness. But then he sees what Manny is seeing.

Hoof prints. A large unshod horse's hoof prints, all around the Theodolite. The prints are deep. It is as if a vast heavy wild horse has danced circles around the machine, around and around in the darkness, and nobody in all the camp heard a thing.

C   (I)   C

Fleming does not mention the hoof prints in his journal entry the next day.

They have made it two-thirds of the way across the southern coast of this island, to a place Joe tells them is called Meelpaeg Lake. "Lake with many coves and bays," he translates.

"I like it," Jack says approvingly. "A beautiful lake. Reminds me of the lochs back home, yes, Fleming, sir?"

"Indeed it does." Fleming wonders if the man is homesick. "Indeed it does."

"Red Indian Lake is to the north," Joe points.

"The Red Indians – do you know anything of them?" Fleming is curious.

Joe shakes his head. "The Beothuk wouldn't talk to us."

The Red Indians are all gone, now. The last of them, a young woman named Shanawdithit, died in St. John's sixteen years before Fleming caught his first glimpse of this island. A tale that does not do the Empire credit.

"You see?" Joe points. On a slight rise, overlooking the vast lake, a tall tree stands alone. Its lower branches have been lopped off, leaving only a tuft at the top, and the bark has been stripped. Long ago it had been painted in red and white stripes, and while the pigment is faded, the colours are, once you notice them, unmistakable. "That is one of theirs."

"The Beothuk?"

Joe nods. "It is a way to communicate."

"Communicate what?" Albert asks.

Joe smiles. "Not what – who. With the world of the spirits."

"Like a lightning rod," Fleming says. It makes him uneasy, for no reason he can discern.

"Good spirits or bad?" Edward shoots back, grinning.

But Jack speaks then. "I might take myself down to that lake," he says. "I think I will, in fact."

"Have a nice time," Edward says, his voice overly polite. The other two boys shuffle their feet and cough, covering their laughs.

Jack, handsome dark-haired Jack, does not appear to notice. He begins to walk down the slope to the lake, then picks up speed until he achieves a bouncing run.

"Well, shall the rest of us get to work?"

Fleming is pleased with the pace of the work that day, even though it goes more slowly than the day before. The terrain is hilly, and rocky outcroppings make the going slow. Finding the best train route will be difficult, although Joe's knowledge of the terrain, coupled with previous geologic maps, assure Fleming that this south coast route will be the best.

It won't please the politicians back in St. John's, who will want to appease citizens outside the city longing for a trunk line to connect them to the rest of the province. Already Fleming knows the government, like the Canadians, will take the cheapest route in terms of engineering – they've already threatened to lay narrow gauge tracks – while making extravagant promises to their citizens. As with Prime Minister John A. Macdonald, and then Alexander Mackenzie, promises will be made that cannot be kept.

Yes, a waking nightmare, politics. But anything is better than nightmares of unanswerable hoof prints and dead-end memories. The image of the lone tree, created by a dead people and staring blindly at the lake, rises unbidden before his mind's eye.

They need to work by "turning" now, as there are so many changes in elevation between the measurement points. Fleming keeps the boys busy with multiple setups and taking levels. "Won't get a nice smooth rail through here, will you, sir?" Albert worries.

"Don't fret, my boy. Dynamite will take care of that," Fleming assures him. "According to our friend Joe, the terrain levels out nicely in only a few miles."

"Yessir." Albert's face is red; it is, by this island's standards, a hot day. He turns and goes back to chopping at the vegetation, which is very thick here, widening the path for the Theodolite.

"It is the business of engineers to make smooth the path on which others are to tread!" Fleming calls out after his retreating back.

Albert turns and gives him a merry grin.

And with his next swipe of the axe, Albert cuts into his own palm.

The flow of blood is instantaneous; so is the boy's shock. Fleming watches Albert's face go white, watches the uncomprehending look down at his own injury, sees even the pupils of the boy's eyes widen, turning his eyes dark, all in the space of mere seconds it takes him to halt the Theodolite, command it to sink, and slide from the saddle. All in time to take the boy into his arms as Albert faints.

It is a matter of a moment for Fleming to wrap the injured hand tight in his neckerchief, to sweep the boy up in his arms and mount the Theodolite. At almost a gallop, chains retracted now so nothing impedes the creature's movement, they ride back to the camp. Albert does not regain consciousness; his head lolls on his neck. Fleming notes in himself a drive, almost an obsession, to care for this boy, for if he does not something terrible will happen. Notes that this desire to rescue, twinned with terror, is perhaps the driving energy of his entire life. Notes this to ponder later.

Albert wakes soon enough, to the pain of alcohol poured on the wound, the tug of stitches taken through skin with a needle. Bites down on a leather belt, does not cry out. Fleming stitches Albert's palm himself. He will suffer no one else to do it.

He will make smooth the path on which others tread.

c ⊙ c

It is near nightfall and Jack has not returned to camp. Emmanuel stays with Albert while Fleming and the others circle the lake, calling. They call until the sun has set and the moon is beginning to rise.

Finally Fleming calls them back to camp. They make a dinner of hard bread and bacon and sit, disconsolate, disturbed.

"Not a footprint," Joe says.

"Could he have drowned?" Andrew quavers.

"Now, no talk like that. Jack is a solitary man, and has probably taken himself off for a time. We'll find him here in the morning, cooking our breakfast." Fleming himself does not believe a word of it. Dull anger at his fellow Scotsman beats in his breast. "How's your hand, Albert?"

"Fine, sir."

He's lying.

They all go off, subdued, to their tents and try to sleep.

c   ⟨⟩   c

That night, he cannot move. Again, his mother's voice: *Sandford, stay away from the water!*

The cries of children are more distinct now, and he sees them: his three boyhood friends, Albert, Andrew, and Edward.

No, those weren't their names; those are the boys here, now, on the survey. Andrew, yes, but the other two were Robert and David.

They'd all three of them drowned in the river.

He'd been a wee lad, only four years old at the time. Nothing had ever been found of the other boys, only some guts washed up on the shore.

His hand had been burnt. That was true. How that had happened his parents never said – if they knew – and nobody would speak of it after. There was much that was not spoken of back in Kirkcaldy.

Only, that you are to stay away from the water. Malignant spirits live there. Kelpies, they're called. Three boys, together, carried into the depths. Beautiful black horse, its back extending, longer and longer to accommodate all its little passengers. Its legs would be backwards. One boy would remain on the shore. He would usually pet the horse, but his hand would then stick to its neck. He would have to tear his palm from the horse to free himself. He would survive, but the other children would be carried off and drowned. Only some of their entrails would be found, afterwards.

Fleming awakes in such pain that he cries aloud. His hand is burning. Something heavy and wild circles his tent – not a bear, no, he hears the hollow ringing of hooves on the ground. Don't the others hear? Fleming pours himself from the tent, hand cradled to his chest. Something dances away from him. There, in the fractured moonlight under the trees: a horse. It prances around the crouching Theodolite, inanimate under its cover. A beautiful, powerful black horse.

Its hooves are backwards.

Fleming knows this creature. For he brought it with him, so many years ago. And something about this land, this vast island full of ghosts, has brought it out of him. He is the lightning rod. The angry spirit manifests in a form that he recognizes inside his blood, his bones.

Summoning something from deep within, something one of his savage, unconquered ancestors might have recognized as courage, he roars and runs straight at the creature, arms raised overhead. He will strike it between the eyes.

The horse, with its demonic turned feet, wheels in a circle and gallops into the night.

Unhesitating, Fleming strips the cover from the Theodolite. He scoops coals from the smouldering campfire into the firebox, and blows upon them until he hears the riveted iron boiler begin to stir; the fire tubes are doing their work, transporting the hot gases throughout the water.

He can hear the Kelpie, through the trees, down by the lake. It neighs, a battle cry.

The others do not wake. It no longer surprises Fleming. This is a battle for him alone.

When he is satisfied that the firebox is burning well, he slams shut its door and begins to mount the Theodolite. Then he pauses. He takes the time to find an iron spike, one of the many they have brought to mark surveying points, and throws it into the embers of the campfire. He lets it heat until it glows red. Then, using a stick, he levers it into a steel pan.

Placing the pan with the glowing spike on the saddle, he then mounts the Theodolite.

It is hard to make his way through the trees, in the dark. But the demon calls him on. Shadows loom, branches strike his face. His hand, still wracked with pain, refuses to close properly on the controls. But he limps forward on his steed, until finally he comes out onto a clear place, a beach of smooth rocks next to the vast lake.

The blind tree watches.

The monster is waiting for him.

It rears up on its hind legs, lands, and charges.

Fleming is only just able to turn the Theodolite aside in time, steel feet screeching on the rocks with the speed of his scramble.

Another scream of rage from the monster, the horse. Equus. The ancient god.

The Kelpie charges Fleming again.

Again, all Fleming can do is dodge.

He runs the Theodolite down the beach, putting as much space between himself and the Kelpie as he can. The rocks shift beneath the Theodolite's feet and the creature lurches. The hot spike is flung from its pan. Fleming stands in the saddle to catch it, and succeeds; the searing pain in his palm is no worse than the phantom pain he already endures.

The Kelpie is charging. Its eyes glow cold blue in the night.

Fleming stands his ground. He swears he can feel the Theodolite quiver beneath him, wanting to charge, or to flee, he knows not which. But they hold, oh, they hold, and the ebony monster comes with flashing eyes, huge, larger than any horse ever was.

Just as it is about to mow them down, Fleming and the Theodolite spring to the side.

Fleming plunges the hot spike into the Kelpie's flank.

c　◍　c

The next day, Fleming blames the terrible long burn across his palm on an overheating incident with the Theodolite in the night.

"But that's impossible, I raked out her firebox myself!" Manny exclaims. He is worried, shaken, doubts his own capabilities.

How well Fleming knows that feeling. He hates to put Emmanuel Smith there, but he must.

Albert, fetching water down on the beach, finds a pile of white, quivering, melting starch, or something like it. So he says.

By the time the others come down to look, it is gone, all but a trace of white film across the rocks. Conne River Joe looks hard at Fleming, but says nothing.

Jack is never found.

The hands of Albert, the boy, and Fleming, the chief engineer, heal but scars remain. They finish the survey, cutting along the south coast of the island.

Fleming's hand never wholly recovers. The palm remains shiny, livid, devoid of any human lines: heart, head, and life, all seared away. The pain continues to haunt him.

But he accepts it, accepts the price. One must have a railroad to enter the modern era. It leashes the land, renders the unknown known, the irrational rational. There are no uncertain dreams, no vengeful gods, in a land circumscribed by a railroad.

GOLD MOUNTAIN

KARIN LOWACHEE

Here in the snow, your handprint. Rabbit small and delicate white, limned by blue shadow and the scrape of spruce branches. Here in the snow, your handprint leading me to hearth, as if you'd been crawling on your knees to start the fire.

I thought at first you were a trapper, surrounded by cabin walls you'd hewn by hand. I was going to discover animal skins tacked to the wood and fur lining your face, feral and savage. Chimney smoke trailed up toward the sky like it was singing a song, every twist of grey a note brought high by the air. It sounded like refuge. My eyelashes jewelled by frost, the ends of my hair brittle with cold. Surely, only a huntsman like my husband buried himself so deep in the woods, clinging to the mountainside that hid you from distant paths, long forgotten by iron tracks below.

When I touched the wooden panels of the door, the grain gave a warmth that sank through my woollen mitten, as if the tree you'd decimated was somehow yet alive, transfused by blood.

c ◑ c

"Please open the door." My voice in the emptiness of a winter forest fell first into the drifts. Everything dampened. Here, you could bury yourself as if you were beneath a blanket and hope the darkness didn't see you.

The latch lifted on the other side. A sliver of light and a gust of that warmth from within. A dark eye not framed by fox fur, but fox-like just the same. Angular and golden, as if it had fetched the fire burning behind you and trapped it. Peering at me, wary in your den.

"Please." I grasped the collar of my coat, squeezing the lapels together against the biting air. "You're the first person I've seen up here and I know it's going to storm." Even the animals were digging holes.

I should've stayed out. I had climbed this far to live and die as the animals. But the tracks in the snow pulled me forward. The scent of smoke. And a part of me thought I would see my husband Sam on the other side of this door. He would apologize for not being able to come down the mountain. He would say he was waiting for the spring thaw.

But it wasn't my husband.

The door eased wider. The dark eye, lit with fire, blinked twice. More warmth spilled out and took hold of me, drew me in.

c   ⟨⟩   c

You even walked like a fox, gentle steps across floorboards that stretched a little warped, curling at the edges. Rough but sturdy, like your hands when you loaded the pot-bellied stove and poked at the flames. Hair black as ink and tied in a knot at the top of your head, pulling your face back to make every stare a scrutiny into the wind. Long cheekbones, burnished skin. Like you'd stood too close to the fire or been hammered out from the elements. I couldn't see your muscles from beneath the grey and brown layers, but you carried the cast-iron cauldron full of water as if it were a picnic basket woven from straw.

I sat with knees to the fire like a child begging for attention. The shadows flung around the walls and corners of the cabin and I tracked them. Barely ten feet in any direction, but that just meant every whorl and eddy of wood lay exposed to this heat. No skins or furs anywhere. No guns. How did you survive in the wild without guns? I watched your hands.

A raised box in the corner must have been a bed; it was strewn with piles of blankets both colourful and dun.

You dropped leaves into the water pot, and things that looked like tiny twigs, and some sort of powder. Soon the aromatic half-notes of spice and salt wafted to my seeking breaths. This was tea. Or broth. I didn't care which. I'd run out of hard tack a day ago.

I took the offered mug with both hands. You passed it to me with the same, nodding twice. We hadn't spoken once in the diligence of your hospitality.

The only seat in the cabin and I sat upon it. You squatted in front of the light and held your own cup, encircled by strong fingers. We sipped and said nothing until enough of the soothing tea had thawed out my thoughts.

"Thank you."

Only a dip of the chin in return.

"My name is Jules." I didn't hold out my hand. I knew this wasn't the ritual of Chinamen, and that was who you were. A Chinaman alone in the middle of the mountains. They came in droves to the mountain and the gold fields, for the rush and then the railway. Set up tents and communities, speaking their strident song language, wary of strangers.

I understood that inclination.

"Lin," you said, nodding again. That was all.

Coolies, we called the Chinese. Some were only boys but they took the voyage from the Far East – actually west of this western side of the country – desperate for a new land or better wages or some opportunity they couldn't find in their home. Escape. Didn't we all come here for that? Except for those who'd been here first. I knew some Indians, no less wary than the Chinamen with just as much reason to despise, if not more.

You passed your palm over the drifts of steam rising from your mug, and the white curls seemed to dance between your fingers. Following them.

"How do you survive up here, Lin?" On frozen berries and herbs and mushrooms? How was it that you survived up here and my husband did not – a man who had made work of thirty-five years in rough country, crossing environments like an explorer until he settled into mine?

You just wafted more of the steam into your eyes, like a tribal chieftain in a smudging ritual.

My skin warmed, some heated delirium after so much cold causing my thoughts to wander to the fantastic. Maybe my husband had transformed. Maybe he was beneath the blankets here. Maybe you could explain how the bones of the Earth dared to latch onto something living. Like we latched onto the dead.

"Why do you live up here?"

Not that I couldn't see the appeal. I'd implored Sam to bring me to these heights, build a cabin like this one, live out the rest of our days away from the tent cities. It was always something to do next spring, next summer, just a little more time.

You sipped your tea as if you hadn't heard. Maybe you hadn't understood.

But then you spoke with a soft accent and a sad bend of your gaze. "I am poisoned."

c ◑ c

We all saw them, the Chinamen, laying track and exploding rocks, serving the unrelenting bridge between one province and the next. Eventually, all the way to the opposite coast if the rail barons had their way. Maybe the Chinese thought if they built far enough, travelling east into the rising sun, they would meet their own country once again.

But we were without country here. We were blown across the land, broken away from our mother homes like shale in a storm.

I am poisoned.

From what?

You just shook your head.

You built me a fort of blankets on that bed and gestured for me to lie down. I was too weary to argue. From beneath the layers I watched you crouch by the belly fire, your palms open to the flames.

c ◑ c

I woke up to a conversation of weather outside the door. There were no windows so I just listened, woollen blankets up to my eyes, as snow and wind made the trees moan and the mountain creak. The buffeting across the log-bound roof sounded a little like war drums. A storm like this howled, as wild as a wolf, and nature rooted to the earth answered back. The whip of branches, the shudder of scrub. And from above, the Lord's impatient fingers tapping a staccato of hail.

You still sat in front of the fire, feeding it.

I thought I saw the flames stretch toward you, dance over your sleeve, then retreat back into the iron. I thought I saw you rise and walk the floorboards, a blossom of fire in your palm, and you went to each dark, cold corner and took the warmth there.

You stood over me, holding fire, and spoke in a different tongue. The heavy heat wore down my eyes until they shut.

c   ⟨⟩   c

I dreamed.

Three-masted sailing ships traversing the wine-dark ocean. Below decks, men and boys lined so tightly behind closed hatches that the cabins felt more like coffins. Your father died on the journey.

Spilled onto the shore of the island, this new world was bewildering. Cold. Like promises.

Your people called the ultimate destination Gold Mountain like it was a place of sunlight and fair wages. Instead it was backbreaking, dollar-a-day toiling and you never complained.

Food, clothing, tents. None of it provided. Nothing left over to send back home. You had your hands, though.

You possessed a quiet:

In the winter, you set your palm to rock and dissolved it.

You could move mountains.

The energy of your body was the energy of nature.

Your hands and feet made patterns into the ground, through the air, passing through fire and stone, some strength born from the world in your chest, and from the quiet. More stable than the explosives they made you use, where country-men fell and died beneath cascading rock and collapsing tunnels. Unreported and ignored, only carried in the memories of those still alive.

And each life lost was a drop of poison in your veins.

So you went headfirst into the canyons. You touched the stone and the sediment. You commanded trees. Under moon-

light, when none of the white workers could see you. Shifting
nature, compelling the breeze.

And the iron laid in your wake was a damning shadow that
followed you all the way up this mountain.

Despite all you did to hold back the earth, men like your
father still perished. The iron was consumed in their blood
and in yours.

You could not hold back every avalanche.

I stood beside you in the dream, overlooking the dark valley. Wishing for green. Where you were silent, I screamed.

c ⬡ c

How did it end?

I only heard from a hunter who came down the following spring. He said Sam had been caught in the winter avalanche. Of course he hadn't left me of his own will, even if
men like him tended to follow tracks most women could
never find.

I heard the words but nothing else. I became deaf to all
but that reality. It was like newsprint that wouldn't wash off
my fingers, no matter how hard I scrubbed. *Man dies in avalanche, leaves wife behind.* Man will never smile again. Man
will never be found. Man was lost somewhere in the wilderness, alone, and the woman refuses to believe. If there was no
body, how could they be sure of death? Death at least owed
me the conclusion, some confirming dream, a deer with a
scrap of wolf fur in its mouth, a bear with blood on its teeth
and a tale to tell.

Suffocated by snow is not how it ended. I wouldn't
believe, even if a part of me trekked up the incline and
through the storm to follow his trail. A part of me sinking into
the snow with every step.

Is that why you climbed the mountain too? Are you chasing your dead?

For everything built, something must be destroyed.

c   (1)   c

Because you didn't speak, I did. It wasn't common to volunteer one's story, but who would you tell? I'd been carrying these words so far deep inside my chest that they were separated from syllable. Emotion existed before language, and without language we were babies, mewling and screaming for expression. Sometimes, experience piled up enough to knock you back into infancy.

A husband buried in the snow. Ours had been a love of truth, perhaps rare in this climate of so much cold and covering up. He came down from the mountain like a roving bear, though he wasn't so large beneath the fur. Blond beard sprouted from pale cheeks. He seemed bleached from the weather but his smile was wide. It took weeks to warm up to him, serving him drinks, letting his eyes march over my back when it was turned to him on purpose. He could have been as rough as the others, and in some ways he was, but there was a sense of honour about him that didn't quite fit this untamed land.

He lived up here. He died up here.

We lose to the weather. We attempt to quell the temper of the Earth. But there is no protection, and once my husband was swallowed by the mountain, I wanted no more of the gold towns. No more of that greed and mud and cold. Season after season, until he became a memory pushed beneath layers of ice. I would not let him turn into an effigy.

You listened. We told our hearts to the ones with the least comprehension. There, they would be safe.

You watched me, dark eyes alight with golden shards. Maybe you understood. The storm warred with the night, and both of us with some taste of poison on our tongues.

c (I) c

I wondered how long you'd been up here. A solitude surrounded you like night around the moon, but there was no loneliness in your gaze. No grasp for companionship. Nor was there the danger of insanity, as one sometimes found in those who spent too much of their time apart from other people.

When the storm abated you led me into the white world. The trees, thick, green and spinal, were weighted with snow. The ground spread pristine and reflected the sun. My husband loved the green, the encompassing multitude of nature. He knew the winter intimately, but growing up in a place did not mean it wouldn't one day turn on you. There was no taming the bear, though it crawled from its den a cub.

Overhead, the sky was a uniform grey. If it were possible to rise above the globe, I imagined this coast would look like the murky banks of churned river water, where silt and rock turned silver-blue into a blind opaqueness.

I stepped in your footsteps, calf-deep in the snow, arms tucked against my body while you forged ahead further into the forest like you were on a scent. I gave no thought of danger, though you moved with such confident precision, perhaps to abandon me somewhere eventually. Many were suspicious of the Chinese, even afraid, though the ones I'd known had never been anything but industrious and kind. They kept to themselves, but why wouldn't they? When the towns and camps shunned them or worse.

We must have walked for an hour. I stared at your imprints in the snow and pretended I was following my husband to the place he wouldn't lead me. The cold scoured my eyes and bit at the tips of my ears. It dried out even tears.

But this wasn't Sam. Your soft footfalls melted the snow in your going. I did not believe it until the more I followed, the more green I saw beneath our feet. Damp, deep green, and wet fallen leaves, and the brush and the dirt of this mountain, the underbelly of a spring that was still months away. You touched the icy branch of a weighed-down pine, swaying it from our path, and water melted off your fingers when you let go. As if some silent burning furnace emanated from your palms.

"Wait."

But you either didn't hear, didn't understand, or chose to ignore. The air around us had grown warm. At first I thought it was from the exertion of our walk, but now it seemed more like you were releasing it, this heat, something that crackled the ends of your hair and seeped through the layers of your clothes to bury deep into the earth.

I had no way to explain it and we had gone far enough that I lost my bearings.

You stopped so suddenly I almost tread on your heels. You did not sweat, yet your cheeks were burnished with warmth and I felt it rising off of you to cling to me, carrying with it a scent not unlike a metal forge. I wanted to ask, yet did not want to know.

You pointed through the blue shadows and I shuffled closer to the break in the forest.

A cabin, this one a little bigger than the one we came from. You looked at me and I shook my head.

"Go," you said.

"Who's in there?" My thought was a white hunter. Someone that would take care of me and release you from any stranger obligation.

"Go," you said, and you touched my arm. It burned like I was too long near a flame, forcing me to take a step away. "I wait."

And just like that, it was inevitable. Once aboard the ship, there was no disembarking until landfall. Between you and this cabin was an ocean voyage.

Every step I took was tiny, hemmed in. Coffin steps carrying me deeper into the cold.

No answer to a knock. Three knocks and silence. I had to shove the door with all of my weight, until it burst in on shadows and a dance of dust in the light that lanced in from the doorway.

In the middle of the room, a block bed.

On top of the bed, covered in blankets, my Sam.

Behind me the mountain was silent.

My steps grew heavier the closer I drew. Until I was looking down into drawn lids covered by ice. His face was wrapped in a scarf but I knew the grey wolf fur on his shoulders and the blond curling around his ears, pale like sunlight.

Here he lay, as if he waited.

A cruel dream.

c   ⑴   c

You told me in lilting English that you'd found my husband beneath the snow. You tried to revive him, your hands on his chest, on his cheeks, over his mouth where breath should've pushed. You carried his body, twice your size, through the snow. And when you could carry him no more, you crawled and pulled until you'd taken him to your door. Your hands in the snow, burning the cold.

But he was already dead.

So you built another cabin and you took him back.

You laid him to rest so he wasn't buried.

You wanted to set him on fire but something told you to wait. Something said I would be coming. Because you would have gone too, if you could have. Your father dead on the voyage over the ocean, your family lost back in China. Your hands worked to the bone for an iron will.

Some things should be reclaimed.

And here I was.

C   ()   C

My hands wrung in the fur and leather and cloth, an attempt to tear his body from this death. And you said words and they stuck onto my skin like ink, emblazoned there like history that would forever be repeated, indelible and true, long after my inability to make sense of the meaning.

The mountain crashed itself upon me like a wave, like a rock slide, like a crushing cave compounded by darkness, swallowing up the only avenue of escape. You can drown in pain – we know this now – like a fire sucking breath and a storm covering sight.

I had wanted to know for certain, but who was to say it wasn't better just remaining in the dark?

Loss was no less loss when it was touched.

"You go home now," you said.

Maybe that was your answer because you never could.

Woman climbs mountain after dead husband.

Woman dies on mountain with dead husband.

This woman stood by the encircling trees and watched you set your hand on the cabin wall. She watched you melt the wood with the fire that arose from the palm of your hand. Fire hot enough to explode stone and forge iron.

For everything built, something must be destroyed.

I would die up here with you, but I knew you would not let me. It wasn't in you, to allow things to die.

You carried my husband's name in your hands, like all of the men and boys who'd died before him at the feet of these mountains, in the valleys, in the canyons. One killed by a rock slide. Another smothered to death in a cave-in. One knocked off a bluff by a hail of stones.

"You go home now," you said, when morning brought ash.

Blackened ash against low white ridges and burnt autumn green.

The long shadows of dawn.

And where you were silent, I still screamed.

KOMAGATA MARU

RATI MEHROTRA

Gurdit Singh leaned against the starboard side of the Japanese steamship and inhaled deeply. Cold and clean the night air, soft the swell of waves. From behind him came sounds of laughter and happy shrieks as children chased each other on the crowded deck. Tomorrow, May 23, 1914, they would dock at Vancouver's Burrard Inlet. The grace of the Almighty had brought them so far. Surely they would not fail now.

A hand touched his shoulder. Gurdit turned. "Daljit," he acknowledged. "Is everything all right?"

Daljit was his secretary; the young man had helped sell tickets in Hong Kong for the voyage of the *Komagata Maru* to Canada. He shifted now, looking uncomfortable. "As well as can be, Baba," he said at last. "But I am worried. Suppose it does not work?"

"It will work," said Gurdit. "Do you not trust me?"

"Of course," said Daljit. "But we have over four hundred people on board, including women and children."

"I know," said Gurdit. "They are my responsibility – mine and Captain Akhiro's. I hired him for a reason, Daljit. Akhiro is an expert and believes in our cause." He looked over Daljit's shoulder at the boy hovering behind him. "Yes, Balwant?"

"Pitaji," said his son, waving a slip of paper, "Captain Akhiro says we have received a wireless message of headlines from the Vancouver newspaper, *The Province*. He asked if you wanted to see it."

Gurdit knew what the headlines would say, but it was better to have the worst out in the open, to be prepared for the reception they would get in Vancouver. "Go ahead," he said. "Read it out to me."

Balwant cleared his throat. "Boat Loads of Hindus on Way to Vancouver," he recited. "Hindus Cover Dead Bodies with Butter. Stop Hindu Invasion of Canada." He looked up at his father with anxious eyes.

"Three hundred and forty Sikhs, twenty-four Muslims and twelve Hindus," said Daljit bitterly. "Not that it makes any difference to them. We're all brown dirt to the Englishman."

"Daljit," said Gurdit, keeping his voice calm yet authoritative, "I will have no talk like that. We are going to find a new home for our people. No matter what happens tomorrow, I need you to be positive. Do your job and leave the rest to God. You are my right-hand man; the passengers look to us for guidance. Do not fail me."

A moment of silence passed between them, then Daljit nodded and left. Gurdit heard his cheerful voice tease one of the children, and exhaled with relief. He didn't blame Daljit or any of the other hot-headed young men on the ship. They all longed for the same thing – a home where they could be safe, where they could plant and grow food or work for honest wages, and be free from the ever-present threat of imprisonment by their British overlords. A place where they could be equal to their fellowman, no matter the colour of their skin or the language of their birth. That place was not Vancouver. Perhaps one day it would be – but not now, not in 1914.

Canada, proud Dominion of the British Empire, was not yet the land of the free.

Gurdit looked at Balwant and felt a pang. Balwant's mother had refused to come; she had clung to her son and begged them not to go. Gurdit – a successful ship engineer who had carved a new life for his family in Hong Kong – had no need to put everything at risk for the hundreds of poor Sikh men desperately looking for a ship to Canada. Not in the current political climate, with every Punjabi suspected of being a Ghadar Party sympathizer, bent on overthrowing British rule. Not with the current anti-Indian immigration policy of Canada that demanded every Indian arrive with two hundred dollars in his pocket, direct from India without stopovers. Even the steamship companies had been ordered not to sell passage to Asians.

But wasn't this precisely why it was important to do something *now*, to play a role, to make a statement that would reverberate around the world?

We are here. We matter.

"Go, Balwant," he told his son. "Thank Captain Akhiro and then get some food and rest. Tomorrow is a big day."

"Yes, Pitaji."

His son left and Gurdit turned back to face the Pacific. The same ocean, given different names from the start of their journey in Hong Kong to the end of their journey in Vancouver. Naming it did not change its nature. God was like that too. Pity that more people did not understand this.

Despite his outward assurances, a needle of doubt pierced his core. Daljit's worry was well founded. What Gurdit and Captain Akhiro were planning had never been attempted before. The ship was untested – a secret experiment born in a Kobe shipyard, plans drawn up by Gurdit's own exacting hands. The passengers knew the risk, but they had been willing to take it. Anything was better than the years of hardship they had suffered.

There was always the tiny possibility that they would actually be allowed to disembark in Vancouver. There was the larger possibility that they would be forced to turn back and return to Calcutta, where the British waited with loaded guns to greet them. And then there was the third possibility, which Gurdit could not bear to contemplate: the failure of the experiment and the burning of the *Komagata Maru* with all four hundred passengers on board.

So fragile, the vessel of their hope. Gurdit closed his eyes and prayed. *"Ik Onkar."* There is one God. *"Satnam."* His Name is Truth. *"Nirbhao."* He fears none. *"Nirvair."* He hates none.

C (I) C

The next day dawned clear and bright. As the *Komagata Maru* chugged into Burrard Inlet, the passengers crowded the upper deck, pointing excitedly at the tall buildings of the city rising opposite. After a two-month voyage, everyone was packed and ready to go ashore, wearing their best clothes, such as they were. Gurdit moved among them, exchanging greetings, ruffling the hair of the children, answering questions in his patient voice. He had slept little last night, tossing and turning in the tiny cabin he shared with his son.

The *Komagata Maru* dropped anchor on the far side of the inlet. Daljit gripped his arm. "Look Baba," he said. "We are being met."

Gurdit raised his eyes. An immigration launch was headed towards them. There were armed guards on its deck. *And so it begins*, he thought, and his chest tightened.

The launch came up alongside the ship, and the crew tied it and lowered the walkway. Daljit made everyone else back away and leave a circular space for Gurdit and Captain Akhiro. Gurdit stood and waited, thinking of everything he could say, everything he had already said to news reporters in Hong Kong and Shanghai. Would it make a difference to these hard-eyed men climbing up the walkway? Would it change their minds?

Two tall men, one swarthy and clean-shaven, the other pallid and moustached, came to a halt before him. Behind them were two guards. The rest of the party remained on the launch below.

"Gurdit Singh?" demanded the swarthy man. "I'm Hopkinson and this is Reid. We are the chief immigration inspectors for the Vancouver port. I'm afraid there has been a terrible mistake. You do not have permission to disembark here."

"We are British citizens," said Gurdit, "and we have the right to visit any part of the British Empire."

"Your ship has violated the Continuous Journey Regulation," said Reid. "None of you have come direct from the country of your birth. We telegraphed the governor of Hong Kong to prevent your ship from leaving port, but unfortunately our message arrived too late."

"That is an unfair regulation," said Gurdit. "It is impossible to travel from India without stopping in Japan or Hawaii. You know this."

"And we doubt you are carrying the minimum required amount of two hundred dollars per person," continued Hopkinson, as if Gurdit had not spoken. "You are aware of the rules governing Canadian immigration, and yet you dragged these people on a fruitless journey. How much did they pay you for the false hope you gave them?"

"How dare you!" shouted Daljit. "We all contributed what we could…"

"Quiet, Daljit," said Gurdit, and his secretary fell silent. Behind him, he could feel the hot glares of some of the men, the anxiety of the others. He turned back to the immigration inspectors. "There are less than thirteen hundred Indians in Canada," he said. "But there are several hundred thousand British in India. Consider this a test case. What is done with my shipload of people will determine whether there is any peace in the British Empire."

Hopkinson's lip curled. "Ghadar Party, just as I thought. You may as well plan your route back, because no court will allow you to stay. Just yesterday there was a protest by the citizens of Vancouver in front of the mayor's office, demanding that Asians be expelled from our city. No one wants you Indians – don't you understand?"

"Our men are strong and work hard," said Gurdit. "The lumber yards and mills will be happy to employ them. Besides, we do not have supplies for a return voyage."

Reid shrugged. "Not our problem. You will leave today. If you're not gone by tomorrow morning, a military ship will escort you out of the harbour."

The men left. Gurdit watched them go with a heavy heart. It was what he had expected, but a part of him had hoped for less intransigence.

The ship doctor came up to him. "It's all right, Baba," he said quietly. "Do what you have to do. I will talk to the men."

Gurdit nodded and glanced at Captain Akhiro, who had stood immobile as stone while the inspectors were on board. "When, Captain?" he asked.

Captain Akhiro considered. "Midnight," he said. "Tell them to lose every bit of extra weight, including the benches of the lower deck."

"And to pray," said Gurdit.

The captain laughed. "Do you think prayers will keep the *Komagata Maru* from exploding?"

"Why not, Captain?" said Gurdit. "Why not?"

The rest of the day, Gurdit threw himself into preparations, even though the captain and the doctor urged him to rest. He would know no rest until their journey was over, one way or another.

Everyone ate heartily, for what was their last meal on board the *Komagata Maru*. When dusk fell, men went below deck to pry everything loose. There was no furniture apart from four hundred wooden benches; this was to their advantage now as they worked to clear the area.

Under the cover of darkness, pre-arranged groups dropped all the benches, packed suitcases, lifeboats, and supplies overboard. Only a single coal stove and the bare minimum provisions were retained.

Some wept to lose their belongings, which were all they had in the world, but most, Gurdit was glad to see, were stoical about it. Once everyone was back below, and a check had been done to make sure no one had kept any personal items, Gurdit, Daljit, Balwant, and the ship doctor joined Captain Akhiro at the crowded pilot house on the bridge. All the crew were present here, their faces taut and expectant. Maps gleamed on the walls, red lines showing the route by which they had arrived in Vancouver, and green lines showing the path they yet had to travel.

"Everything on schedule, Captain?" asked Gurdit. Things had been set in motion; it was out of his hands now.

"Ballast seven has been emptied," replied the captain. "We have but to empty eight and nine, and then we can start divestment and inflation." He turned to the first officer. "Make sure the upper deck is clear and everyone is safe below."

The ship rose as the ballasts emptied, pitching and rolling even in the quiet harbour. The first officer returned to report all was clear.

Captain Akhiro grinned. "All set, gentlemen?" he asked, and without waiting for a response, commanded, "Start divestment procedure."

The first officer turned a massive wheel, grunting with effort. For a few moments nothing happened, and Gurdit held his breath. Then with an enormous clanking noise, the railings of the upper deck fell away, dropping into the water. The ship shuddered as she shed her weight. Balwant squeezed his eyes shut. They were all hanging on for dear life, but Gurdit realized he himself was singing. *Singing.*

> *The sky will be my home*
> *The sun and moon my lamps*
> *To light Your face.*

"Open deck," said Captain Akhiro. The middle of the upper deck cranked open, revealing gleaming pistons and valves layered into the middle deck.

"Gas board operational!"

The *Komagata Maru* shook and juddered as a vast, dark material billowed out of the open deck – gel-cotton, light and strong, that Gurdit had designed by simple use of film gelatine between two layers of cotton. Valves pumped hydrogen and the envelope ballooned above them, blotting out the starry sky.

Balwant's mouth was open in a silent scream. Daljit's lips moved as if in prayer. Gurdit hugged them both, trying to communicate his love, his conviction.

Daljit's expression changed to horror as he looked over Gurdit's shoulder. Gurdit twisted around to see what had alarmed him.

A military launch, bullhorn blaring, guards angrily gesticulating: *Stop.* Their illicit manoeuvre had finally caught the attention of the Port authority.

Daljit cupped his hands and shouted, "Do you think they will shoot?"

Gurdit shook his head. *I don't know. I hope not.* It was not a possibility he had allowed himself to consider until this moment. Would the immigration guards be willing to have the death of four hundred innocent souls on their conscience? He had wagered all their lives on that answer.

"Start the engines," yelled Captain Akhiro, his hat askew.

A deep vibration passed through the ship's body and travelled up Gurdit's, as if they were one and the same, the ship and its designer. Roaring filled his ears and the *Komagata Maru* rose above the water, carried aloft by two million cubic feet of inflammable hydrogen gas. Water wheels repurposed into giant propellers whirred beneath them.

"We did it," gasped Daljit. "We're flying!"

Gurdit crawled to the rim of the deck and peered below. Balwant caught hold of his legs and whimpered, "Pitaji, be careful."

His heart leaped. Daljit was right. *They were flying.* About a hundred metres up, Gurdit judged, the dark swell of the Pacific to their left and the lights of Vancouver to their right. The launch below grew smaller, a tiny speck bobbing futilely in the harbour. A few moments more and they had left it far behind.

Gurdit drew back and stood to embrace Captain Akhiro, who was smiling smugly. "Congratulations, Captain," he said.

"Now all you have to do is guide the ship to the prairies, vent the gas and land us safely."

Captain Akhiro laughed. "I will guide the ship, if you will guide the people. Yes?"

Gurdit thought of the hardships just ahead – the northern wilderness, the dark winters, the struggle to survive – and smiled. "Yes," he promised. "As long as I live free."

The *Komagata Maru* flew into the night, carrying its frail cargo of human lives and hopes.

BONES OF BRONZE, LIMBS LIKE IRON

RHEA ROSE

I remember being a young child the first time I saw a steam locomotive thick with the exhalation of its hot, giant clouds of breath. The engine, embroiled in its own storm, spewed and billowed wave after wave of white mist; a bell clanged and the giant black Cyclops rolled across the earth like a mountain falling down a valley. The train's wheels screamed as if they were large trees ripped asunder by lightning, and the ground shook to the horizon. Headlights like meteors came to burn and blind us, and its tail grew into an endless line of cars that stretched to the other end of the world.

A woman, as terrified as me, stood nearby reciting something biblical. *"Behold, Behemoth, which I made as I made you; he eats grass like an ox. Behold his strength in his loins, and his power in the muscles of his belly..."* I remember stepping behind her blowing skirt, a thin veil of fabric, for protection from the rolling monster.

c ◑ c

This morning a red barn mysteriously appeared in an unused field.

The fallow land around the barn formed a bevy of graceful swells. These small hills were equally mysterious, having
appeared over the last few weeks.

Tim, a helpful young man, was my neighbour's son; each
morning he gave me a ride to school on his horse and wagon.
Tim went to town to do chores while I went to work as a
teacher of a one-room schoolhouse.

When Tim eventually noticed the barn, he eased up on
the horse. We examined the building. I regarded it through
my spectacles. Tim blocked out the light to get a better look.

The barn sat quietly, red, round-roofed. Its slick and
smooth metallic doors revealed some of the more subtle technological design gone into its engineering. I doubted that Tim
had ever seen anything like it.

As strange as the presence of the barn was, to me it
seemed oddly familiar.

Then, without a word, Tim sped up to get away while I
wanted a better look.

There weren't many buildings on the outskirts of the small
town of Port Ingles in the late 1800s, in North West Saskatch-
ewan. The school where I taught stood tiny but strong. Ten
years and I still worked with the farmers' and the miners' children, teaching them how to spell and read, encouraging them
to broaden their horizons, to further their education, so that
they need not be held to this land.

c (l) c

I pushed the dust away from my apron and adjusted my bonnet as I walked into the school building, and when I looked
up a strange man stood in the small room. He stood comfortably and read the school's handbook.

I was tall, but he stood much taller.

I pulled out the curls at the side of my bonnet.

He seemed a quiet man, a bit of a dandy with his dark hair and grey bowler on his head. This suggested that he'd come from town. He wore suspenders over his pinstriped high-necked shirt and over that he wore a grey tweed jacket; the hue matched his hat exactly, and from his jacket pocket hung a watch chain. He had sharp eyes that were blue and made larger by the wire-framed specs he wore. He ran his hand up and down one suspender while he held the school handbook in the other. He liked a closely trimmed, black beard. His smile finally acknowledged my presence.

"Good morning," I said, sounding overly cheerful, even to myself.

"Susanna?" He closed the book and put it down on a student's table.

"*Mrs*. Susanna," I corrected. He smiled as if I'd said something funny.

"Of course."

Did he know me? Perhaps he was a relative of one of my charges and not a teacher.

He was strangely familiar.

"Grant," he said, "Mr. Grant," and held out his large hand to me. I didn't know what to do with that hand, so I did nothing.

We were silent a moment as we sized each other up.

"Three…" I said, an attempt to break the tension and awkwardness of the situation.

"Three?" he repeated, and then looked puzzled.

"Wishes!" I said. "Grant – me three wishes," I said, and hoped he had a sense of humour.

"Never heard that one before," he replied with polite sarcasm.

He had a bit of an accent, an unidentifiable drawl that suggested warmer lands, perhaps slower days. Even though his dress suggested city slicker, I guessed that this was not his first encounter with small-town life.

I had no idea why a second teacher was dispatched to our small one-room school.

But secretly I was pleased.

I showed Mr. Grant the extra desk hidden in storage, and together we pulled it free and set it up in an appropriate place near my own.

"I'm to instruct the young men in games," he said.

"Games?"

"Outdoor activities," he explained.

I *did remember* a letter sent by the board of education. Sports activities were to become part of the curriculum.

"I see," I said, then noticed a few small personal items of Mr. Grant's on his desk. In the chaos of his minutiae, I observed a small figurine – a tiny, black glass dragon warming itself in a beam of sun streaking through the window. Light twinkled in the magical refraction of the dragon's sheen, causing the dragon's reddish and golden glow.

When Grant wasn't looking, I put my hand around the beautiful little dragon and slipped it into my pocket.

c (l) c

I went home that evening and made chicken pie and served cut greens from the garden. My family loved my dandelion salad. They gobbled the meal without comment. My two beautiful boys, ages fourteen and fifteen, did not attend my one-room class. My husband, the area doctor and veterinarian, drove them by wagon into town each day for their studies and to learn trades; a forty-five minute ride east.

"There's a new teacher. A Mr. Grant," I said to my husband. "He's – teaching the boys games."

My husband nodded. He continued to read the almanac. "He gonna preach on Sundays?" he asked.

c　ⓘ　c

One day in the supply room, while I searched for the ever-elusive supply of ink bottles, Mr. Grant found me there.

"Tight squeeze," he said, manoeuvring by me, careful not to make contact in the close closet.

"Yes," I agreed. "Can't you wait until I'm done?" I asked, feeling a little annoyed at his impertinence. I very nearly tipped the box of black ink bottles. "And you should really take that hat off when you're in the school teaching," I said, sounding more harsh than I'd intended.

He stopped his reach toward an upper shelf. He looked at me as if he saw me for the first time. In the cramped quarters with only the lantern for light, he resembled a spirit, something the local medicine man had called out of a dream to the land of the living.

"Trust me, Susanna. You and I, we – I'm different. I'm not from here. Please don't be frightened. Do you – ever feel as if you've known…as if you know me?" he asked.

I did feel that way.

I knew him somehow.

I fished through my pocket for something. I didn't know what I was looking for – a distraction of some sort. I found the black glass dragon.

I kept it hidden in my pocket as I turned it over and over.

c　ⓘ　c

That night I went home and my thoughts raced. What could he possibly mean? *I shouldn't know Grant* – and, yet, I did. I liked him. To quiet my mind I reread the school's rulebook. It mentioned nothing about male teachers and hats. Then I read a hundred pages of an old bible I flipped through at random, but none of these gave me the comfort I sought. I stared at my sons and husband as they ate dinner. They seemed distant.

The black glass figurine I'd taken from Grant's desk came to mind, and with it a vision of the red barn.

c   ⊕   c

I thought of Grant all night. He haunted my dreams. I wrote him a few love poems, which I then crumpled and stuffed into the far end of my pillowcase.

c   ⊕   c

A few days after our brush in the supply closet, Mr. Grant sat reading the local paper. On the front page was a picture of the mysterious barn. I was about to read the accompanying article over Mr. Grant's shoulder when we were disturbed by Tim. He rushed in, his wagon parked awkwardly outside.

"Your husband dispatched me. He'll pick up the boys this afternoon from their studies, take them to dinner and stay in the next town this evening and the next two evenings. Your sons will participate in the early morning weekend marching practices. I'm to offer you a ride home after school."

It was Friday.

"Thank you, Tim, but I have my bicycle in the shed."

Tim took this in.

Tim glanced at Mr. Grant, nodded a cursory hello and good-bye then fled down the stairs he'd rushed up. His britches white with road dust.

The two men could not have been more different. Tim, short, fair and a little heavy in old thin jeans, work shoes caked with dried mud. Mr. Grant, tall and well groomed, pressed pants, bow tie and teacher's jacket and bowler. Not only were they from different stations in life, they seemed out of time with each other.

I caught Grant staring at me, regarding me as if I were a project he still needed to pull out of a box and put together.

"I can walk you home, Susanna."

My heart pounded through my rib cage. I glanced at the newspaper in his hands.

"There's a second bike, if you'd like. I'll read the paper to you. Sit here." He sat on the wooden bench, an old donated church pew. He patted the empty space beside him, which caused a miniature cloud of chalk dust to rise.

"The barn," he said, pointing to the picture in the paper. I took the paper from him and I quickly read. The railroaders accused the barn builders of sneaking in to stake a land claim.

"You're a railroad man?"

"In a way."

I stayed quiet, wanting to know more.

"I've borrowed some of their railroad material – you might say – but I'm not really like any of them," he said very mysteriously. "I need to show you something special. I made it for you."

"I'm not sure," I said. I got up and took a step away from him, but he followed closely. His eyes held my attention as he cornered me.

Grant slowly shook his head. "Remember, even just a little. There's no time left," he said in a desperate tone. "Mrs. Susanna. I'm from the future – we're from the future, you and

I, the twenty-fifth century – thirty billion are trying to survive there. There's nowhere to go but backwards."

And then he took a small step back.

He pulled out his pocket watch and glanced at it.

"Backwards?" I asked, having nearly lost my voice with fear. My heart pounded.

"Immigration – backwards – in time. It will start soon. There's no room in the future; it only gets more populated. Resources nearly extinguished. There's room here, in Port Ingles, we've made it a retro-temporal hub for now. There are other time-habitats – but these stops are temporary. There's another world, a planet beyond this one, many can go to – but it's far – very far," he said, impassioned.

Finally, he stopped talking and stepped aside.

c ⦿ c

At the end of a long day teaching, we headed for the shed where the bicycles were stored. We didn't speak. Grant pulled the old wooden door open. It took a few moments for my eyes to adjust to the cool dark. He took a few steps inside and banged into something.

"Damn it."

I blushed at his language. He took my hand and pulled me in after him. The door swung shut behind us.

I became very still, quiet, as I lost my sense of bearing.

"Susanna, I know you took my desk ornament."

I pulled my hand from him.

"It's alright. I made it for you."

"Me?" *Incredulous*, I thought.

"Yes. I build things, make things," he said. His voice was ahead and above me in the dark.

"Like barns?" I asked.

"Like barns, but other things, too."

"What other things?"

"Transport – to distant places."

The small light from the cracks in the walls gave me my bearings, the sheen on his bowler, a glint from his watch chain. I reached into my pocket and touched the figurine right away.

"It's glowing," I said, truly amazed, as I pulled it out.

"Yes, it is. The radium, tritium makes it glow." He put his hand over the exquisite ornament and put it into my tote.

"I've missed you," he whispered.

c ◖ c

As we approached the barn on our bikes he slowed down. The barn looked exactly the same, deserted, the sky overcast.

He looked at me.

"Did you really build it?" I straddled my bike, both feet planted firmly on the ground. He nodded a quick, small smile. He stopped his roll forward and whispered in my ear, "With love," he said.

"Why? Who am I then, if I'm not Susanna?" I asked, bewildered.

He parked his bicycle and walked all the way to the barn doors, then he went inside and I waited.

Two minutes passed.

Finally, I headed to the barn.

c ◖ c

The faint smell of lavender and something else – Grant called it ozone – wafted through the barn's interior. I inhaled deeply soft lavender breezes, then ozone, which made me think of thunderstorms.

"It isn't a barn at all," I exclaimed.

Grant locked the doors behind us. The interior looked crammed with junk, neatly organized forests of metal parts, iron logs and metal barrels in which two people might sit comfortably, but nothing was assembled. "This," he said, and pointed to a beautiful brass tub, "is a firebox and this, over here, is a boiler." I looked around and saw that the mechanical components Grant pointed out sat inside small animal pens. Within the pens, near several bales of hay, lay black iron bolts, the size of small frying pans; many heavy, metal wheels, much larger than the ones on our bicycles, rested on the floor outside the pens. Metal tubes, long and narrow like the naked trunks of poplar trees, leaned against a wall, while several brass boxes, bronze rails, rivets and wrought-iron knobs were scattered like rocks. Grant pressed a lever near the locked barn doors, and the barn's incredible electric lights began to glow and cast low shadows. "There are fields in this area with huge caverns below them," he said.

He had me follow him downstairs.

"The immigrations will start soon. You're the first. You volunteered. Once, upon a time, you were my wife – we worked together," he said, his voice trailing off. Then, "Do you hear that?" he asked, his finger pointed to the dark corner of the cellar.

He moved to a trough where water trickled through a dark half-pipe. He rolled up his sleeve. "Stand close, but don't touch the water." He hung his fingers over the water – slowly dipped them in, then his palm and wrist. "Look into the stream."

I did and, of course, his hand was still there. Then he dipped his forearm up to his elbow into the stream.

I reached toward the water.

"Don't!" He held me back with his free hand.

"What's going on?" I asked half in wonder, half in fear.

"You'll get wet," he said, laughing. "There's an underground stream here, actually, several of them, and I've rerouted them to feed my creation. I require a great deal of water. For effect." Then he pulled his hand from the water and licked the tips of his fingers. He touched my cheek with his cooled hand. "Don't be afraid. You knew once – about the search – for a place to move populations. We found just the right planet with plenty of water, and that world is massive."

"What is this all about?" I asked, feeling again a little fearful, even though I wanted to be brave.

"Your three wishes. I'm here to give you the last one, like we'd agreed."

c ⊕ c

"Why am I in Port Ingles, of all places, if I'm an immigrant from the future?" I asked, feeling distraught. "What about my memories? My childhood?"

"You chose those," he said, "from a book. You made three wishes. Port Ingles was your first wish."

"I…" Of course I didn't believe him and he saw that.

"And my second wish?" I asked in disbelief.

"A barn," he said without hesitation. "You wanted children, boys and a barn. We – you and I have no children. It's not done," he said, more subdued.

"Not done? No children?"

"Very few are allowed."

I mulled these revelations. "My third wish must have been to be a teacher?" I guessed.

"No!" He laughed loudly. "In the future you were much less practical."

"I can't imagine."

"You *can* imagine. Remember, I know you're having some memories. You have to fight for them."

Grant was right. Things about him – us, felt as if they'd happened last week, or only yesterday. He was becoming as familiar as the annuals in my garden.

I crinkled my face at him. All this talk in the cellar full of shadows.

"If you can't remember then I'll show you," he said.

I hesitated.

"Is it possible to ride to a star – I mean in the future – where we're from?" I asked.

He turned to me; a look of astonishment.

"Yes," he said," but—"

"But?"

"You don't get to come back."

c (1) c

On the last evening of that weekend, at the barn, a hot summer night, we stared up at the black sky. We lingered in the dry grassy field and lay down to count shooting stars. I made more idle wishes. As I lay there finding faces in the star patterns, I felt something move beneath me.

A long, low slide like a giant serpent gliding, vibrating under the earth's surface.

"Don't you feel it?" I asked.

The Earth groaned and moved for a long time. I stared at Grant. He smiled back at me, as if he knew all along what was going on.

"He's awake," he said. "Your final wish."

c (1) c

"The barn is a hypercube," he explained as we walked back to it. "New settlers will arrive through it. This isn't the only 'barn' and this isn't the only place in time they'll arrive at, but this is the only one you must attend to."

Thrilled and terrified at the prospect, I asked, "What will they look like?" The possibility of hoards of strangers arriving on Port Ingles' doorstep frightened and overwhelmed me.

"Not to worry. They'll look like everyone here. They'll forget who they were and where they're from. The veil does that. Their old lives will become a *déjà vu* of dreams and nightmares. They'll fit in. The way you have. They'll arrive with little and make their way. You'll teach and help them."

"And you? What will you attend to? Why don't you forget the future as I have?" I asked, not wanting to know answers.

"We loved each other in the future, but we had a – a decision to make – you and I. I'm a builder – an inventor and a maker, and it is my job – and yours – to try and save the human race, or as many as possible. You are, were, a field biologist, an organic chemist and a specialist in genetically modified organisms. Some of that knowledge remains with you, but you wanted a chance to be – a mother."

My heart shifted in my chest. My eyes stung.

He continued. "I'm one of the few allowed the resources and energy to transfer my entire memory at full strength. I need my mind, my memories, but there's a price—"

I took his hand.

"This is our last time – forever," he said.

A small tremor under our feet made us both freeze a moment.

"...*he makes his tail stiff like a cedar; the sinews of his thighs are knit together. His bones are tubes of bronze, his limbs like bars of iron.*"

c ◊ c

The beast rose out from under the ground where it existed in stasis, its girth gurgled in the wet tanks of water under the barn, fed by the ample Port Ingles springs.

We ran up the short flight of stairs from the barn's cellar to the surface, then burst through a small side door, raced across the fields, stumbled, fell, and scrambled to stay upright in the uneven earth.

"Watch the stars," he said over and over, between breaths. But I noticed the swells of the field moving slowly, snaking ahead of us. Astounded, I believed I was running for my life, yet, for some reason, laughed joyfully. We took a quick glance at each other then ran until we came to the next road between fields.

c ◊ c

Over two fields the beast's body emerged black and serpentine. When it first broke through from the underground lair it rose like a wet, articulated eel; it had lain coiled and kinked underneath the fields. Its iron and bronze and brass and steel penetrated the horizon with an endless roar. We watched it squeeze itself from its earthy sheath, heard its metal girth groan and clank. It shed massive clots of dirt like a serpent sheds an old skin, and ascended and then rocketed rapidly into the night sky. When its wings unfurled and flapped for the first time, a hurricane of wind snatched Grant's hat, and my bonnet. The beast eclipsed the Milky Way, a dark, sinew of cloud. The dragon breathed its fire once, lighting up the Earth's corona as if a million shooting stars exploded there. Then the creature pierced the atmosphere, boomed like a mountain tearing down a valley, and shed the pull of Earth's gravity.

Gone, through the veil.

"How can it do that?" I asked.

"Fission – lots of uranium in this part of the world, at this time. You love the old-timey energy stuff, so I put it all to work in your Steam Dragon."

"Will it return?" I asked.

"That's what it was designed to do. Once the bugs are worked out, *Emergence* will take only the immigrants from each temporal-hub on its generational voyage. It will return – to collect those waiting here."

"And you'll ride it?"

"Yes, as many will ride it to the stars as those who come through the barns to immigrate, and they need me to keep it all working. Eventually, hopefully, a population will make it to the planet. I can't come back. I oversee what goes on up there, as you will here – that was your wish."

He put an arm around my shoulders.

c (l) c

I asked Grant if I'd ever really remember him, my life from the future and all that had transpired between us there. He said I would not; the real memories would always be a struggle. "You might start collecting little dragons, or something obsessive like that," he'd said. We were at school, cleaning out his desk. The time had come for him to leave. The steam dragon waited for him somewhere in orbit. He planned to go to it and search for this new world, with a new future. He stopped his tidying, reached for me. "Close your eyes. Hold out your hand." When I opened my eyes, another small, black glass dragon sat in my palm. Exquisitely detailed, it shimmered when I passed it through the sun shining in the window, its tail in its mouth.

c   (I)   c

Now, decades after my sons have grown into adults, their childhoods forgotten, and their father long dead, after I've helped thousands find their way in this new world of old ways, I often take the wagon out to the pristine red barn, then to the edge of the long fields. I park and stare out at the sparkling night. I place my dragons beside me on the seat, make a wish, and watch the Milky Way for a long time. Once in a while a dark shadow eclipses the powdery spill of stardust. I hope that somewhere in the future Grant wishes upon the same stars.

ABOUT THE AUTHORS

COLLEEN ANDERSON of Vancouver has published over 200 pieces of fiction and poetry. She co-edited *Tesseracts 17*, and co-edited with Ursula Pflug the previous anthology in this series, *Playground of Lost Toys*. Twice nominated for the Aurora Award, she has also been longlisted for the Stoker Award, and has received honourable mentions in the Year's Best anthologies. Some of her new and forthcoming works are in *nEvermore!: Tales of Murder, Mystery and the Macabre*, *Best of Horror Library*, *Exile Book of New Canadian Noir*, *On Spec*, *Second Contact*, *The Beauty of Death* anthology, *Polu Texni*, and *Blood in the Rain*. www.colleenanderson.wordpress.com

CHARLOTTE ASHLEY of Toronto is a writer, editor, critic, and bookseller. Her work has appeared in *The Magazine of Fantasy & Science Fiction*, *The Sockdolager*, *Kaleidotrope*, and a number of anthologies. www.once-and-future.com

CHANTAL BOUDREAU lives by the ocean in Nova Scotia with her husband and two children. She is an accountant by day and an author/illustrator during evenings and weekends. In addition to being a CMA-MBA, she has a BA with a major in English from Dalhousie University. A writer of all varieties of speculative fiction, she has had several of her stories published in a variety of anthologies, online journals and magazines. Her more recent publications include stories in the anthologies *My Favorite Apocalypse*, *Strangely Funny 2*, and *Return to Deathlehem*. www.chantellyb.wordpress.com

TERRI FAVRO of Toronto grew up in "immigrant Niagara" (Ontario) in the shadow of Laura Secord, Sir Isaac Brock, the

Catholic Church and Buffalo TV stations. She is the author of the novella *The Proxy Bride* and co-creator of the *Bella* comic books. Her work has appeared in *Prism, Geist, Humber Literary Review* and *Room*, among others, and shortlisted for the CBC Literary Prize in Non-Fiction and *Broken Pencil* Indie Death Match. Two new novels, *Sputnik's Daughter* and *Once Upon a Time in West Toronto*, will be published in 2017.

www.terrifavro.ca

KATE HEARTFIELD of Ottawa is a newspaper journalist and fiction writer. Her short stories, many of which explore some aspect of Canadian history, have appeared in publications like *Strange Horizons, Podcastle, Daily Science Fiction* and *Lackington's*.   www.heartfieldfiction.com

www.twitter.com/kateheartfield

CLAIRE HUMPHREY of Toronto works in the book business. She has had stories appear in many magazines, including *Apex, Beneath Ceaseless Skies,* and *Strange Horizons*, as well as anthologies including the World-Fantasy-Award-nominated *Long Hidden*. Her first novel, *Spells of Blood and Kin*, is coming out in June 2016.

www.clairehumphrey.ca   www.twitter.com/clairebmused

KARIN LOWACHEE was born in South America, grew up in Canada, and worked in the Arctic. Her first novel *Warchild* won the 2001 Warner Aspect First Novel Contest. Both *Warchild* (2002) and her third novel *Cagebird* (2005) were finalists for the Philip K. Dick Award. *Cagebird* won the Prix Aurora Award in 2006 for Best Long-Form Work in English. Her books have been translated into French, Hebrew, and Japanese, and her short stories have appeared in anthologies edited by Julie Czerneda, Nalo Hopkinson, John Joseph Adams and Ann VanderMeer.

www.karinlowachee.com   www.twitter.com/karinlow

RATI MEHROTRA is a Toronto-based speculative fiction writer whose short stories have appeared in *AE–The Canadian Science Fiction Review*, *Apex Magazine*, *Abyss & Apex*, *Inscription Magazine*, and more. Her debut novel, *Markswoman*, is based in a post-apocalyptic, alternative version of Asia, and will be published in early 2018.

www.ratiwrites.com   www.twitter.com/Rati_Mehrotra

BRENT NICHOLS of Calgary is a science fiction and fantasy writer and man about town. He likes good beer, bad puns, high adventure, and low comedy. He is a member of the Imaginative Fiction Writers Association and is the author of the *Gears of a Mad God* steampunk/Lovecraft novellas and the *War of the Necromancer* trilogy of sword and sorcery novels. His stories have appeared in anthologies like *Shanghai Steam* and *Capes and Clockwork*.   www.steampunch.com

DOMINIK PARISIEN (the editor) of Toronto is a poet and writer. He is the co-editor, with Navah Wolfe, of *The Starlit Wood* and several other anthologies forthcoming from Simon & Schuster's Saga Press. He has worked on anthologies with Ann and Jeff VanderMeer, including *The Time Traveler's Almanac, Sisters of the Revolution,* and *The Bestiary*. His fiction and poetry have appeared in *Strange Horizons, Uncanny Magazine, Shock Totem, Lackington's, Imaginarium 2013, Exile: The Literary Quarterly,* the anthology *Playground of Lost Toys,* and other venues. www.dominikparisien.wordpress.com
www.twitter.com/domparisien

TONY PI of Toronto was shortlisted for the 2009 John W. Campbell Award for Best New Writer, and is a frequent finalist for the Aurora Awards. His work appears in many anthologies and magazines, and further adventures of Professor Voss can be found in *Ages of Wonder* (DAW anthology), *Abyss & Apex Magazine*, and *Beneath Ceaseless Skies Magazine*.

www.tonypi.com

RHEA ROSE of Vancouver has published speculative fiction and poetry in *Evolve, Tesseracts 1, 2, 6, 9, 10, 17, On Spec, Talebones, Northwest Passages, Masked Mosaic,* and Exile Editions' *Dead North.* She has received honourable mentions in the 2014, 2010 and 2007 Year's Best Horror and Fantasy anthologies, appeared in *Christmas Forever,* twice made the preliminaries for the Nebula Award, and was twice an Aurora nomine. She is a teacher of creative writing, holds an MFA in creative writing, has edited poetry for Edge Press, and hosted the Vancouver Science Fiction and Fantasy (V-Con) writers' workshops. Her most recent works include *Second Contact, Art Song Lab,* and three Indie novels, *The Final Catch: A Tarot Sorceress* series.   www.twitter.com/rheaerose1

HOLLY SCHOFIELD lives in rural British Columbia and has had fiction published in *Lightspeed, Crossed Genres, Tesseracts 17,* and many other venues throughout the world. Her stories recently appeared in the anthologies *Second Contacts, Coulrophobia* and *Scarecrow.*

www.hollyschofield.wordpress.com

KATE STORY of Peterborough, Ontario, is a writer and performer originally from Newfoundland, and she was the 2015 recipient of the K.M. Hunter Artist Award for her work in theatre. Her first novel, *Blasted,* received a Sunburst Award honourable mention for Canadian Literature of the Fantastic, and was longlisted for a ReLit Award. *Wrecked Upon This Shore* is her second novel. Recent publications include stories in *Carbide Tipped Pens,* the 21st-century bestiary *Gods, Memes, and Monsters, Imaginarium 4: The Best Canadian Speculative Writing,* and in Exile Editions' *Playground of Lost Toys.*

www.katestory.com

HAROLD R. THOMPSON of Nova Scotia is the author of the *Empire and Honor* series of historical adventure novels, which include *Dudley's Fusiliers, Guns of Sevastopol,* and *Sword of the Mogul.* He also writes short science fiction, fantasy, and historical fiction, and occasional combinations of these genres.   www.haroldrossthompson.com

MICHAL WOJCIK of Whitehorse, Yukon, was born in Poland, raised in the Yukon territory, and educated in Edmonton and Montreal. He holds an MA in history from McGill University, where he studied witchcraft trials, medieval necromancers, and, occasionally, 17th-century texts about enchanted wheels of cheese. His short fiction has appeared in *On Spec, The Book Smugglers, Pornokitsch,* and *Daily Science Fiction.*

STEVE MENARD (cover) is from Minneapolis, Minnesota, USA.
wwwFineArtAmerica.com – under Putterhug Studio
www.RedBubble.com – under Shutterbug2010

ACKOWLEDGEMENTS

First, I would like to thank the authors who submitted the terrific stories that make up this book. Thanks to Ann & Jeff VanderMeer for many wonderful opportunities, to the steampunk communities around the world, to Helen Marshall for introductions, and to Michael Callaghan and the people at Exile Editions for believing in this book. Thanks to friends and loved ones for their support, especially Nicole Kornher-Stace, Mike Allen, Derek Newman-Stille, John O'Neill, the PstD folks, Kaitlin Tremblay, and my family. Thanks to Marianne LeBreton for her support over the years. Thanks to Kelsi Morris for listening to me ramble on about this project over and over, and for her many great thoughts. Finally, thanks to my frequent collaborator, Navah Wolfe, for her invaluable insight.

Dominik Parisien

EXILE SPEC FIC

THE EXILE BOOK OF ANTHOLOGY SERIES

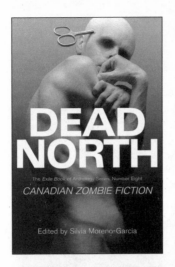

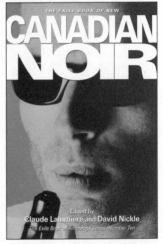

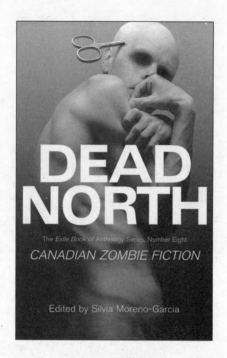

DEAD NORTH:
CANADIAN ZOMBIE FICTION

EDITED BY SILVIA MORENO-GARCIA

"Every time I listen to the yearly edition of *Canada Reads* on CBC, so much attention seems to be drawn to the fact that the author is Canadian, that being Canadian becomes a gimmick. *Dead North*, a collection of zombie short stories by exclusively Canadian authors, is the first of its kind that I've seen to buck this trend, using the diverse cultural mythology of the Great White North to put a number of unique spins on an otherwise over-saturated genre."—*Bookshelf Reviews*

Featuring stories by Chantal Boudreau, Tessa J. Brown, Richard Van Camp, Kevin Cockle, Jacques L. Condor, Carrie-Lea Côté, Linda DeMeulemeester, Brian Dolton, Gemma Files, Ada Hoffmann, Tyler Keevil, Claude Lalumière, Jamie Mason, Michael Matheson, Ursula Pflug, Rhea Rose, Simon Strantzas, E. Catherine Tobler, Beth Wodzinski, Melissa Yuan-Ines

FRACTURED:
TALES OF THE CANADIAN POST-APOCALYPSE

EDITED BY SILVIA MORENO-GARCIA

"The 23 stories in *Fractured* cover incredible breadth, from the last man alive in Haida Gwaii to a dying Matthew waiting for his Anne in PEI. All the usual apocalyptic suspects are here – climate change, disease, alien invasion – alongside less familiar scenarios such as a ghost apocalypse and an invasion of shadows. Stories range from the immediate aftermath of society's collapse to distant futures in which humanity has been significantly reduced, but the same sense of struggle and survival against the odds permeates most of the pieces in the collection… What *Fractured* really drives home is how perfect Canada is as a setting for the post-apocalypse. Vast tracts of wilderness, intense weather, and the potentially sinister consequences of environmental devastation provide ample inspiration for imagining both humanity's destruction and its rugged survival." —*Quill & Quire*

Featuring stories by T.S. Bazelli, GMB Chomichuk, A.M. Dellamonica, dvsduncan, Geoff Gander, Orrin Grey, David Huebert, John Jantunen, H.N. Janzen, Arun Jiwa, Claude Lalumière, Jamie Mason, Michael Matheson, Christine Ottoni, Miriam Oudin, Michael S. Pack, Morgan M. Page, Steve Stanton, Amanda M. Taylor, E. Catherine Tobler, Jean-Louis Trudel, Frank Westcott , A.C. Wise.

The Exile Book of Anthology Series
Number Eleven

playground
of
LOST
toys

Edited by Colleen Anderson and Ursula Pflug

PLAYGROUND OF LOST TOYS

EDITED BY COLLEEN ANDERSON AND URSULA PFLUG

A dynamic collection of stories that explore the mystery, awe and dread that we may have felt as children when encountering a special toy. But it goes further, to the edges of space, where games are for keeps and where the mind plays its own games. We enter a world where the magic may not have been lost, where a toy or computers or gods vie for the upper hand. Wooden games of skill, ancient artifacts misinterpreted, dolls, stuffed animals, wand items that seek a life or even revenge – these lost toys and games bring tales of companionship, loss, revenge, hope, murder, cunning, and love, to be unearthed in the sandbox.

Featuring stories by Chris Kuriata, Joe Davies, Catherine MacLeod, Kate Story, Meagan Whan, Candas Jane Dorsey, Rati Mehrotra, Nathan Adler, Rhonda Eikamp, Robert Runté, Linda DeMeulemeester, Kevin Cockle, Claude Lalumière, Dominik Parisien, dvsduncan, Christine Daigle, Melissa Yuan-Innes, Shane Simmons, Lisa Carreiro, Karen Abrahamson, Geoffrey W. Cole, Alex C. Renwick; Afterword by Derek Newman-Stille

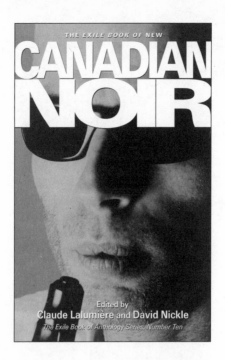

NEW CANADIAN NOIR

EDITED BY CLAUDE LALUMIÈRE AND DAVID NICKLE

"Everything is in the title. These are all new stories – no novel extracts – selected by Claude Lalumière and David Nickle from an open call. They're Canadian-authored, but this is not an invitation for national introspection. Some Canadian locales get the noir treatment, which is fun, since, as Nickle notes in his afterword, noir, with its regard for the underbelly, seems like an un-Canadian thing to write. But the main question *New Canadian Noir* asks isn't "Where is here?" it's "What can noir be?" These stories push past the formulaic to explore noir's far reaches as a mood and aesthetic. In Nickle's words, "Noir is a state of mind – an exploration of corruptibility, ultimately an expression of humanity in all its terrible frailty." The resulting literary alchemy – from horror to fantasy, science fiction to literary realism, romance to, yes, crime – spanning the darkly funny to the stomach-queasy horrific, provides consistently entertaining rewards." —*Globe and Mail*

Featuring stories by Corey Redekop, Joel Thomas Hynes, Silvia Moreno-Garcia, Chadwick Ginther, Michael Mirolla, Simon Strantzas, Steve Vernon, Kevin Cockle, Colleen Anderson, Shane Simmons, Laird Long, Dale L. Sproule, Alex C. Renwick, Ada Hoffmann, Kieth Cadieux, Michael S. Chong, Rich Larson, Kelly Robson, Edward McDermott, Hermine Robinson, David Menear, Patrick Fleming.

SAME SERIES: DIFFERENT GREAT WRITING

THE STORIES THAT ARE GREAT WITHIN US
Edited by Barry Callaghan
Over the last 60 years, Toronto has been turned upside down and inside out
– and over the decades the city's storytellers have given vibrant voice to
the city's characters.

NATIVE CANADIAN FICTION AND DRAMA
Edited by Daniel David Moses
Tomson Highway, Niigonwedom James Sinclair, Joseph Boyden, Joseph A.
Dandurand, Alootook Ipellie, Thomas King, Yvette Nolan, Richard Van Camp,
Floyd Favel, Robert Arthur Alexie, Daniel David Moses, Katharina Vermette.

CANADIAN DOG STORIES
Edited by Richard Teleky
"Twenty-eight stories that run the breadth of adventure, drama, satire,
and even fantasy, and will appeal to dog lovers on both sides of the
[Canada/US] border."–*Modern Dog Magazine*

CANADIAN SPORTS STORIES
Edited by Priscila Uppal
Clarke Blaise, George Bowering, Dionne Brand, Barry Callaghan,
Morley Callaghan, Roch Carrier, Matt Cohen, Steven Heighton,
W.P. Kinsella, Stephen Leacock, Barry Milliken, L.M. Montgomery,
Susanna Moodie, Mordecai Richler, Guy Vanderhaeghe and more.

PRIESTS, PASTORS, NUNS AND PENTECOSTALS
Edited by Joe Fiorito
Mary Frances Coady, Barry Callaghan, Leon Rooke, Roch Carrier,
Jacques Ferron, Seá n Virgo, Marie-Claire Blais, Hugh Hood, Morley Callaghan,
Hugh Garner, Diane Keating, Alden Nowlan, Gloria Sawai,
Eric McCormack, Yves Thériault, Margaret Laurence, Alice Munro.

20 CANADIAN POETS TAKE ON THE WORLD ~ Mulitlingual
Edited by Priscila Uppal
20 Canadian poets translate the works of Nobel laureates through classic
favourites. Each poet provides an introduction to the translated work.

THE EXILE BOOK OF YIDDISH WOMEN WRITERS
Edited by Frieda Johles Foreman
2014 WINNER of the Helen and Stan Vine Canadian Jewish Book Award.
The first collection of Yiddish writing to emphasize the work of Canadian-
Yiddish women writers, like Chava Rosenfarb, Rachel Korn and Ida Maze.

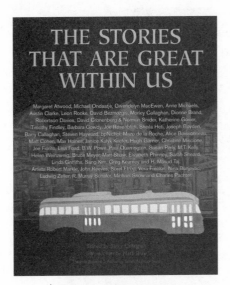

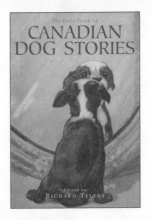
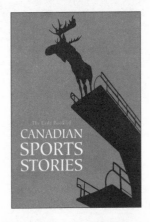
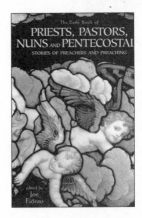
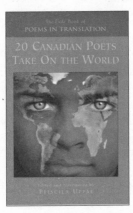
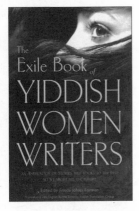

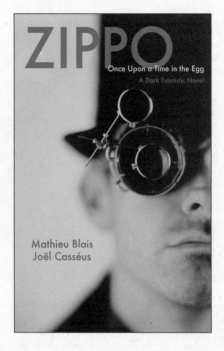

ZIPPO

MATHIEU BLAIS & JOËL CASSÉUS (translated from the French)

"More than just a dark futuristic novel, ZIPPO sits at the rarely visited border between the detective story and science fiction. Here is a striking testimonial on the stormy beginning of our new century. The elliptic, well-worked, stylized and poetic writing quickly wins us over, regardless of syntactic conventions: the sentence is often severed from its subject and syncopated as if as it was the very reflection of this tattered, tense universe." —*Solaris*

A science fiction, dark thriller, written with language as sharp as the crack of an automatic weapon, meant to shake us awake and make us think: In a North American city in the not too distant future, a great economic summit is getting under way and Nuovo Kahid is the journalist assigned to cover it. When the economy goes well, they say, everything goes well. But Villanueva is a city physically divided into haves and have-nots. The pornopros are disappearing, the old gum-clackers teeth are on edge and the authorities are showing the city's disenfranchised no mercy. The city is falling into ruin. And to add insult to injury, a meteor is heading straight for the Earth. What more is needed to tell us that the end of the world as we know it is nigh? Kahid, mourning the loss of the beautiful A***, fills his days smoking lungspitters and getting drunk on buzz-juice, trying to remember the details of one fateful night before it's all too late.

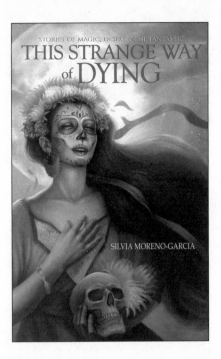

THIS STRANGE WAY OF DYING

SILVIA MORENO-GARCIA

This book is a collection of short stories and it's rather unlike any I've read before. In some ways I don't think "stories" is the correct way to refer to these entries… Every story has the best atmosphere. It is creepy with a capital CREEP. What is alien is alien and the settings around Mexico and especially in Mexico City are really powerful. You get an excellent sense of time and place even though they're only thumbnails in short stories, they're very elegantly described– not overwritten but not sparse and very much aware that the atmosphere is vital for these stories… In all, this is an excellent book and a refreshing change from so much of what we normally see in the genre. I think it's a great book to read in bite-size pieces, a few stories here, a few there, picking a random one out when it appeals, rather than in one setting. Read three or four at a time and be transported by the atmosphere and folklore that so very rarely has the chance to be told."

—*Fangs for the Fantasy*

"This genre defying collection of short stories are all of the fantastic – sometimes leaning more towards horror, other times more sci-fi tinged. One of the reasons I remain dedicated to diverse literature is that it's almost always a subversion of common tropes. The Mexican folklore weaves its way beautifully through the stories, even as it gave me new things to be terrified of.." —*Galactic Tides*

Exile's $15,000 Carter V. Cooper Short Fiction Competition

FOR CANADIAN WRITERS ONLY

$10,000 for the Best Story by an Emerging Writer
$5,000 for the Best Story by a Writer at Any Career Point

The 12 shortlisted are published in the annual *CVC Short Fiction Anthology* series and *ELQ/Exile: The Literary Quarterly*

WITHDRAWN

Exile's $3,000 Gwendolyn MacEwen Poetry Competition

FOR CANADIAN WRITERS ONLY

$1,500 for the Best Suite of Poetry
$1,000 for the Best Suite by an Emerging Writer
$500 for the Best Poem

Winners are published in *ELQ/Exile: The Literary Quarterly*

These annual competitions open in October & November
details at: www.TheExileWriters.com